Almost Demon
Chamber One of the Sigil Cycle

AJ Salem

To J.

I love it when authors share their playlists. So here is what I was listening to while I wrote.

1. Stripes - FM Belfast
2. Strict Machines - Goldfrapp
3. The Greeks - Is Tropical
4. Secret Alphabets - Kasabian
5. Madness - Muse
6. Corduroy - Pearl Jam
7. Echoes - The Rapture
8. First Wave Intact - Secret Machines
9. No Good Trying - Syd Barrett
10. Hearing Damage - Thom Yorke
11. Heads Will Roll - Yeah Yeah Yeahs
12. You Lot - Orbital
13. Eat Raw Meat = Blood Drool - The Editors
14. You're Lost Little Girl - The Doors
15. Television Rules The Nation - Daft Punk
16. Fainting Spells - Crystal Castles
17. Don't Worry Baby - The Beach Boys
18. Jimmy James - Beastie Boys

CHAPTER ONE

My cheerleading uniform hung from the top of the closet door like a corpse. I took another brief look at it before slipping into a pair of gray sweatpants and an oversized t-shirt emblazoned with the word Alaska. I shoved each foot into a worn sneaker, not bothering to unlace them. My bedroom was still enveloped in darkness. Pulling back one of the red curtain sheers, I watched as the only hint of dawn was still fastened to the horizon line and I was glad to see that the morning dew had already settled onto the ground and no longer littered the air. I reset the alarm on my cellphone, left it on my night table and walked out the front door.

The cool breeze held the distinct smell of autumn and the flock of waterfowl overhead was loud, already busy practicing formations. I wound my way around the patio, waved to the ghost reclining on the chaise and headed east for the dirt trail that began at the forest line and curved its way deep into Mohonk State

Park. I meditated on my breathing, controlling the tempo until I lost myself in the blissful mindlessness.

Each time the heel of my foot connected with the earth, I plunged deeper into a place devoid of pitiful looks and harsh accusations. Unfortunately, my legs couldn't carry me forever and after an hour I was back home, stretching on the lawn and having a staring contest with the black wispy blob that had now joined me on the grass.

All it did was sit there. I've tried talking to it, ever since the faceless wraith showed up on my doorstep the day after I was discharged from the hospital. Haven't gotten so much as a peep out of it. Once I felt the heeby-jeebies coming on, I decided it was time for a shower.

"Bye," I said and got up.

I stepped through the sliding glass door, kicked off my shoes, and peeled away my socks that were supposedly sweat-proof -so claimed the perky assistant manager at the Sports Authority. The cool tile felt good on my swollen feet but I winced as my back decompressed and my right shin throbbed. I rubbed the scar that ran the length of my leg. I filled up the coffee pot with tap water and watched through the window as the ghost settled back into the chaise.

Knowing that good old Mr. Coffee was doing his job, I got ready for the first day of school. After settling on a floral peasant top and black jeans, I rounded the corner of the hallway back into the kitchen.

"Dad!" I said, unable to hide the hint of surprise in my voice. He rarely slept at home. I pulled two mugs from the cabinet hanging over the breakfast bar and took the pot of fresh brew from his hand.

"Good morning, Gem. You sleep well?" His blond streaked hair gave him more of an aged-surfer look.

"Like a baby." I stared straight into his brown eyes and faked the most genuine smile I could muster. I started analyzing the split ends at the mop of mousy dark brown hair that was in desperate need of conditioner as I poured him and myself a cup of coffee.

He was already dressed in his daily uniform: navy suit, white collared shirt, no tie. His lab coat was slung over the back of his chair. A pair of chrome-tinted aviators was tucked in his front jacket pocket behind a white plastic photo ID for Moab Pharmaceuticals. Dark circles bruised his lower lids and I wondered if he had slept at all.

"Excited about your first day of senior year?" he asked. I set his coffee in front of him and went to grab the newspaper I had tossed in earlier. "Gem?"

"I'm not sure, Daddy." I thought about the micropleated skirt hanging in the closet, still encased in flimsy plastic, and then looked down at my legs. Should I go blonde? Maybe then I'd feel like having more fun.

"If you're not up to it…"

"No, it's fine," I blurted.

He smiled and then went on to read the day's news. The rest of our time together was spent in familiar silence while I made eggs and toast for two.

"I'm going to be late tonight."

"I know the drill." I took another sip from my mug before getting up to dump the rest of my food in the trash. The thought of walking through the halls of my school had my stomach in knots and although the idea of hiding out in the bathroom all day appealed to me, I just wanted to get the whole ordeal over with.

"You would tell me if there was something bothering you, right, pumpkin?"

"Sure, I would tell you. Not some therapist." I added the latter for good measure.

"It might do you some good. Talking to someone."

"I have you, Daddy." I put my arms around him and gave him a peck on the cheek, inhaling the comforting smell of his pine- scented soap.

"Don't worry about the dishes," he said as I grabbed my keys and tote.

"Wasn't going to." I laughed.

"It's nice to hear you in a good mood. Need a ride?" my dad asked from behind the local sports section.

I pawed through my book bag and edged my way closer to the front door.

"Gem?"

"Bye, Dad." I couldn't hide the disappointment in my voice.

I walked out into the sun knowing that he wouldn't come out to follow me.

As soon as the front door slammed behind me, I felt awful, leaving on such a sour note. My guilt quickly turned bitter and I was angry that he even suggested I get in a car. He knew how I felt. Even angrier that he hadn't come running out of the house, groveling. I took a deep breath and brushed away the negative thoughts. Maybe tomorrow I would run for a bit longer. For now, the walk to school would have to do

Hudson Valley is an eclectic part of New York State, filled with hippies who rooted themselves to the area surrounding Woodstock and Manhattanites yearning for more square footage to meet the needs of their growing families. Chic renovated farmhouses and mansions on secluded twenty-acre plots were popping up with more frequency but the landscape was mostly wooded, littered with neat ranch homes and vinyl siding.

Harrisport is right in the midst of the Shawagunk and Catskill mountains, lending the area to a good amount of tourism for the B&B types who want to do a bit of hiking and antiquing. Once off the thruway, a good twenty minutes away from the nearest strip mall, much of the town is a cluster of paved roads all leading to Main Street.

I made the long way downhill on Old Farm Road and hung a left when I reached the end of the large football field. Harrisport High came into view.

"Ohmygod, Gemma. I didn't think you would make it."

"Good to see you too, Charlotte."

"Did that come out wrong?" she asked, her voice getting higher the more nervous she became. Charlotte was supposed to be my best friend. We've known each other since the third grade. She was my exact opposite: blonde to my brunette, petite and curvy to my lankiness.

"Long time no see." I sorted through my textbooks, trying to conceal the tears welling up in my eyes.

"I'm really, really sorry, Gem. I meant to come see you in the hospital but first I had that internship abroad thing and I had no idea what had happened and by the time I got back, I felt weird about being away and I didn't even know if you wanted visitors and then it got to the point where it was too awkward to even call."

I pulled her into a hug. Part of me wanted to hold a grudge but I didn't really feel like shutting everyone out of my life. Everyone in town blamed me for the accident. I really didn't need another person cursing me under their breath.

"It's alright, Charlotte. It's not like I was taking any visitors anyway."

"Really? You mean it?" Her crystal blue eyes grew wider as she squealed in delight.

"Heads up."

A football came hurtling towards me and made contact with my locker, slamming it shut. I jumped back, the crash of metal startling me. I felt the heat of blood rushing to my face.

"Seriously, Matt?" Charlotte screamed, picking up the ball and tossing it back while trying to keep her balance in her four-inch wedge sneakers. I was starting to remember why we were always friends. I made her happy and she dealt with everything else while dressed to kill. "Go bother someone else, you jocktard."

I caught Matt's gaze from across the way. The crowd parted for him as he headed towards me and I mentally prepared myself for an extremely awkward and difficult conversation.

"He is a total asshole," Charlotte said.

"Leave it. I deserved it."

"I'm going to stay out of this. But I need details."

"You got it," I replied. "Later."

"Hey Gem," Matt said, folding his arms across his broad muscled chest. He leaned against the lockers, blocking my access to Charlotte.

"Matt." I continued to arrange my books according to height.

"I'm waiting."

"Listen." I turned finally, looking at him straight on. "I'm really sorry for not taking any of your calls but I thought you would understand."

"Why?" His voice was pained. "Why would you think that I would understand that my girlfriend didn't want to see me after she had been in a freaking car accident?"

I forced down the bile in my throat. There was no explanation and I didn't want to make up some bullshit story just so he would feel better.

"Just leave me alone."

"That's not what I want, Gem. I want to fix things. Like how they were before."

"You know what I want?" I said angrily. "I want you to go away."

"You sure about that?" he said, giving me one last expectant look and then punched the locker beside mine.

"Oh wow, Matt, just leave it," Charlotte said, positioning herself between his body and mine.

"Fine." He snorted and walked away.

"Gemmy," Charlotte started, "I know I've been a crappy best friend but I am so here for you now. Wanna meet up at lunch? I don't think we have any classes together this semester." We both looked down at our schedules and grimaced.

"Sure. That sounds nice."

Minutes later, the bell rang and Charlotte walked me to homeroom. My half-broken heart swelled a bit at the thought that someone was still by my side.

The feeling of acceptance didn't last long. I sat in the front row, thinking that if anyone was going to be giving me dirty looks, I would at least be oblivious to them. I was, however, left sitting with an empty desk on either side. Having leprosy might have made me more popular.

Principal Kelly stood right at the door, her back to the room, blocking my view of whomever it was she arguing with.

"Please, ma'am. I know I can do it. Just give me a chance," the voice in the hallway pleaded.

"But you aren't qualified to teach here," she replied.

"I'm only twenty hours' worth of student teaching away from certification. Otherwise, consider me a university grad."

I couldn't make out the rest of the conversation but after a few more minutes of watching Principal Kelly shake her head, she moved aside and let the mystery man walk in.

"Class, welcome to homeroom 313. I'm Mr. Flynn and I'm new, so please bear with me."

Mr. Flynn was handsome in a restrained British sort of way. He looked fresh out of college, had a full head of side-swept brown hair and eyes that were nearly black. His red flannel shirt looked a bit Paul Bunyan but the tan cord blazer toned it down a few notches.

He parked himself right in front of me. I looked up, trying to keep my eyes away from the direct view I had of his crotch. He smiled, handed me a stack of papers and said, with a distinguished accent, "Take one and pass them back."

I did as I was told and then examined the sheets in front of me. A parental waiver that needed a signature if you wanted to use the computer lab, a schedule of events for September/October, and a sign-up sheet for extra-curricular activities.

"Aside from being your homeroom and an English lit teacher, I will also be hosting an after-school reading club on Fridays. Look-y here on the bottom of the orange page. The first few sessions will focus on Homer and the Greek Myths."

Silence.

"Settle down. Don't get too excited."

A few giggles resounded from the back.

"Do keep in mind that it looks great at a college interview when you can recite a little Virgil or Frost on the fly. Any questions?"

The loudspeaker interrupted and let out the single tone meant for school-wide announcements. There was some reverb followed by a pert female voice.

"Ladies and gentlemen, good morning. This is Principal Kelly speaking. I would like to take this opportunity to welcome you all back to another productive year of higher learning. However, we must all take a moment to reflect on those who will not be returning to these halls. Please join me, as well as the esteemed members of the faculty, in a memorial dedication in honor of three shining stars that were extinguished too soon in a senseless car accident:

Mimi Yin, Jenny Goodwin, and Brian Pope. We will commence before first lunch in the auditorium. There are also additional counselors on staff this week for anyone who needs it."

My pulse sped up to a break neck speed. I couldn't believe it.

"Freak!" I felt something wet hit the side of my cheek. I wiped off the wad of paper encased, no doubt, with a million germs, and kept my eyes on my planner.

"All right then. Let me call roll before you all run out of here." The familiar drumbeat of panic began throbbing in my head. No way was I going to survive the assembly.

"Gemma Pope."

"Here," I replied.

I looked up at the clock perched above the threshold and groaned. It was only forty-five minutes into the school day and I was already fuming. Someone could have warned me about the production the school was going to make, starring my dead brother.

CHAPTER TWO

My brother was born two minutes ahead of me and never let me forget it. He was perfect. Everyone wanted to bask in his presence, including me. I went as far as joining the cheerleading squad with my subpar gymnastic skills just so I could spend extra time with him. Brian Pope, quarterback, honor roll, member of the debate team, all neatly packaged with my dad's good looks. Harrisport's potential claim to fame. And I loved him more than life.

I squirmed in the plastic bucket seat while Brian looked out at me from the blown-up junior yearbook picture projected on the screen alongside Mimi's and Jenny's.

"What are you ladies up to?" Brian barged into my room and flung himself on my bed, sending me to the floor and getting more than a few chuckles out of my friends. He propped himself on his elbows and gave us all a signature smile. The kind with dimples.

"Well," Mimi started, "we're trying to decide if we should

bother heading down to the city or go local."

"Sounds like a plan. I'm in."

"Brian, don't you have other things to do? Like Allison?" I said, sticking my finger in my mouth in a fake gag.

"Gem, I am deeply offended." He placed my hand to his heart. "You are my other half. Can't I spend some quality time with you?"

I rolled my eyes, the irony of the situation was not lost on me. I was usually the one hanging on to him for a social life.

"Fine."

"Let's just go to the lake. My dad always keeps the garage unlocked. We can grab a few kayaks," Jenny interjected.

"Sounds like a plan," Brian added. "What about Matt?"

"Well, this had started out as a girls' only kind of day," Mimi said.

"The lake it is," I said reluctantly. I had hoped to get a little birthday shopping done since it was always so hard picking something out for Brian and keeping it a secret. Pushing it off until the week before didn't seem like such a good idea now with him throwing a big fat wrench into my plans.

"But no boyfriends today. Or girlfriends. Agreed?" Jenny said.

"Yeah sure, fine," I said.

"Yay," Mimi squeaked, her straight black bob swaying back and forth with glee.

"This is going to be a beautiful day, Gem," Brian said as he put one arm around my shoulder and pulled my head in for a noogie.

And it was.

"Gem, you mind if I sit next to you?" My daydream was cut short.

I looked up and nodded, relieved to see Charlotte.

"You think you can even sit through this? I mean, if you just want to bail and go get a slice, I am one hundred percent with you."

If I left, it would look even worse, I thought. I would just have to bear it despite the nest of snakes swirling around my stomach.

"Thanks, but I think I can manage," I replied.

"Meanwhile, did you see Allison? Barf; crying crocodile tears all through math. She is definitely milking this. O'Brian already exempted her from any work in the foreseeable future."

"Listen," I said. "She was Brian's girlfriend. She obviously is having trouble dealing with it."

"Yeah. She sure is heartbroken."

Charlotte nodded her head to the left where Allison was seated with her crew. She gave me a pert smile. We were never friends, but we were at least friendly. The overhead lights dimmed, followed by the sound of a throat clearing over the auditorium speakers.

"Students, faculty." Principal Kelly never came off as an ordinary principal. The best way I could describe her was a hippie. Her thick black hair was secured to the back of her head with oriental hair combs and her eyes had an uncanny way of letting you know they were green from across the room. They almost glowed. The rest of her was hidden between layers of mismatched floral prints and Bakelite bangles. Today's ensemble looked straight out of Past & Presents, one of a string of throwback shops that liked to sell anything second-hand and call it antique.

"Today we have come together to cast light on these bright souls." I watched as the fringes on her suede vest swayed back and forth in perfect sync. I had to suppress an inappropriate chuckle as I watched the audience, enraptured by her clichéd speech. The light on the rear projector went on and thus began the torture. "The best way we can keep them alive is by keeping Brian, Mimi and Jenny close in our thoughts." The click of the remote echoed through the room while the hum of machinery drowned out any other noise.

"Let's journey through the last few years and let these photos tell their story."

"Is she serious?" Charlotte whispered in my ear.

All I could do was shrug my shoulders as I watched each jumbo Megatron-sized photo fade into the next. Static poses from three of the most important people in my life on display.

"Why do I feel like she's showing naked photos of me up there?" I said.

My fingers gripped the armrests and I looked down to watch my knuckles go white instead of the fiasco happening on stage.

"Screw this, I can't watch." I kept my voice low.

I bolted out of my seat and mumbled a string of Excuse me's as I made my way down the row and out of the auditorium. I shut the door behind me and tried to forget all the negative looks as I made my way out of the choking situation. I leaned my head on the cool steel door and closed my eyes, trying to control the heat creeping up my neck. My temper ran hot and cold these days. I tried to push my mind back to the empty feeling I get while running but all I could see were the happy smiles staring back at me from those sterile school pictures.

I was beginning to forget what Brian sounded like. The way his hands and feet looked. Things absent from photos. One measly video on my phone was all I had. I started looking through my bag, desperate for the comfort of seeing Brian alive on the tiny screen as I held back the flood of tears desperate to break through the wall of steel I had erected around my feelings.

The thud of the door slamming rang through my ears. I was expecting to see Charlotte. Instead, I was face to face with Allison.

"Nice job."

"Hey." I managed to squeak out.

"I can't even begin to tell you how much you've royally effed up my life," she started. Her face was uncomfortably close to mine. "I think it's about time I started messing up yours."

"Allison, I understand you're angry with me."

"Brian and I had plans. We were applying to Cornell together. We were going to get an apartment and date through college until we got married. We were going to have two kids." The words were dripping from her mouth. "You ruined it. If he wasn't always trying to make sure you were okay then he would still be here. Poor Gem, he would tell me, she's so lonely."

"Allison, I don't really know what to say."

"All you had to do was tell him no. You had to be a codependent sniveling baby and drag him around with you that day. Did you know that we had plans that night?" She had worked herself up to the point where her shrill voice was clawing it's way into my head.

That's when she starting using her fists. A shove of my shoulder, a palm to my chin, a knee between my legs to keep me from running. *Just take it. I'm tired of beating myself up, maybe it was time someone else took over for a change.*

I braced myself for more impact but the punch never came. From the corner of my eye, I watched as a pillar of black smoke took human form, save for its face, which bulged and elongated until it reminded me of the man in The Scream. It drew up its arm trailing wispy tendrils of fog across the floor, and at the end of this mystical rope was Allison, who was now walking away from me and making her way to the row of lockers opposite me.

"Hey!" I yelled.

Just then, the apparition aimed its other arm at me and the air burst out from my lungs. All that was left was the silence. It spread its inky hand across my chest and held me in place.

I felt like I was back in my dreams, trying to scream for help but nothing would come out. I tried harder and pushed with all my strength until tears were streaming down my face from the force and the realization that I was helpless. It whipped its other arm around and Allison spun on a dime like a puppet. The locker behind her was open and in her hand, I saw a jump rope.

"Poor, poor, Gemma."

Allison waved the rope back and forth as she looped the other end through into a noose. A gray mist began filling the entire hallway until all that was left were our two faces, the ghostly friend and the orange handle in Allison's hand that shone like a beacon.

Is this the part where I started praying? Our family stopped going to church the day my mother walked out the door and never came back. If I gave in, it would all go away. Everything would stop, including the pain, and I wouldn't have to figure out what came next.

The small voice in the back of my head that always sounded like Brian told me to get over it. There was no way I was giving up. That's when my instincts kicked in. Allison was inching her way towards me. Picturing Brian's face, I gathered up all of my remaining strength and released the mournful dirge that had been bottled up inside me. I kept the stream going until the being's grip was loosened, freeing my arms. The steady drone of my voice filled my ears and I wrestled out of the spirit's hold.

The dark ghost refocused its attention on Allison. She picked up her pace as the fog around her grew thicker. I huddled closer to the ground, away from the battering wind that was surrounding her.

I kept screaming, hoping someone would come to help but it continued to swirl, creating a vortex of endless energy. With every spin, it delved deeper into Allison's body. And then everything stopped. The haze cleared and the air settled. The spirit was no longer standing in the hallway but peering at me from behind Allison's eyes, which had turned from hazel to a black as thick as ink.

"Hey, what's going on?" A voice came from down the hall. Someone was coming.

I watched as the newly-possessed Allison flung the jump rope onto her shoulder.

"Hey there, hot stuff," she replied. "Just showing Gem here some moves. Since her leg is all messed up."

When he turned the corner, I got my first look at the mystery guy and was relieved. His board shorts hung low on his lean waist and the slight tan coupled with his azure eyes conjured images of sand and surf. I watched as he ran a hand through his black hair.

"Hey," he said, tilting his head towards me. His biceps flexed beneath his white tee.

"Hey, yourself," Allison smoothed down the front of her gray crepe blouse and did a signature flip of her long auburn hair. "You're new." The corner of her lip turned up in a half smile and I watched the shadow in her eyes dissipate. As Allison walked away, I felt the tension in the air release. I gripped the sides of my arms and massaged the cold dread that had me pinned to the wall only seconds ago.

"I couldn't help noticing you and your friend there." he answered.

"Right, friend." I watched as Allison walked her fingers across his forearm. "I'm Allison.

He pulled back and I caught his gaze. "Ian." His eyes softened.

Before I could form a coherent thought, Allison, obviously in search of my brother's replacement, threaded her arm through Ian's and spun him around, leading him away. He looked back over his shoulder but continued walking while Allison blabbed about the town and her upcoming back-to-school party. I made no move to follow them. This was the first time I had seen the blackness do anything other than sit on its proverbial behind and, for now, I was staying very far away from Allison.

Slowly, I peeled myself off the concrete wall and checked the hallway. Empty. The school bell rang, followed by the usual bustle of students out into the hallway. I felt a hand rest on my shoulder and jumped. Books went flying from my arms, including a math textbook, which made contact with my ankle. I knelt down to rub the tender spot.

"Are you okay, Gem?"

I looked up and saw Charlotte, who immediately knelt down to help collect my things, including my AP English workbook that I had left on the seat next to her.

"Thanks, Char."

"Are you sure you're alright, Gem? You're definitely on edge. I worry."

We both stood up and I tried to chase the fear out of my voice. "I'm fine. Really. Where are you next period?"

"Well, I was trying to keep it a secret but in this town that's close to impossible. I'm joining the Drama Troupe. I know. Doesn't really fit with my image but I decided that if anyone is going to take my dream of being an actress seriously, I'd have to bite the bullet and join the geeks."

"Real sensitive. I wouldn't call them that to their faces." I adjusted the strap of my bag and started walking down the corridor with Charlotte by my side.

"So I'm going to just come out and say it. Are you coming to practice?"

I thought about the uniform I had refused to put on this morning. "I don't know."

"No pressure. You have a spot on the team

whenever you're ready. Whatever I say goes. I'm captain now." She smiled and I envied her for the ease with which she could see the good things in life. It was easy to assume that everything was fine and dandy at the Harris home. It was anything but. I could count the number of times I'd been to her house on one hand. She kept everyone away from her bickering parents: her father the Senator and her mother the drunk, and the reason why Charlotte wasn't with us the day of the crash.

"I'll think about it," I said.

"We'd get to spend more time together." There was a flatness to her voice that someone else would miss, but not me. I tried to get the courage to push away all the reasons I didn't want to show up on the football field ever again and try to be normal again. I just couldn't.

"Like I said, I'll think about it. I have to check what days I'm going to be at the library."

"Why do you insist on working for free?"

"It's better than sitting in an empty house," I said.

"Yeah, but I told you that I'd come hang out. Plus, I'm sure Senator Harris would love to pay you to make his coffee."

"Sorry, Charlotte, but a paycheck cannot make spending time with your Dad any more enticing," I said, patting her on the back.

We both laughed and it seemed for a moment that everything just might go back to normal.

CHAPTER THREE

"Charlotte!" I called out, waving out the passenger side window of Mimi's Prius. There was no room to park the car in the large circular driveway in front of her palatial home. There were cars parked everywhere, even on the lawn. She was waiting near the wrought-iron gate at the front of the property, wearing something that could only be referred to as a frock.

"What are you wearing?" Jenny called out.

After smoothing her hand on the crisp cotton of her dress, Charlotte pushed off the wall and approached the car, walking gracefully in heeled sandals over gravel.

"I'm sorry, guys. I can't come."

"Why?" I asked. "I thought you cleared it with your parents already."

"Last minute fund raiser. Dutiful daughter must attend." Her voice cracked from the sarcasm and I could only guess what was going on between her parents at home to have gotten her this upset. Charlotte never wanted to be the reason that they were at each other's throats. I kept telling her she might as well be, that would mean she was at least living life the way she

wanted to.

"Are you sure?" I asked, reaching out to tug the hem of her bright cornflower blue skirt.

"I'm just trying to get through the summer. As soon as school starts, they won't even notice when I'm out of the house. You know how it is. Don't worry, go have fun without me. We'll catch up later. My flight isn't until ten."

"Will you be joining us today, Miss Pope?"

"Uh, sorry?" I turned to face Mr. Flynn and was immediately struck by how attractive he was, and confused at how I hadn't noticed it earlier.

Must have been distracted.

"AP English. Will you be joining?" He had one hand on the doorknob and motioned me in with the other. I don't recall actually walking to my seat but there I was, in the front row again.

"Tick tock," Mr. Flynn said, glancing at the clock and tapping the white board a few times. "We are here to wax poetic about Shakespeare and Chaucer and let's throw an American in there for good show, Fitzgerald."

As he passed out the syllabus, I scanned the reading list and groaned. My entire course load had been scheduled at the end of last year under the expectation that I would have Brian helping me. So much for plans.

"Excuse me."

The temporary bedlam in the classroom drowned out my voice. *Now would be the perfect time to sneak out.* I gathered my things, my intentions fully focused on trying to get out of this advanced English class and into something better suited for me.

Mr. Flynn stopped me mid-stride and blocked my exit.

"I think I'm in the wrong class," I whispered, pleading with my eyes.

He stared back unwavering and replied, "That is where you're wrong, Miss Pope. I am pretty confident that I saw your name on the roll."

"Oh don't worry, Mr. Flynn, nobody would mind if Gemma wasn't here." Allison's voice carried across the room. "Or if she fell off the face of the planet."

I resisted the urge to respond amidst the half-concealed giggles and mumbles that followed her comment. "Well, you see, I just don't think I'll be needing the credits so I'll just go settle it with the office."

"One day. Just give me a chance. I'm not too horrible." His smile was warm and disarming in its imperfection, one front tooth protruding slightly in front of the other.

I settled back into my chair and for the rest of the period kept my focus on note taking. With fifteen minutes left to the class, and only three spitballs to pull out of my hair, I was relieved to find that I enjoyed listening to Mr. Flynn's enthusiasm for old books.

My gaze wandered to the door. There was no one there but I couldn't shake off the sense that someone had been staring into the classroom. I rubbed my eyes and checked the clock. Fourteen minutes to freedom.

Looking back at the door again, I caught the slow movement of black tendrils creeping in from the spaces along the jambs. I inhaled with an audible gasp.

"Is everything alright there, Miss Pope?" Mr. Flynn

asked.

The black pillar now clung to the corner of the room and remained motionless. The pain in my hands called me back to myself and I watched as blood erupted from the surface of my palms in the shape of four crescents each. I looked back up and saw that the entity was still there and had taken on a more opaque blackness. The muscles in my neck coiled with tension and I looked around to see if anyone else had noticed the strange creature.

Just then, the door slammed open, hitting the wall behind it in the process.

It was Ian.

"Hey, sorry I'm late." He gave Mr. Flynn a meek smile.

"Fascinating." Mr. Flynn nodded towards the empty seat to my left. "Just don't make it a habit."

Ian sidled right in. "Hey," he said.

"Hey." My mind was spinning between the black spirits and the hottie sitting next to me.

It had started after the crash. The doctors insisted that the only injury I had sustained was to my leg but they had run the gamut of tests to check for any damage to the brain.

I mentioned these "black spots" to my dad as soon as I regained consciousness. There were three of them standing in a row, as if they were waiting for me to wake up. No one refused him but after what seemed like an inordinate amount of MRIs, CT scans and even ultrasounds, the doctors spoke to my dad in hushed tones, spitting our terms like "psychosomatic" and "PTSD."

Until now, they hadn't bothered me much. I passed

one every day on my run and saw a few more near the library and bank. This was the first day that I felt they were stalking me.

The final bell rang and after a bit of mingling, only a few stragglers were left behind. Allison made it a point to pass by and scratch her long fake acrylic nails against my desk. She winked and said, "Bye, Ian. Catch you later."

I tried to check for any signs of the spirit, though nothing in her appearance clued me in. It was possible that it was no longer with her. I hadn't seen her for the rest of the day, keeping my promise to Charlotte to run out and get some pizza. Then again, it was also possible that I had been hallucinating.

When Allison was finally out of earshot, Ian let out a sigh and said, "She's a handful."

"Yeah." I laughed. "That's an understatement."

"You alright? From before, in the hallway. It looked like she was about to give you a hard time."

He offered me his hand as he stood up, but I brushed it away, bracing my hand on the desk and lifting myself out of the chair to take the stress off my back.

"I…yeah, I'm fine."

The words came out harsher than I had expected so I made a mental note to stop letting the pain affect my mood.

"Just making sure." His smile was a mixture of sly and endearing. "You never know."

We started to head out when Mr. Flynn called out to us. "Are either of you interested in the book club?"

"Book club?" Ian responded.

"You know, those pesky things with a back and

front and a bunch of pages stuck in the middle."

I smiled at Mr. Flynn's attempt at a joke.

"Not my style," Ian answered. "I'll catch you around. Gemma, right?" He put his hand on my shoulder and I felt the tingly sensation of energy pass through my body.

"Yeah," I replied and took an extra moment to marvel at the deep green blue shade of his irises.

"How about you, Miss Pope?"

"I don't know. I'm not really the studious type. That was more my brother's thing. I kind of just followed his lead."

"Let's make a deal then. We'll consider it extra credit. This way you'll feel comfortable staying on through the AP course for the rest of the year. How does that sound?"

I caught my lower lip between my teeth. My eyes wandered back to the spot where the darkness had held on to the wall. I couldn't tell if it was still there, the open door was blocking my view.

"I can help you with that problem of yours as well."

"Excuse me?"

"Those pesky bogies that have been hanging about." He waved both hands in the air. "We must do something about them." Back at his desk, he opened his attaché, pulled out a worn hardcover book. "Let me show you something."

I moved closer to the desk. The book felt like it had its own gravitational pull.

"You see this symbol?" He pointed to the gold embossed circle on the cover of the book. It was adorned with a medallion created by a series of circles and lines but other than that, the gray leather was blank.

"Looks fancy," I said.

"That's the first time I've heard that word used to describe this book."

"So what is it then?" I asked.

"Meet me for the book club tomorrow afternoon and I'll tell you all about it."

"I'm not sure. I don't know what my schedule is going to be like."

"Listen, Gemma." It was the first time he had called me by my first name. I watched as the next words rolled off his tongue and onto his full smooth lips. I definitely needed to get my head straight and ignore the unnatural amount of new hotness that had moved into the neighborhood. "I want you to start living and doing. If it doesn't work out, that's fine, but you ought to give yourself another chance."

"How did you…?"

"It doesn't take a genius to figure it out. And I saw you run out of the memorial ceremony this morning. You come tomorrow to English class and afterwards I'll show you how to put things right."

"Sure. Tomorrow."

"That's the spirit." The look of approval on his face was worth whatever torture I would be subjected to listening to long-winded lectures for an hour a day in Allison's presence.

"Can I ask you a question?"

"Anything."

"What are they? Or what is it? The black smoke."

"Oh well, that's easy, luv. It's all in here." He tapped the book. "But you'll have to be here tomorrow to get your answer." And without any further explanation, Mr. Flynn, his book, and all sense of reality left the building.

Chapter Four

The next two hours were spent shelving books at the public library, where I went to great lengths to avoid the two spirits flanking either side of the information desk.

"Are you alright, Gemma?"

"That seems to be the question of the day." I laughed.

Seeing the confusion on Ms. Halle's face, I rephrased my answer. "Thanks. Just peachy. Beats sitting at home alone," I said to the librarian. I pulled the trolley of reference books out from behind her desk and got into the elevator.

The fluorescent bulbs on the second floor flickered overhead, the artificial light reflecting against the metallic shelving units. I went from aisle to aisle, reorganizing books that had been pulled out of place as well as the ones from my cart.

Starting at the left most wall, I began by rearranging the biographies and then wove my way through the stacks, oblivious to my surroundings and enjoying the quiet repetition of the job.

When I was down to my last book, I got on my tiptoes and reached for the upper shelf, making room for Volume 9 of the Encyclopedia Britannica. *Who even uses these anymore?* I stretched my arms as far as they could reach and tilted the book forward into its spot.

Out of nowhere, a pair of hands grabbed me by the waist and pulled. I screamed and then rammed my elbow into the body behind me, sending us both flailing to the ground.

"Ow, what gives? It's just me."

I lifted my head up off the wall of steel pecs beneath me and looked back to find Ian in a fit of laughter. He flashed me his killer smile and let his hands wander up the side of my body. I rolled off him and jumped to my feet, ignoring the hotness sprawled before me on the floor and went on to adjust the hem of my shirt, trying to hide the flush on my face as best as I could.

"What are you doing here?" I said.

"I could ask you the same." His voice casual, the smile still on his face.

"That's not an answer." I leaned on the trolley, pushed off and made my way down the narrow corridor until I was back at the elevator. I pressed my index finger on the down button again and again, knowing full well that it wasn't getting here any sooner, no matter how hard I willed it. The building hadn't been renovated since the sixties and that meant the lift that serviced the two-level drab structure moved at a snail's pace. Ian was soon by my side.

"Hey, I didn't mean to scare you."

My expression hardened. "Listen," I started, "I'm really busy now. If you need any help, Ms. Halle's downstairs."

When the steel door opened, I stepped right in. *Please don't follow me.*

But he did.

"Look, can we start over? If I upset you in any way, I'm sorry," he said, shifting from one foot to the next.

"You know September in upstate New York is a bit brisk for shorts," I said with a smile.

"I'm going to take that as apology accepted."

He smelled good. Not like too many layers of body spray. There were hints of cinnamon coupled with layers of spice wafting through the air of the cramped space.

"Who are you?" I couldn't pretend to be angry any longer.

"I dare you to find out." He winked and I noticed how dark his lashes were against his light eyes and skin. This in turn sent my stomach doing flip-flops.

We were back on the first floor and Ian helped me stow away the trolley. Ms. Halle was halfway through *The Tale of Peter Rabbit*, and the handful of children seated on the circle time rug were listening intently, while a few of the younger ones wandered around, never straying too far from their parents. Ms. Halle's long silver hair swung down over her shoulder in a thick braid and she appeared content sitting on the floor, her feet tucked beneath her long denim skirt.

"This way," I whispered and waved for Ian to follow. In the back room, boxes of new books were waiting to be catalogued, invading much of the space meant to be an employee break room.

"Let me just grab my bag and we can go." I leaned over a stack of new best-sellers and pulled my tote out from my secret spot between the wall and the desk.

"Where are we going?"

"You're going to walk me home. That's what guys around here do. And you had the serendipitous timing of scaring the hell out of me at the end of my shift so now I'm afraid to go alone," I replied.

As I grabbed my jacket from its hanger, there was a loud thud followed by terrified screams. "What was that?" Ian asked.

"No idea."

What the hell was going on? I peered out, expecting to find a rational explanation for what was happening in the main room. Instead, Ms. Halle was standing on her desk with a blank look on her face and a rifle in her hands. The orange glow of the sunset filtering through the windows cast a sinister light on her as she reached into the delicate eyelet-trimmed front pocket of her blouse, opened the chamber of the gun and placed a large bullet inside.

Mothers were screaming as they scooped up their children and ran to the exit. Ms. Halle remained composed, uninterested in the melee and remained focused on her weapon.

Ian hurried towards the front, herding the patrons out the door while I speed-walked unseen to the far end of the room where the media centers were. I looked left and then right, making sure that there were no more people in harm's way.

I was shocked to find Ian when I back-tracked to

where Ms. Halle stood, in the hopes that I could placate her.

"Put the gun down, Ms. Halle," he said, his voice strong in the face of danger, his posture unthreatening but firm.

"You'll do just fine." Her voice was not her own. She aimed the barrel of the rifle at his forehead. The sweet-hearted librarian was definitely off her rocker.

I looked to the left, expecting to see the two spirits, only to find they were gone.

"I said put down the gun." This time, Ian's voice held an extra layer that I couldn't identify. It reverberated with power and I watched as Ms. Halle hesitated. With a quick yank, Ian pulled the rifle out of her hand and tossed it to the far end of the room.

The sound of sirens grew closer and I remained frozen in place as Ian grabbed Ms. Halle by the legs, sending her onto her behind. Her ass hit the desk with a loud smack, followed by a high-pitched shriek as she resisted Ian's requests to calm down.

The doors burst open and the rush of footsteps beat across the navy commercial grade carpeting. "Police. Hands in the air!"

I let out a sigh of relief.

Two officers were by my side in a flash, hustling me away from the crime scene. Outside, I tried my best to answer questions in spite of being distracted beyond belief.

When Ms. Halle was escorted out of the building, hands behind her back, her eyes full of tears, she cried out, "I'm sorry. I'm so sorry."

A group of onlookers had already flooded the street from neighboring buildings. I leaned away from the black and white squad car, hoping to catch Ms. Halle's attention. When she passed by, I craned my neck between the wall of patrolmen. Our eyes met and the shadow passed over her eyes. She was possessed.

"Miss? Can I give you a ride home?"

"Huh?" *If one of the spirits was inhabiting Ms. Halle's body then where was the other one?*

"We'll probably need you to come down to the station for some questioning but that can wait until tomorrow. Your father will need to bring you in. I can give you a ride home if you want?"

"No. It's okay."

At last, I saw Ian come out. He nodded to me and turned down the street, heading west in the direction of Main Street.

"Are you sure?" one of the detectives asked, not noticing Ian slip past.

"Yeah. I'm fine." I smiled for good measure, hoping that the officer would feel comfortable enough to let me leave. When he gave me the go ahead, I pulled the ends of my jacket closed in one hand and held on to the shoulder straps of my bag with the other as I rushed away from the scene.

"What happened in there?" I asked, my breath visible in the air. The temperature had dropped a considerable amount since the sun had gone done. Soon the clocks would go back and the nights would last even longer.

"Come on. Let me take you home," Ian answered, ignoring the question, frustrating me to no end.

We walked through the parking lot of a convenience store in companionable silence. No questions about my well-being or how my father was "holding up" like I got from most people around town. No awkward pauses. No forced chatter. We stopped in front of an empty block of land, which was overgrown with weeds and surrounded by a chain fence six feet high.

"Where are we going?"

"You'll see." He yanked at the master lock, which easily gave, and swung the hinges open. Placing his hand at the small of my back, he ushered me through, closing the gate behind us.

The dandelions, quackgrass, and woodsorrel fell beneath our feet as we traversed the abandoned yard, littered with broken appliances, old tires and a large porcelain bathtub filled to the brim with rusted gears and pistons.

"Is this the part where you break out the hockey mask and chainsaw?" I said, trying to sound snarky and hoping that it hid the fear that had my voice wavering.

We stopped by a large yew, the diameter of its trunk standing more than four people wide.

"We're here," Ian said.

"I can see we are here." I looked around. "But why?"

The tree was ominous, wider than it was tall, its branches stretching up towards the sky and small red berries that radiated between the shadows cast by its flat thin leaves. Quiet blanketed the area; not even a car horn disturbed the eerie peace that surrounded us.

We stood side by side and watched the tree sway and come to life. I felt dwarfed by its size, as well as by Ian's, who was a good six inches taller than my five feet eight.

"I told you, I'm taking you home."

"Excuse me. I think I'm missing something here. One," I said, "I don't live here. Two, last time I checked, tree wasn't a popular mode of transportation."

He gave me another of his wicked smiles and placed the palm of his hand on the soft soil at the base of the tree. I was becoming familiar with the crinkle of his eyes that hinted at knowledge beyond my own.

Before I could say a word, the ground began to tremble, shooting pulses of red light up through the grooves of the bark. I brought my hand up to my face, shielding my eyes against the heat.

"It's okay, Gemma," Ian said. I felt the wisp of his breath tickle my neck and felt safe enough to look.

Where before there had been a haphazard pattern of brown scaling bark, there now lay a door of polished smooth onyx with nothing but a knocker of brushed nickel in the shape of a curved ram's horn on it.

"You've got to be kidding," I said, in awe of the enigmatic display of the arcane.

He picked up the solid horn and dropped it, letting out a large resonant whack. The door creaked open in response and I was left with a choice to make.

"Your chariot awaits," Ian said.

The inside of my nose tickled and I sneezed at the strong smell of sulfur that wafted towards us. Entranced, I moved forward, taking Ian's hand for support and following him through the opening.

The pull was furious, sucking us in like the hose of

a vacuum cleaner. Ash sprayed my eyes and filled my mouth as my body propelled through a series of loops. I couldn't distinguish between up and down, left and right. We were being launched at near Mach-speed through an ephemeris tunnel. My insides churned from the pressure and I gripped tighter to Ian's hand, holding on for dear life. I felt my hold on him loosen. No longer able to grasp his palm, I clutched onto the pads of his fingers. He grabbed my other wrist and I calmed amidst the rolling waves of soot and wind.

We decelerated, came to a slow stop and then hovered above dozens of sinkholes cluttering the phosphorescent landscape, rolling dunes of sand that moved in an endless expanse within this cavern.

And then there was the sun. Not the sun seen on Earth that nourished its inhabitants but a brilliant blue and white gaseous ball that shone like a diamond and was just as icy.

"That's the one." Ian pointed to the black hole below.

When we touched ground, the wooden soles of my lace-up boots clicked.

"I don't understand," I said, circling around and breaking out in what bit of tap dance I could still remember. "It looks like sand."

"That's just how things work here." He crouched down and stuck his arm into the pit until it disappeared. After a bit of maneuvering and hoisting, he was able to pull out a massive length of leather cord.

I leaned over his shoulder in order to get a better view of things. Instead, I was distracted by the curve of his collarbone peeking out of the V-neck of his thin white cotton tee.

"Watch." He grinned. I was pretty sure that meant *I know you were checking me out.*

I knelt beside him, too embarrassed to sneak any more looks at my Adonis and watched as the cord in his hold jerked away, curving itself to form a head. Then, without warning, it split into a spiral of thinner strips. A portion wound itself around his forearm and embedded deep into the skin until it resembled a tattoo while the remainder rippled back into the shadows of the hole.

He yanked at the cord and it became taut, shivering with energy. "Hold on tight," Ian said as he wrapped his free arm around my waist.

And off we went, riding into the dark abyss, his laughter echoing behind us.

"We're here."

Those were the first words I heard after being shoved through a wall of viscous goop.

I stared, dumbfounded at the sight of Ian sitting on the stoop with my ghost beside him, awash in the light of the flood lamp above my front door.

"Who's this?" he asked, pointing to the apparition.

"Wait a minute." I spun around and saw the lawn, and the hazy silhouette of the mailbox and hedges that lined our property.

"It's a one-way trip," Ian replied to my unasked question. "You can't get back in from here."

"Yeah, but how did you know where I live?"

"Do you really want an explanation? It's sort of long- winded and doesn't make any difference,

Meanwhile, what's up with Casper?"

"Who?"

"You know, the friendly ghost?" He pointed to Ghosty, who remained inert.

"It's been here ever since I came home from the hospital. I've been seeing them everywhere."

"Were you sick or something?" he asked. Concern drew lines around his mouth.

"Do you really want an explanation? It's sort of long-winded and doesn't make any difference." I avoided his gaze and found my bag on the floor. I picked it up and dusted it off before making my way up the stairs, keys in hand.

"Well, goodnight. I'll see you tomorrow," Ian said, hopping to his feet.

My mind was buzzing with questions about what I had just seen and experienced. All I wanted to say was *"No, don't go. Come inside. Tell me everything,"* but the words got stuck in my throat. The part of me that would have confided in him had already switched off.

I started to put my key in the lock when Ian called out.

"Oh, and Gemma."

"What?" I said.

"I've been seeing them since I was born." And then he left.

CHAPTER FIVE

The next morning, I immersed myself in routine. Wake, run, shower, eat. This time though, I had had a late start. My mind kept racing in circles. First to Miss Halle's psychotic break then to Ian's trippy way home, leaving me sleeping all through the entire length of Freddie Mercury's operatic styling of "Bohemian Rhapsody" I had set as my alarm.

"Good Morning, pumpkin." My dad stood next to the counter with his coat on, rifling through stacks of papers and yesterday's mail.

"Morning." My voice was hoarse. *Must have been the pound of sand I swallowed following Ian into Never Never Land.*

"I got a call last night at the office about what happened yesterday."

Thanks for calling to check up on me, Dad. "No biggie," I replied and began shoveling Cheerios into my mouth so that I wouldn't say something stupid.

He fiddled around with his briefcase, transferred a

bunch of manila folders, and rearranged them until he seemed satisfied with the way they fit. "No, it is a big deal, honey," he said, looking up from his papers.

Finally, he is going to realize I'm alone.

"But I really had to work late and you know how it is when I get busy."

Ah, the two big b's: but and busy.

"Sure, Dad," I answered. My head ached and I wasn't in the mood for a confrontation. I've had my fill.

"Can you describe these black spots for me, Gemma?"

This was a new doctor. A pediatric neurology specialist flown in from the Boston Children's Hospital after a lot of arm-twisting.

"They're more like shadows." I flicked the first aid tape that held my IV in place and played with the end as it began to curl.

"Can you be a little more specific? It's important we find out exactly what you're seeing so you can get a proper diagnosis. The sooner we can give you a clean bill of health, the sooner you can go home."

"Um… Can I get some water?" I asked. If I stalled long enough, maybe he would give up and leave. The thought of going home petrified me. Four weeks in the hospital had me wrapped in a cocoon of fear and complacency.

"Gemma," my dad barked.

"What? I'm thirsty."

"I'll get the water." He stuck his index finger in my face. "You answer Dr. Volpe's questions."

But I didn't.

Instead, I lay there, staring at the small television screen, ignoring Dr. Volpe until he made up some excuse about checking my MRI results again and left.

"Gemma, please." My father's pleas stole through the wall I had erected to shut everyone out so I reinforced it and sealed myself tighter while the nurses dragged my screaming father out of the room.

"Gem?"

"Hmm?" I looked at my dad and knew by the strain in his neck that he had caught me zoning out.

"Is that okay?"

"Is what okay?" I mumbled as I tilted the bowl to my face, slurping up some of the milk.

"We'll drive down to the station now so we can wrap up your statement to the police and then you won't miss too much class."

"I don't think so." My heart hit the floor.

"Gemma, it's about time you got over your fear. You can't let these kinds of things dictate your life." The vein on the side of his forehead reared its ugly head and I knew he was frustrated. My dad the control freak couldn't get me to do anything these days. With Brian it was different. I had a partner and it was easy getting things done - homework, studying, practice, even chores.

"These kinds of things?" My voice was harsh and I nearly spewed a mouthful of cereal into his face. "I was in an accident. My brother died. My two best friends died. And I'm just supposed to paint on a happy face and get on with my life so you can feel better?"

"That's not what I meant, Gem." He let out a sigh.

I pushed my bowl into the sink and stalked off to the coat closet where I wrenched my jacket off its hanger and pulled my tote off the floor.

"Gem, I'm sorry. I'm just trying to help. It isn't healthy to let life's rough spots stop you from living."

"Oh, just like when Mom left." I threw my arms up in the air. "You had no problems leaving us with baby-sitters and getting right back to your research. Or how about now? Do you even notice that Brian is gone?"

"What happened with your mother was different." His eyes grew cold. "You'll understand when you have kids of your own."

"Sure," I scoffed.

He held the front door open for me and I stormed off towards his car. I grabbed the door handle and took a deep breath. My father paused and smiled before getting into the driver's seat. The ignition started and the car rumbled to life.

Frantically, I rapped my knuckles against the plate glass window. When there was enough of an opening, I blurted, "I'll meet you there," and ran down the driveway.

I managed to get to the police station fifteen minutes after my dad, which I thought was great timing. He did not. I could tell by the number of times he checked his watch. This happened to work to my benefit since the detective on the case decided to spare me additional parental torture by keeping the interview short and sweet.

He explained that Ms. Halle was still in custody and was awaiting arraignment. The city was pressing charges but her lawyer had requested a mental health evaluation.

When I strode into gym class, with only ten

minutes left to the period, I had the pleasure of being the target of a barrage of dodge balls.

After changing out of my gym clothes, I met Charlotte in the hallway. She had opted for a more demure look of skin-tight jeans and a red velvet corset top. Definitely, the most clothing I'd seen her on her in school since fourth grade.

"Guess what?" she said.

"Your cleavage got cast as the lead in the school play?"

She had started developing first. I was still in the process of catching up.

"Shut up. No, really. Try to guess." Her pout was accentuated by high gloss pink lipstick.

"I hate it when you pout," I replied as I took out my wallet and shoved the rest of my bag in my locker.

"Well, aside from everyone talking about how you pulled a gun on the old librarian, I got the lead in the Broadway Revue."

"I did not. It was the other way around!" I slammed the door to my locker and went straight to the cafeteria, dragging Charlotte along.

"Just forget it, Gem."

"Easy for you to say." I joined the line and ended up with a bagel and cream cheese while Charlotte got her usual chicken Caesar salad.

"Let's go sit and you can vent to me all you like," she said.

As I was unwrapping the wax paper from my sandwich, someone elbowed me, sending my food underneath the table to my right.

"Please don't shoot," Allison said in mock terror. Her friends giggled like a cackle of hyenas. She parked herself on the bench while Matt took the empty spot next to her. I couldn't get to my lunch now even if I was willing to salvage it. Which I wasn't. The dust bunnies hiding under the baseboard heater and around the legs of the table extinguished any plans to follow the five-second rule.

"Hey, Matt," I said, my voice low.

He didn't reply and continued to inhale his meatball sub. I had always teased him about slowing down.

"Go away, Gemma," Allison snapped.

Not having enough money to get something else, I gave up on the thought of lunch and joined Charlotte, who had snagged a spot in the back near the emergency exit doors and the window with the view of the field.

"Why do you even listen to that bitch?" Charlotte asked, stabbing a crouton with her fork.

"I can't bring myself to be mean to her, no matter how badly I want to be. She's kind of one of the only connections to Brian I have left. Hopefully, she'll come around and stop being a perpetual hag." I sighed, picking a piece of grilled chicken from her bowl. "But I don't want to be a downer. Tell me about the play."

I managed to find a smile for her, which sent Charlotte into a flurry of dialogue about the audition after drama class and the casting list that had been tacked up on the bulletin board first thing this morning.

"Who knew so much work went into these things? But apparently Marcus really likes to put on a semi-professional production so he made everyone audition right away." Her demeanor had turned remarkably serious.

Marcus, whom we all knew was born Marc Torres, was a fixture in Harrisport, always with the same olive green scarf around his neck, regardless of the weather, and newsboy hat concealing his male pattern baldness. He directed the two school performances and ran the Roundabout Community Theater. This year, with the help of private funding, Principal Kelly was able to add a drama class to the curriculum.

"I'm proud of you, Char."

The rest of the day passed by in a slow wave of boredom. I spent my time analyzing my supernatural trip with Ian, who was nowhere to be found, and wondering if I should mention any of it to Charlotte.

I did perk up as soon as it was time for Mr. Flynn's class, excited at the prospect of getting any information out of him that would help get rid of the ghosts that were beginning to become more of a nuisance. I sat down and rummaged through the endless stuff in my bag in search of a pen.

"Hey." Out of the corner of my eye, I could make out Ian taking the same seat as yesterday.

"One sec. Got it." I held my ballpoint up in glee and ran my gaze from the tip of his black Chuck Taylors, over his fitted black cargos, to the waffle knit Henley until I reached those charming eyes. *They're greener today.*

"Good afternoon, class." Mr. Flynn marched into the classroom, satchel tucked under his arm, wearing white tennis shoes with dark wash jeans. *Eek.* "Today, we will begin our unit on Lies and Deceit with *Hamlet*." He walked over to the closet at the far end of the room and pulled out three stacks of paperback editions of Shakespeare's classic. "Allison, will you please help me distribute the books."

"My pleasure, Mr. Flynn." I could have sworn I heard her purr like a cat.

With the class busy, I leaned over to Ian and said, "About yesterday."

"What about it?" he said looking like he had just eaten the canary.

"Well," I was grasping for the right words, "what exactly was all that?"

He slid his desk closer to mine until I was able to make out the slight stubble on his jaw that trailed down his neck and smell the intoxicating scent that clung to him like second skin.

"You didn't seem eager to talk afterwards. I could only assume you weren't too impressed." He was still smiling, the only indication that I shouldn't take him seriously.

"Well, I was waiting for you to ditch the surfer look. I'm finding this 'you' a bit more irresistible." *Did that just come out of my mouth?*

His laughter was melodic but contained. "I'm more than willing to catch up later."

I groaned at my own disappointment. "I can't. I promised Mr. Flynn I would join his book club. For extra credit. I kind of need it, just in case."

"In case of what?"

"I fail my tests miserably."

Just then, Mr. Flynn rapped on his white board with a long metallic pointer and pulled up a series of slides. "These are your notes," he said in a militaristic tone. "Please copy them from the board. These are the only notes I want you taking. When everyone is finished, I expect your full attention. Then I will regale you with many fascinating facts about William Shakespeare."

The lecture ended up being more interesting than anticipated. Listening to his accent could have been the reason why Mr. Flynn had everyone enraptured, or his captivating theatrics. Nevertheless, time flew by and before long, the bell rang, signaling the end of the day.

"Here's my number." Ian slipped a scrap of paper into my tote and went for the door.

Allison was on his heels in moments. I watched as she shoved her way passed a few people just to get to him and then proceeded to paw at his arms. The look on his face remained benign in spite of the effort she was making, so I couldn't tell if he was interested in her or not.

My heart fluttered when he looked me in the eyes. And it just as quickly deflated when he nodded to Allison and let her lead him away.

"So, Miss Pope, are you ready for your first lesson?" I turned to Mr. Flynn's voice, who had taken Ian's place beside me. The class had quickly emptied out.

"Yes, I am." *At least I hope so.*

CHAPTER SIX

The so-called book club was noticeably lacking membership. Mr. Flynn and I were the only ones who stayed after class and my apprehension was evident.

"No worries. I can't be teaching you the secrets of the universe with an audience. I postponed it due to a scheduling conflict." He added air quotes.

"So, these secrets. How do you know about them?"

"You can consider me an expert of sorts." He stiffened his spine, unbuttoned his blazer to reveal his retro batman t-shirt and took on a boyish appearance with his goofy smile.

"Let's have it then." I was in the mood for a challenge.

"First things first. Let me allay your fears and tell you that the things you've seen lurking about are not a figment of your imagination."

"And that's supposed to make me feel better?" I asked.

"Yes, because you want to know that all your

faculties are intact when I tell you the rest."

"I'm listening."

"Brilliant! Let's begin." He got up and closed the door. When he sat back down, I understood why.

"That," he pointed to the black splotch on the wall, "is one of the Dybbuk."

"Of course," I singsonged.

"Cheeky, aren't you? Go ahead, go on and touch it."

"I don't think so." I scrunched my nose up in distaste.

"Miss Pope, let me explain to you how this is going to work. We are forming a relationship wherein you and I," he motioned his hand in a give and take gesture, "are working to a mutually beneficial goal." His eyebrows did a little dance as he said those words.

"And?"

"And in order for you to understand what this goal is in the scope of things, you need to do as I say."

"That doesn't sound like much of a partnership."

"It isn't. I'm the one holding most of the cards."

"Well, I may not know much," I replied, "but if my hand didn't trump yours, you wouldn't have me sitting here."

"Touché." He stood up and walked back towards the Dybbuk, placing his hand over what I could imagine as its head. "See," he continued. "Nothing. And this is why: the Dybbuk is a collective, a group of lost souls denied entrance to the Otherworld. Unable to find peace, they roam the Earth in search of a living thing, of their choosing, to attach themselves to. Once they have taken possession of this human, animal, or plant, they begin to alter that being's behavior to suit their needs."

"So why am I seeing them?" I asked.

"Usually, a trip to the Otherworld can make you a bit screwy. Crossing the veil can open your eyes just a bit wider."

"My accident." I rubbed the back of neck.

"Correct. But there is something else, which I can't figure out, and that's where you come in." He went over to his desk, unlocked the bottom drawer, and lifted out the   gray leather- bound tome I had glimpsed the day before. He set the book in front of me, keeping it closed with his hands clenched on either side of the worn cover.

"I need to know you're with me." His eyes pleaded with me and I couldn't help but stare at his beautiful lips while I thought of what to say next. *How could I say no?*

"I'm in."

Relief smoothed the worry lines from his forehead. He flipped the cover open and then began to pace.

"For some reason, this town has become a hotbed for these spirits. There is an abnormal amount of activity up until about a ten-mile radius beyond the city limits."

"Lucky us." I laughed, nervously.

"Indeed." He pointed to the title page. "And this is where we arrive at the *Lemegaton*."

"The what?"

"The Lesser Keys of Solomon. It contains the seventy-two true names of the demons that are said to have been bound to the king in servitude. Upon his death they were freed but this book is a legacy of his knowledge. Now all we need is to summon one and ask them why the Dybbuk have decided to come for the people of Harrisport."

I ran my hand over the pristine white parchment. "That easy, huh?"

The light extinguished from his face. "Unfortunately, things get a little complicated." He turned to the next page. "Let's not dwell on the negatives. Look here." He pointed to the large flower-shaped image. "The image on the top is some sort of cipher to break codes."

I pointed to the alphabet listed with its corresponding numerical value. "What's on the other pages?"

"The summoning names of these demons," he said, tapping on the list at the bottom. "Their position in the hierarchy, and their special talents."

"Demons?"

"And angels. There are two facets to sigil magic." He cleared his throat. "A sigil is a symbolic representation of a demon or an angel. One can draw upon the powers of a certain being or energy or one can summon the actual entity. To summon the actual demon, you need to know its true name."

"But why summon them at all if you can just draw its power?"

"For any number of reasons. The main one being etiquette."

"Seriously?" I was flabbergasted. "I must have misplaced my copy of Emily Post's *Guide to Demonic Encounters*."

His nostrils flared. "This is serious and I am only going to tell you this once. Otherwise, you cannot be trusted and I am wasting my time." He raised his voice. "When you create a sigil without purpose, there are severe repercussions. Energy is not created. It's all there but everything has its source and essentially any power you are using is channeled from elsewhere. You will under no circumstances draw power from unknown sources, is that clear?"

"Yeah, sure." I wasn't sure what I was agreeing to but I thought it prudent to keep things calm. "Can I ask a question?"

"Go ahead."

"What's your first name?"

"Thom." His curt reply filled me with a mixture of hope and doubt. I was fascinated by this energetic man who, in one fell swoop, had turned my world upside down with this forbidden knowledge. "Are you ready to continue?" he said.

"I think so."

"I hope I'm not keeping you from something more important."

"Like what? If you haven't noticed, there isn't much to do around here, and my after-school job is kind of on indefinite hiatus."

"Very well. Where was I?"

"Summoning demons," I reminded him.

"The next step is what is referred to as charging. The summoner focuses on these symbols until the power is drawn into them."

"So what exactly are these symbols?" I asked, excited by the knowledge that there was more to this world and comforted by the belief that Brian might be somewhere better. Not just gone.

"Yes. Let's first move a step back. The power of the written word is infinite. Letters have the capacity to affect our surroundings, aside from magic. Letters form words that in turn form ideas that every person projects into the universe. Once spoken. they carry the burden of returning to their source."

"Like karma."

"Exactly. You say something positive it boomerangs backs. Unfortunately, negativity accrues compound interest and returns threefold."

"So how does using this magic not rebound on the user?"

"That is where names come in to play. Using a demon's true name creates a conduit for the energy. The sorcerer knows where it's coming from and can funnel it back to its source. We'll get into the details another time. For now, I just want you to learn how sigils are drawn."

He ripped out a blank sheet from my binder and set it before me. Using the back of a pencil, he pointed to the rosette on the cover page of the book.

"This is a template." He placed the paper over the book and started circling letters and connecting them together with lines. "You start with the first letter of the name and draw a circle. From there you draw a line to each consecutive letter until you reach the end, where you close the sigil with a perpendicular line. Try one."

I scanned the list for anything familiar. I recognized one of the first ones from a cheesy horror movie I had seen once and placed my paper on top of Mr. Flynn's. Our fingers touched briefly and I noticed the warmth emanating from him. Pushing those thoughts away, I started at the A in the center ring, went back and forth between it and the Z, next was the E and finally the L.

"Azazel," I said and put the pen back on the table.

He picked it up and circled the symbol. "Good. After you have created the designated sigil, you encircle it and add a pentacle within. This will activate its ritual function."

"That's it?"

"Simply put, yes. But in time you will learn that when done with more finesse, sigils become more powerful and easier to control. That, however, only comes with practice."

"So where is he?"

"Azazel?" He chuckled. "He's not very likely to show up. The demon of sorcery would need a lot more pomp and circumstance."

"So demons can control whether or not they appear?"

"To some extent. Otherwise, every Goth kid around would be able to summon a prince of hell. Keep in mind that it is prudent to be courteous. A demon will act as civilly as you treat them."

"Why bother showing up at all?"

"They usually want something and are always on the lookout for a good bargain. This leads me to rule number two: never promise a demon something that you cannot deliver. Otherwise, the ball is in their court and you are in debt to them until they see fit to release you."

"Sounds serious."

"It usually is."

"Any other numbered rules?" I asked.

"One more for now. Always store your sigils in a

safe place and never destroy them."

"So how do they actually work?"

"That's for our next lesson. For now, take the grimoire and practice. Familiarize yourself with those we will possibly be dealing with. We need to get a handle on the Dybbuk flying about."

"Cool."

"And with that I must go."

"Already?" I checked my watch. It was already six thirty. "I just don't understand one thing. Why do you need me?"

"You can see them," he said in a matter-of-fact way. "Only humans who have the sight can harness the power of the demonic arts." He grabbed his satchel and was gone before I could reply. I sat there eyeing the tracing in front of me, curious about my ability to help Thom. *What was I getting myself into and how come he could see them?*

CHAPTER SEVEN

The house was empty and dark. I flicked the switches on the control panel in the kitchen, illuminating the pendant lamps that hung over the breakfast bar and the recessed lighting that staggered through the small formal dining area down to the sunken living room that opened up to the backyard.

I opened the freezer, took out a pizza, and tossed it into the oven. After setting the temperature, I sprawled out on the couch and turned on the television with the intention of finishing my homework at a normal hour.

My eyes wandered from the flashing screen to the page of math equations I was loathe to finish to my bag, thrown casually onto the round glass coffee table. Its contents had spilled out, and I could see the corner of the grimoire.

He did say I needed to practice.

I pushed my work aside with promises that it would get done in homeroom and placed the antiquated text in my lap. The calligraphy was beautiful and the illustrations fierce–pictures depicting beings that were part human, part animal, riding astride beasts, brandishing vicious weapons, baring their teeth. There were kings, princes, dukes, marquises, and counts, each with their own army of lesser demons. Their job descriptions ranged from inciting jealousy to deforming the young.

"Barbatos, Duke of the Legion of Thirty, Eighth Demon of the Lesser Key. Yields the power to speak with animals. Sees both Futures and Pasts. Uncovers that which has been hidden with Magick."

Interesting.

When I heard the jangle of keys in the door, I ran to my room and shoved the mystical book under my bed, adjusting the bed skirt so that it didn't look like I was hiding something under there. Back in the kitchen the oven timer chimed that dinner was ready.

"Hi Dad," I said, grabbing the mitts and pulling the hot pie of melted cheesy goodness out of the hot oven and setting it on a trivet.

"Hey, pumpkin. How was school?"

"Fine."

He unloaded the armful of groceries onto the counter and placed a kiss on the top of my head. I helped put the canned goods and boxed meals away while waiting for dinner to cool. I slid two slices of pizza onto a plate, grabbed a bottle of seltzer from the fridge, and made my way down the hall.

I paused in front of Brian's door, the one directly across from mine. *Change of plans.* I toed the door open and settled into the brown leather bean chair he used while playing video games. Nothing was out of place. Everything was just as it was the day we went out.

"I promise you, he always leaves it unlocked," Jenny said, as we all piled out of her tiny car and started up the winding road that led from the cabin to the shed by the water. Somehow, Brian and I, the tallest out of the four, were stuck in the back with no legroom for the two-hour drive to Lake George.

"Race you." I tagged Brian and catapulted forward, the soles of my sneakers skidding on the gravel.

"You're no match for me," he said, yanking on my ponytail and throwing me off balance.

When we had all reached the large blue shed, Jenny tried the door. "It's stuck," she said.

"Let the man try," Brian said. Brian gave it a good pull.

"It's not stuck, Jenny. It's locked. Did you think to mention it to your dad that we were coming?"

"He never locks the shed. Just the cabin." She pulled out her cellphone. "Let me call him. I'm sure there's a spare key somewhere."

"I'll be right back. I think Jenny has some blankets in the trunk. We can just hang out," Mimi said.

Jenny never reached her father. We spent the afternoon lazing around on the grass behind the dock instead, watching the boats speed by and the sun sparkle on the water's crystal surface.

When Brian and Mimi made up some story about looking for some skipping stones, I decided to put Jenny on the spot. "What's going on with them?" I asked, when I was sure Mimi and Brian were out of earshot.

She grimaced. "What do you mean?" Jenny was a terrible liar.

"Spill it," I said. "I've been watching them give each other googly eyes all day."

"Mimi said she wanted to tell you herself. She said she wouldn't do it if she didn't get your permission."

"Do what?"

"Date Brian."

"What do you mean, date Brian? He has a girlfriend. Not that I like her all that much but Brian isn't the type to cheat."

"He told Mimi that if she was willing, he'd break it off with Allison. She said she would think about it and told me that she wanted to ask you first."

I wiped the crumbs on my jeans, left the plate on the desk and crawled into a fetal position beneath the plaid patchwork quilt of Brian's bed. The sheets still smelled like him. I turned my face into the pillow and inhaled. *Not too deeply. Can't have the scent of him disappear just yet.* I clenched the edges of the blanket. Tears streamed down my face and I opened my mouth wide in a silent scream.

It was midnight when I woke up. I picked up the dish of stale leftover crusts and went out to drop it in the kitchen sink.

The television glowed but the volume had been muted. With no sign of my dad, I padded to my own room and shut the door. I got out of my clothes and into leggings and a sweatshirt. I lay in bed, thinking about the last few days and how the outrageous events had to be part of a major, concussive hallucination.

Leaning over my bed, I grappled in the dark for the book. When I felt it beneath my fingers, the doubtful thoughts in my head melted away. I relaxed back into the mattress and went back to sleep.

* * *

"How's it hanging?" I asked Ghosty, as I adjusted my position to stretch out my hamstrings.

As usual, the black Dybbuk, as Mr. Flynn referred to these inky spirits, sat motionless on the grass. After seeing Allison's strange behavior and Ms. Halle's psychotic break, I knew I should keep a distance but for some reason, this one felt different. It felt more lost, not as malicious.

When I got back into the house after my run, my dad was already gone. So said the hot pink sticky note on the fridge with the words Be Home Late.

After the well-deserved shower, I stood in front of the open closet, staring at my clothes. I caught my reflection in the mirror and began to trace the ridges of my scar that ran from the middle of my shin, over my knee and to the top of my thigh. *Jeans it is.*

Pleased with my choice of a red plaid shirt and boot cut denim, I made sure to retrieve the grimoire from beneath my bed before starting out for school. Charlotte, my rock, was waiting for me at our usual spot.

"Hey, Gem." She was already wearing her cheerleading uniform beneath the matching navy letter cardigan.

"We need to talk," I said, not able to resist the urge to spill all the nitty-gritty details of the past two days.

"Let's go." She checked her phone. "Ten minutes to homeroom." She took me by the hand and dragged me to the girl's bathroom.

She dropped her mammoth-sized velvet purse on the counter and took out her make-up arsenal. The black vinyl case had a handle and everything, and was filled to the top with every mascara, powder, eyeshadow, and liner known to woman.

"Want some?" she said, handing me a tube of mascara.

"Isn't that unhygienic?"

"It's new. Can you believe I entered one of those online giveaways and I won a box full of new make-up." Her smile brightened the room. "Take it. You could use some."

"Uh thanks. I think."

"So?" she asked, swiping an extra layer of cherry red gloss on her lips. "What's up?"

Chalk it up to nerves or good sense but I suddenly thought it unwise to mention anything dealing with the supernatural.

"It's Ian," I said. "I think I really like him. A lot."

"Ooh. I've seen him. Definitely a keeper," she gushed.

"I just don't know if I'm ready to get into that yet."

"Listen, Gem," she said. "You just have to jump in. No one is going to hold it against you."

"They already are. Matt won't even talk to me."

"They'll all get over it." She turned to me and grabbed both sides of my face. "Come to practice today. Just watch. No pressure."

"Okay," I said, unsure if I was sincere or not.

The bell rang through the intercoms. I put my arms around Charlotte and squeezed.

"And you better get your hands on Ian before Allison does. I've seen her trying," she added. "Wow, I got to get to class."

Before walking out, I spent an extra minute in front of the mirror until finally I gave in and decided to put on some of the makeup Charlotte had unloaded on me.

When I walked into homeroom, I was surprised to see Ian there. Everyone else had already clustered in groups, either copying homework or deep in conversation. Mr. Flynn acknowledged my presence, checked off my name on the roster, and went right back to attacking a stack of papers without saying so much as a word.

I didn't let his mood sink into mine and put on a smile with a bit of fake confidence. I psyched myself up for what I was about to say to Ian. "So, I was thinking we could catch up after school today."

That wasn't too hard.

"Oh hey, I'm sorry, Gemma, but I was planning on going to try-outs. You could come watch."

This was a problem. I really didn't want to say no and not just because he looked yummy in his hunter green zip-front sweater. I needed some sort of answers from him if I didn't want to implode from the stress of not having anyone to talk to about any of the surreal experiences I've been having. "I'm not sure," I said.

"Come on. Don't start playing hard to get." His grin was full of mischief.

"It's not that, I swear. I just haven't been on that field since last year. My brother used to be quarterback."

His face remained blank.

"Before he died," I added.

His expression softened.

"Why don't you come watch and then you can tell me all about him after, over some food. My treat." He placed his hand over mine and I practically melted.

"Yeah. That sounds nice."

The day went on as usual, including the shoves in between classes and snide remarks that seemed to be my new normal. During English, Mr. Flynn was evasive, never glancing my way and not calling on me the couple of times I actually raised my hand. So I spent the hour sneaking glances at Ian, watching the way he would spin his pen around in one hand or how his face would take on a far-off look like his mind was millions of miles away.

"I'll see you soon," Ian said when the bell rang.

"Yeah."

"Great." He smiled and took off. "Gotta run."

It was pretty lonely out on the bleachers. Everyone there was trying out for the team or squad or watching from the sidelines. I was happy to see that Charlotte had her hands full, weeding through the freshmen for potential junior varsity candidates.

I spent my time scrolling through news articles, even though the grimoire was burning a proverbial hole in my bag.

National:

Seventy-six dead in train derailment outside OK City.
Eight point two earthquake in Japan threatens tsunami.
Syria declares martial law in wake of rebel incursions.

Local:

Harrisport librarian charged, mental health a concern.
Local pet hoarder found dead, 200 cats.

Entertainment:

Kat Von D engaged. Again?

An hour went by before Ian sat beside me, freshly showered and wearing a black military cut jacket, the collar upturned and framing his strong jaw. "How was it?" he asked.

"You were great. I mean, I couldn't tell which one was you after all the helmets went on but I'm sure that you did a great job."

"No, I mean, how was it being here. You seemed nervous about it."

The sun was beginning to set, spraying veins of oranges and pinks beneath the stretches of cirrus clouds that accentuated the curvature of the sky. I thought about how I hadn't really had anyone to talk to about Brian or the ghosts. At least Ian and I had shared a common, albeit freaky, trip through the matrix.

"I couldn't go to his funeral," I muttered. "Brian's. I was awake after the accident but during my surgery, I slipped into a coma. For two weeks. My father buried him. The whole town apparently showed up. Just not me."

"The two of you were close, huh?"

"Twinsies." I laughed, trying hard not to cry.

"Let's get out of here." He took me by the hand and we walked away.

We ended up not far from the empty lot with the magical mystery tree, at a diner called McCloone's, which was known for its short segment on one of those food channel specials about local eateries and their strange delicacies.

"Try the mac and cheese," I said as he scanned the menu. "It's famous. Or the bluefish sandwich."

"Mac and cheese it is." He smiled.

The restaurant was a throwback to a much earlier era. It had made its mark as a popular truck stop and kept to its roots by only making necessary improvements to its vintage chromed-out railcar housing. This meant that there were only about ten tables in all. Another few weeks and the place would be packed with tourists making stops along their fall-foliage driving tours.

The pink and blue neon lights of the sign outside streaked across the window pane and crept onto our booth. I hugged my tote while we waited for the waitress.

"You going to stay a while?" he asked.

"Sorry?"

"You're still wearing your jacket. And by the way you're clutching your bag, it looks like you're gonna bolt any minute now." His laugh was warm and deep.

"Oh, I'm sorry." I grinned and placed my bag down, along with my thin black windbreaker. "Habit."

"Hey guys, what can I get you today?" our waitress, Missy, asked. She was wearing the new McCloone's logo t-shirts that Harry the owner was making all the employees wear since making their national television debut.

"The lady says I should try the mac and cheese," Ian said, the ever-present grin on his face.

"Good choice. What about you, Gem?"

"I'll have the cheeseburger, well done."

She cringed. "Are you sure? You know how Harry gets when people ask for it that way."

"Just tell him back there that I like it charred to perfection. And the customer is always right."

"Alright. But consider this fair warning if he comes running out the kitchen with a spatula."

The three of us laughed as Missy went to put in

our orders.

"So," I started, "are we going to talk about the enormous elephant in the room?"

"Where?" He turned his head in surprise.

"You know what I mean."

"Well, if you're talking about our little joy ride, it's difficult to explain."

"Try me," I said, leaning my elbow on the table. *Wow, his eyes are really magnificent.*

"Suppose there are places in this world that are hidden from most. Other dimensions. And to see them you just have to know where to look." He pulled a breadstick out from the small basket Missy had set before us.

"So how did you find them?"

"Someone else showed me. Just like I showed you."

"Why me?" I asked, as a flush of embarrassment warmed my cheeks.

"You seemed a bit lost. I thought you could use some fun."

Missy interrupted us with our plates but quickly left to take care of a new patron. I took a bite of my food and thought about Ian's last words.

"You might be right," I continued. "But I wasn't always like this."

"Losing family can do that." He looked down at his food and struggled with some extra gooey strands of cheese.

I snorted the mouthful of water as I watched the goofy way he tried grasping at the unseen food hanging from his chin.

"So what about your family?" I moved on to my fries.

"What are you dipping your fries in?" he asked.

"Tartar sauce."

"That's just weird."

"This is a judgment-free zone," I said, squaring off the width of our table, unable to control the fit of laughter that followed.

"I'm staying with my uncle for senior year. After that, who knows?"

"I have no clue what I'm doing." I stirred the straw around my cup aimlessly. "Brian always had the answers."

"There is way too much pressure. How does anyone expect us to know what we're going to do with our lives? Most thirty year olds can't move out of their parent's house." He spoke with passion, which made him seem more mature for his age.

"At least you have an escape route." I took another bite of my food and enjoyed the way it warmed my stomach. *They don't call it comfort food for nothing.*

"Don't worry," he said. "I'll teach you everything I know. We'll catch another trip soon."

The invitation left my mind filled with wild dreams that he would take me with him wherever it was he was going, and I was starting to feel free once again.

CHAPTER EIGHT

The next day, for the first time in a long while, I woke up with a smile on my face. And then I felt guilty for it. I lingered in bed, savoring the pleasure of Saturday morning as I thought back to my evening with Ian; the small talk made over dessert and coffee, the walk home where I did most of the talking, and the tension as he walked me to the door. I sighed. *I should have just kissed him.*

I caught up on some homework and tried my best to act normal for my father, who had decided to use one of his rare days away from the office to do yard work.

When my eyes began to cross at the sight of ellipses and hyperboles, I picked up the phone and called Charlotte. "Hey, I'm bored," I said.

"You didn't look too bored last night."

"What does that mean?"

"Stop being so paranoid, Gem. I saw you and Ian walk into McCloone's, that's all."

"It was nice. We talked. He walked me home."

"Whatever it is, it's good. At least it'll give Matt a hint."

"He's been hanging on Allison ever since I told him off the other day. He's over it."

"I heard from Emma who heard from Candice, whose boyfriend Gage is on the team and overhead him telling Scott, that he was definitely going to get you back."

"Fat chance." I sighed.

"Oh wow," she squealed on the other end. "I just got two VIP passes to The Creeps tonight. You in?"

"That concert's been sold out for months. Were you born with a lucky gene?"

"I know. I can't believe it either," she said, the pitch of her voice rising higher. "Sheila just texted me saying she got into a fight with Patrick and that she only bought the stupid tickets because it's his favorite band. Not hers."

"I think I'll pass. It's a long walk to Foxwoods." Not even one of my favorite live acts could get me over my current vehicular phobia.

"Oh Gem, I wish you would tell me how I can help."

"You're doing just fine, Charlotte. Just be yourself," I said. "Bye, Char."

As soon as the conversation was over, I went to work practicing sigils, knowing that it was the type of busy work that kept my mind blissfully blank. The demonic world was filled with pretty strange names: Leviathan, Beelzebub, Gaap, Vual.

There was no way anyone could commit all the information to memory so I took great care in keeping my best sigils in a notebook, just as Mr. Flynn suggested. When it was break time, I walked over to the window and looked out as I stretched my neck. From the corner of my eye, I glimpsed a cluster of black shadows sailing across the tops of the trees.

I hope there really is something to all this. I have a feeling we're going to need it.

On Monday, Mr. Flynn stopped me before homeroom. "I'd like you to stay after class today, Miss Pope." His left eyebrow arched in anticipation of an answer.

"Sure," I replied. "I just didn't know what you wanted. I mean, Friday you weren't really paying any attention to me."

Great job running your mouth off, Gemma.

"Ah, attention." There was amusement in his tone and I couldn't look him in the eye as he stared down at me. "I gave you an assignment. I hope you've done your homework."

He walked into the classroom before I had a chance to redeem some of my pride. I stood in the hallway for a few minutes to regain my bearings. Mr. Flynn had a way of setting me off balance, and I kind of liked it.

Late that afternoon I was excited to show Mr. Flynn what I had been working on. Maybe it would make up for sounding like an idiot earlier.

"We need to find someone who's gone a bit rogue," Mr. Flynn said as he fingered the pages of the grimoire.

"Rogue?" I asked.

"Flying under the radar. Not checking in with superiors. Toying with humans without following proper protocol. Avoiding contact with other demons of your rank." He picked up the large book and moved to his desk, where he sat on the edge, keeping one foot on the ground.

"There's protocol for tormenting people? Like paperwork?"

"Nothing like that, unless you've entered into a contract. But the Dybbuk are gaining strength and that kind of coordination could only mean they are getting support from down below. We need to find someone who'll spill the beans."

He was back to his giddy boyish self, rubbing his hands in excitement. I made a show of flipping through some of my practice sigils that I had worked on all day Sunday but in reality I was peeking through my fingers and checking out his ass as he reached over to his jacket. *Stop it, he's a teacher. Not really, he's student teaching, that's different. Yeah, that's so much different, Gemma.*

"Is there some sort of demon social media page out there? We can check who hasn't updated their status in a while."

"I'm afraid not." He chuckled. "We've got to do it the old-fashioned way. A good old summoning."

"Why would any of them help?"

"They aren't automatons. Nor are they evil. They just happen to be on the side opposite of God's."

"Do tell. Sounds interesting and deeply philosophical."

He grinned and pulled one of the desks in front of mine so that we faced each other. "When God

78

created the world, it took him six days. The angels were jealous when He created man in His image. They were even angrier when He created the demons. Now they had two other species to contend with for His attention. The end of the sixth day drew near and He had only begun to form these beings. They were to be like angels, their counterparts. For every good deed a man did, there would be an angel praising him before the gates of heaven. Now there would also be demons monitoring evil doers and preventing unworthy souls from returning to the source. Between the angels and the demons, each soul would be judged fairly upon its return.

"But God didn't have a chance to complete them soon enough. On the seventh day, God rested, leaving the creatures in an agonizing stasis. The angels thought God cruel for leaving divine beings in such a state. They were suffering at the expense of the humans and they worried that they too could be forsaken by Him for these inferior creatures that roamed the planet.

"The angels expected God to resume his work on Sunday. He didn't. Days passed and He watched over Eden with fascination and did nothing else. A group of angels, Lucifer among them, was outraged. They insisted God complete His work but he refused. He said that man would not sin so gravely to deserve such harsh judgment. There would be no need for them. The angels argued that He granted humans free will and that in itself would be their downfall.

" 'It wouldn't be fair,' Lucifer argued, 'to allow the demons to persist in their current form. Man will disappoint You. It is inevitable.'

"For that God hurled these rebellious angels to the Earth. Ultimately, He was forced to complete His work on the demons after Adam and Eve ate the forbidden fruit but by then the fallen angels had organized themselves, calling themselves the Watchers. Their mission was to maintain balance in the world by exploiting man's faults and taking as many souls away from the source as they could, thus proving God wrong. They joined forces with the demons who, by now, were deeply embittered by their painful birth and happily submitted to the Watchers' hierarchy. Watchers and demons have worked like that ever since. You could call that place hell - the opposite of returning to the source."

Mr. Flynn finished the story. "So, what do you think?" he asked.

"Makes things a little less black and white. There doesn't seem to be much difference between the two sides."

"Nothing is perfect. God also lets things slide a bit and takes in souls that are unworthy of heaven. The two factions are in a perpetual war to keep things equal but it's the system that's in place. And it's worked more or less for thousands of years."

"So why would the Dybbuk agree to be used like this and why now?"

"My guess is that they would rather be stuck in hell than roam this planet any longer. Each one is a soul that has not been sentenced yet. Nor will they ever be. Their sins are enough to keep them out of heaven and they usually have something tethering them to this world - unfinished business of sorts, so they cannot even choose to side with hell."

"Sounds like a loophole."

"It very well could be. And we should get on sorting this trouble out." He grabbed the stack of paper I had carefully arranged in a separate folder and looked through my work.

"I'm not so sure about this demon-summoning thing. Maybe an angel would be better for a first try?" I was afraid that he would think I was being silly.

"I guess we could give it a shot." He smiled. "We'll meet again tomorrow." His voice was formal again.

"Sure. Anything I should work on, Mr. Flynn?" I waited expectantly as he collected his things and put on his awful wool-lined denim jacket.

"Figure out which angel it is we'll be summoning," he said, standing at the entrance. He made no move to leave and continued watching me. I sat, not moving a muscle, having a difficult time making eye contact. I finally looked away with the excuse of putting my papers away.

"One more thing," he added.

I looked up.

"Call me Thom."

When I was sure he was gone, I smiled.

In breaking news, it has now been confirmed that members of the infamous cult, Brotherhood of the Spear, have committed mass suicide on their private compound located in North Dakota. Sources tell us that sixty adults are known to have been staying at the secluded complex…

….only two people are known to have survived the crash. No word yet on their condition.

….record level rains in Taipei has caused massive flooding and mudslides.

I sat on the couch tying my laces as my father watched, engrossed in the day's news coverage.

"See you later, Dad," I said, getting ready to leave for school.

"Hold on a minute, Gem. Sit down," he said, turning off the television. "I'm a little concerned about you spending so much time out of the house during the week."

"Wait, since when?" I laughed at the absurdity.

"It was a close call the other day at the library. Things are getting a little crazy lately, even in Harrisport. I need to know that you're safe at home."

"You get home after I do. What difference does it make? Pick up a phone if you're that nervous," I added.

"Gemma, watch your tone. You know it's hard to make phone calls while I'm in the lab."

"What about my book club?"

Take that. In your face. Can't make me stop doing school stuff. Nah nah na nah nah.

"School, book club. Then home. It's enough that you're out there walking. What's going to happen when it starts getting dark out?"

"I don't need you to plan out my day for me. I don't need rides to school. I don't need curfews. I've been handling all that on my own."

All I need is for you to put your arms around me and tell me you still love me.

I grabbed my bag and slammed the door behind me.

Ghosty was standing on the porch today.

"Hey you," I said with a salute, and off I went into the foggy distance, trying to forget the helpless look on my father's face.

CHAPTER NINE

"Gemma, awesome. You're here." Charlotte said, chipper as usual.

"Nice outfit." I had to give her props for the long-sleeved lavender lace top and burgundy wool shorts she was wearing today.

"You look super too, Gem."

I looked down at my boots, jeans, and cotton top. There was a whole section of my closet that lay dormant. Skirts were off the menu because of my huge ugly scar. The rest didn't feel like mine. It belonged to a happier, more carefree Gemma, who liked attention and spending time in the morning trying to impress.

"So listen," she said as she checked herself in the mirror she had strategically placed on her locker door, and slathered on another thick layer of gloss. "I decided that this year I want a sleepover party for my birthday."

"What's the catch?" I asked, knowing that she

always had her mom and dad bend backwards as payment for being stuck with them for parents.

She laughed and threw her arms around me with enough vigor to send us both crashing to the floor.

"Can you two dykes take it somewhere private?"

I heard Allison's voice and then looked up, watching for any sign of the Dybbuk but only a pair of ice cold eyes stared back. Her and her usual gaggle of followers stood around us in a fit of hysterics.

"That's a pretty homophobic comment, coming from the student body president," I muttered under my breath.

"Just try complaining, freak." She spat on the floor next to me and walked away, her clucking friends not far behind.

"Nothing crazy. Just a few girls. And my again best friend," Charlotte said, bringing me back to our conversation. The recent altercation with Allison hadn't even fazed her.

I wish I could do that.

"Sounds fun." I was eager to get Allison out of my head and remembered what I had originally wanted to ask Charlotte. "How was the concert? You weren't here yesterday."

"Super! But I totally needed to catch up on my sleep." She put the cap back on the tube. "Oh, and I got to meet the band. How cool?"

She scrolled through the pictures on her phone and gave me a play by play of the entire night.

"Maybe you could trip on some free pedicures next time." I laughed.

"I'll see what I can do. Just. For. You," she replied, tapping my nose to the beat. The bell rang and I watched Charlotte falter a bit on her five-inch platform wedge booties. *There had to be sensible shoes somewhere in her closet.*

Thing didn't get interesting until lunchtime. Charlotte had rescheduled a test she missed while nursing some post-concert laryngitis, so I was left to fend for myself.

"There's my girl," Ian said, taking the seat in front of me.

My girl. Ohmygod.

"Hey, yourself."

Could I play cool or what?

"I was thinking," his voice was dark and playful, "that we could take another trip soon."

"I'm in," I said, sounding a bit eager. I chose to ignore the entire conversation with my dad from this morning and instead focus on the way that Ian's black-collared shirt made his neck look extra delicious.

"How's tomorrow sound?" he said in between bites of his pizza.

"Great."

"So what's the deal between you and Queen Bee over there?" he said, motioning to Allison who was busy exercising power over her table full of subjects.

"She was my brother's girlfriend." I left it at that.

"There's got to be more to it than that."

"Well," I cleared my throat, "Allison, like everyone else in town, my father included, thinks that the car accident that killed my brother and my two best friends is my fault."

"Why would they think that?"

"I was the one driving." I kept busy with the salad I

had gotten in an effort to eat healthier.

Would dousing it in Ranch dressing be okay?

"And do you think it was your fault?" he asked.

I shrugged my shoulders and didn't answer. He didn't look very convinced by the story.

Senior year was on its own collision course, losing most of its purported luster on the first day. My thoughts were caught in a constant tangle of Ian's smile and worry over what evil intentions the smoke-filled spirits of the Dybbuk had for this town.

Alone again with Mr. Flynn, or should I say Thom, I decided to make a case for the angel I had picked. There was no way I was going to summon a demon if I could get out of it. Visions of red-skinned, horned creatures taunted me at the mere thought.

"So, after reading through the book and doing some research online-" I said.

"Are you daft?" he interrupted, his vowels becoming longer creating a more brogueish accent. "Was this in between searching for Katy Perry's favorite color and pictures of Brad Pitt's arse?"

"Listen." I smacked the desk and stood up, meeting him eye to eye. "I have had with people either telling me what to do or telling me off. I am trying to help. So we're going to lay some ground rules."

Stay strong Gem. Don't wimp out, no matter how scary angry he gets.

His pupils dilated and his jaw became stiff.

This was becoming a showdown.

Don't flinch. Don't flinch. Don't flinch.

The line of his mouth began to curve into a smile.

"Go ahead, Gemma. Tell me about your rules."

Teacher. Teacher. Hot Teacher. Not really. He's just a sub and, technically, he's still in college.

For a moment, I lost myself in the endless pools of Thom's dark eyes but the smirk on his face reminded me that he had just dissed me for my unconventional demonic research methodology.

"One, you have to take my work seriously. I know I'm kind of new to this whole magic thing but I'm at least giving it my best shot."

"Keep going," he said.

"Two, you need to try to be a little more predictable. Between barking orders and ignoring me, I can't tell if all this is real. And three, you can't just run off."

"Pardon?"

"You do it all the time. Say something completely earth- shattering then pick up your stuff and leave."

The clock ticked off a new minute.

"Very well." He circled my desk. I could feel the heat of his body radiating behind me. "But let's make something clear."

His breath tickled the hairs on my neck.

"You will help me at all costs. That means getting your wee little head out of bed at dawn and working long after our little meetings. And this stays between the two of us."

Before I could reply, I caught a glimpse of something black in the corner of my eye. The Dybbuk that had faithfully clung to the wall all week long had detached itself in a flurry of activity, circling around itself until it sped out the door.

I followed it out into the hall and continued down to the end where a large picture window stood overlooking the grassy knoll in front of the school. I looked to my left and right where the hallways continued on, spanning the width of the building.

"Run off, did he?" Thom said. "Curious."

"Is there some way to track them?" I continued to stare outside and caught a flash of discolored shadow weaving through the parking lot. "Over there," I said, pointing to the spot that was now empty.

"They can't be caught if they don't want to be." He placed a hand my shoulder and after a few moments, the heat from his touch became unbearable.

I jerked away and rubbed the spot beneath my shirt, which now felt raw.

"What was that?" I shrieked.

"Let's get to work," he said, his face now a mask of indifference.

In the classroom, it was back to business. I didn't ask about what voodoo powers he may have and he didn't mention them. Instead, he went back to trying not to taunt me too much.

"Please regale me with your findings. I have spent a great deal of time combing through ancient texts. I'd like to know what you came up with from your Google."

It was now or never. If I didn't pull this off with confidence, there was no way I was having a say about anything with him. Ever.

"Ambriel. I figured the angel of communication would, you know, communicate." I flipped open the grimoire to the angel's page. The letters of his name were gilded and illustrated in colored inks, like the ones found in hand-illuminated Bibles from the Middle Ages. They were vertically placed on the left

89

hand side while on the right, small neat calligraphy went on to describe the angel's rank, tasks and abilities along with, what I had discovered online, *yes, online*, was an incantation.

"Let's give a go," Thom replied. "Oh and before I forget." He walked over to his desk and pulled out a package, which he dumped in front me. "That's for you." The way he tapped on the brown paper wrapped box exuded impatience. Anyone else would have me seeing red. From him, it was endearing.

The folds on the edges were so crisp that they must have been scored. I stuck my finger beneath the clear tape and inched it open with great care. After getting all three sides done, I peeled away the paper, revealing a stack of more paper. Cream-colored index card-sized parchment that was as smooth as suede beneath my fingertips.

"It's real goat hide." The pride in his voice was unmistakable.

"Um, wow." I was starting to sound like Charlotte.

"It will absorb the ink better." His elbow brushed my arm as he drew one leaf away from the stack and placed it in front of me with reverence. I felt the warmth rolling off his body.

"Thanks."

"Go ahead." He placed a silver nib fountain pen in front of me.

I picked it up with the same care he used when setting it down and turned to the page with the sigil wheel. I placed a piece of scrap paper over it and circled each of the letters of the angel's name in order. A-M-B-R-I-E-L. Then I drew straight lines attaching the small rings together, doubling back between R and I because of the close proximity between the two on the chart.

"Good." Thom's voice broke the silence. "When you get a little practice in you, you'll know how to add some flourishes. It'll make you stronger and root the power more firmly."

I then took the piece of parchment and copied my design carefully on it, picking up my hand after each smooth stroke to avoid smudges.

"What now?" I asked.

"For an angel, just recite the incantation. For a demon, there's a bit more involved. Summoning circle, candles. Think of *The Craft*."

"Movies? You're on my case for consulting modern man's version of the encyclopedia and you're telling me to get my ritual information from a cheesy, yet very watchable, 90s movie?"

"Just as a familiar reference point." He laughed. "But surprisingly accurate."

"You said yourself that angels and demons are pretty much the same. Why the difference between the summonings?"

He ran a hand through his hair. It settled in a haphazard mop to the left side of his head.

"They're more two sides of the same coin. Demons need the summoning circle to keep them contained until you give them leave to depart. Angels always follow orders and return to where they were prior to the summoning."

"Then I'm glad we're calling an angel," I said.

"Let me know what you think after you speak to him."

I brushed away the confusion at his last remark and

went back to the page with Ambriel's incantation and started at the words.

"Out loud," Thom said with an insisting nudge.

How the hell was he so warm?

I was more embarrassed than anything but decided it was probably easier reciting the ridiculous chant than invoking the wrath of Thom.

"I conjure and pray ye, O Angels of God, to come unto my aid. Come and behold the Signs of Heaven. This being done, let Ambriel arise."

The room remained still. Nothing happened. We sat motionless until I began losing feeling in my leg. I leaned over to give my shin a good rub when Thom yanked at my arm.

"Sit up," he hissed.

"What's your problem?" I asked, bumping my head on the underside of my desk. I was ready to tear him a new one, when the new presence in the room caught my attention.

"Ambriel at your service." There was a mock tip of a nonexistent hat from a squat, freckle-faced red-headed boy who couldn't have been older than eleven. The lapel of his white robe lay crooked on his neck and the hem was in tatters. His feet were bare but clean.

"I was kind of expecting a bit more," I blurted.

"And I was expecting Angelina Jolie." He eyed Thom sitting next to me, winked, and then turned back to me. "Like I said, I'm at your service." He began chewing his nails while I tried to regain some composure.

"So. Ambriel. Um. I was hoping you could help me with a little problem we have going on here."

"Not likely," he answered.

"Why not?" I said, unable to hide the anger in my voice.

"I don't get involved. Sorry." He began walking around the room.

"Why not?"

"Not much finesse in this one," he said to Thom.

"Excuse me, I'm right here." I was starting to sound like a child and decided that a deep breath would do me a world of good.

"Look, girly," Ambriel started. I wanted to wring his little neck. "I can't help you. None of us can. Angels have a strict 'stay out of human business' rule. It would interfere with free will."

"Free will? But the Dybbuk think it's fine to take over other people's bodies and make them go crazy and do things that aren't right," I said.

He put his open palms up in the air in the universal sign of *I can't do anything about it.*

Before I could rail against the lack of justice in this world, the skin on the inside of my wrist began to tingle. I scrunched up the sleeve and watched as the pricking sensation intensified. "What the f-!" I screamed.

A dark mark began to take shape on the thin pale skin, darkening bit by bit until it finally came into focus.

"Tell me this comes off," I continued.

"A small price to pay to be a sorceress. It's a badge of honor." The impudent little mother effer snapped his fingers and disappeared, leaving a hideous stamp of evidence like a calling card on my skin. His sigil.

I scowled and then turned to Thom, letting him

know how pissed off I was at my new tattoo.

It was late by the time I got home. The furniture was cloaked in the blanketing darkness of shorter days. I almost wished to find my dad waiting with his arms crossed and his face in a grimace. The biggest disappointment of the day, though, was Ambriel's refusal to help. Thom had said as much with his retelling of the creation story but I wouldn't believe it until I had seen it. He had known it wasn't going to work. *And he let you do things your way, to be fair. He also left out the bit about getting a tattoo with each new sigil I create.*

I grabbed a stack of cookies from the pantry, forgoing a more traditional frozen dinner. The summoning had drained more energy than I had noticed and the fatigue was settling into my bones. I toed off my boots, kicked them to the side, and headed straight for the bathroom, pausing shortly in front of Brian's room. Thinking of all the crumbs I got on the carpet the other day, I decided against wallowing in my sorrows there and instead went to run the water.

After a bath and another tower of snickerdoodles, I lay in bed, thinking back to Ian's invitation for another ride on the roller coaster of the absurd.

Remembering the scrap of notebook paper he had scribbled on, I went back to the coat closet for my bag, flustered at the idea of storing Ian's number in my phone.

After keying in the digits and double checking for errors, I added Ian to my contacts and toyed with the idea of calling him. Instead, I opted for the coward's way out. Texting.

Me: Hey. It's Gemma.

Ian: Hey! What's up? We still on for tomorrow?

Me: Not really supposed to be going out after school. Daddy said.

Ian: You don't seem the type to care what Daddy thinks.

Me: No, I don't. He either already forgot or doesn't want to bother enforcing his own rules.

Ian: Fear not, my fair damsel. We shall ride again.

Me: Tomorrow. I'm looking forward to it.

Ian: Me too.

Me: Goodnight.

Ian: G'night.

The moon was full and high, spilling bands of white light into my room. I was able to make out the lines of the sigil that had embedded itself to my skin. I traced the lines and my body hummed.

And although I was comforted by the visual reminder that I wasn't imagining any of this, I lay awake, worried what would happen next time. When it would be a demon summoning. And why Thom's touch burned like the sigils on my skin.

CHAPTER TEN

The next morning, I tore through all seven drawers of my double-wide espresso stained dresser in a desperate yet futile attempt to find something that would cover the mark on my arm. Concealer didn't cut it. I stormed into Brian's room and after a bit of rummaging, found the black leather cuff he always wore while playing guitar. It was a bit loose and bore the unmistakable rainbow prism of Pink Floyd but managed to cover the sigil completely.

As soon as I stepped into the kitchen, my father's angry eyes were on me. "What part of our conversation did you misunderstand?" he barked.

"Sorry?" I asked, squashing the urge to laugh in his face.

"Cut the act." He stood up and took a step closer, placing his hands on his waist. I took notice of how wrinkled his lab coat, slacks, and button down shirt were.

He must have been at work all night.

"What act? How could you possibly even know what time I came home?"

"Gemma, you are making things very difficult for me. You've forced me to use some extreme measures. There are some cameras in the house so I can monitor you from the office. And I've activated a tracking device on your phone."

"Well, I'm sorry, Dad. I don't mean to mess up your life but you're doing a great job on mine." I walked around his imposing figure and scooped my bag out from its usual spot in the closet.

"Yeah but you did," he called after me. "It's enough you killed Brian. Can't you just follow my rules?"

The sharp intake of my breath was the only sound in the room. Everything else became fuzzy. I turned to look at my dad through tear-filled eyes to check if he meant what he said. I saw no signs of hesitation. I could usually find weakness when he was unsure of himself. There was none. No chewing the inside of his cheek. No twisting of the hair in the back of his head. No other nervous tactile movements.

"Sure, Dad. Whatever." I tried to keep my voice stone cold but it was hard when the lump of dread was threatening to break free.

I thought I caught a flash of something dark pass over his face.

Could one of the Dybbuk have taken him too?

Just then the clouds passed, sending the morning light in through the vertical blinds. I could make out the deep lines of wrinkles around his mouth and the bags under his eyes. Nope. No supernatural explanation for what he said. Only pure spite.

I left him as he was, standing in the kitchen, waiting

for some kind of daughterly response that probably involved some hugging and a lot of denial.

Outside, I found Ghosty, who seemed to have committed my morning routine to memory. When I went on my run, he waited in his usual spot on the patio and then, two hours later, stood outside the front door.

"Bye, Ghosty." I waved, unsure if his presence confirmed the fact that my father just hated me and had not been possessed by a spiteful and bitchy soul.

Maybe something else had gotten to him. Sure, Gemma, keep telling yourself that. And maybe unicorns do exist.

At school the mood wasn't any better. Everyone seemed to be on edge, snapping at each other for silly reasons. Then again, in high school that was expected.

When I walked into homeroom, Thom was handing out issues of the New York Times. "Good Morning, Miss Pope," he said.

"Good Morning, Mr. Flynn," I said and sat down displaying my covered wrist.

He glanced down and said, "Nice choice."

"You, too," I replied, pointing to the purple-checked shirt he wore today beneath a gray cashmere sweater. He managed to look good even if he insisted on wearing white sneakers every day. His sleeves were rolled up and I noticed how bare they were, save for the dusting of light blond hair.

How come I was the one getting stuck with the body art?

"Class, today we are going to do things a bit differently," Thom said walking to the white board. "In front of you is all the news that's fit to print." He pointed to the paper's banner he had projected. "I would like each of you to read an article and identify instances of bias. Journalism isn't supposed to contain any. However, it happens every day."

I scanned the headlines on the front page and wondered if I was being overly sensitive, thinking that things seemed extra depressing.

"Which one are you doing?" Ian leaned over and asked.

Our conversation from the night before had been short and sweet.

"Maybe I can find some bias in the sports section," I said, reluctant to read anything that could possibly depress me more.

"Are we still on for today?"

"I think so," I replied. "I might have to meet up with Mr. Flynn first. Text me later and I'll have a better idea on the time."

"Sure." He smiled and went back to flipping through the layers of newsprint before him.

I was trying to decide between "Mass Airstrikes on Afghanistan kills Dozens including Allied Soldiers" and "Rebels move towards Capital of Gabon," when I felt the familiar buzz of my phone rattling through the things in my bag.

I peeked inside so as not to call attention to my obvious violation of school rules.

Dad: Gemma. Be home by six. No excuses.

The snort that erupted from my nose came out louder than expected with half the room, including Ian and Thom, looking at me questioningly.

"Is there a problem, Miss Pope?" Thom asked.

"Um, not really."

I thought he would let it go. Instead he motioned

with his finger to come up to his desk. I wrestled with the newspaper, sending a chorus of crackling until I managed to crumble it into some vision of its former self. I looked over at Ian, who was chuckling as he flicked his copy of *The Times*, neatly folded into quadrants and framing the story he was reading.

"Show off," I whispered as I got up and made my way towards the teacher's desk.

"Miss Pope."

It was still a bit disconcerting when Thom, Mr. Flynn, whatever he was at the moment, went all formal on me.

I wonder if he feels as funny around me as I do about him.
"Yes?"

"We will meet today after school."

"I figured," I answered, "I'd let you use the time to explain why you left out a little detail to this whole ritual thing. Does this even come off?" I lowered my voice for the last question.

He looked up at me from his chair and I could see he was holding something back. He looked at the class and then at me with his warm eyes. "We'll discuss it later."

"Fine." I let it go for now, trusting that he would tell me everything when we were alone. If not, I was going to have to pry it out of him with my bare hands.

I went back to my seat and couldn't make sense of the small words that followed one another like rows of marching ants. I looked back from my newspaper to the text my dad had sent and my heart filled with regret.

* * *

"I'll drive this time. Gemma gets shotgun and you two shrimps get to squeeze in the back," Brian stated as he snatched the keys from Jenny's grasp.

The sun was dipping low past the tree line that surrounded the lake. I was busy cleaning up the wrappers and Styrofoam boxes from the little takeout lunch Brian and Mimi were kind enough to go pick up for all of us. As I tied a knot in the plastic bag and looked for any sign of the Goodwins' trashcans, Mimi grabbed the blankets.

With Jenny and Brian busy arguing and clawing their way to the top of the hill, I was engaged in a fervent prayer that Mimi would not use this time to broach the subject of dating my brother.

"Gem?" Mimi started.

"Hmm?" I replied, pretending to be engrossed in my search for the holy grail of trash receptacles.

"I don't know how to ask you this."

She didn't continue until I turned to face her. Mimi was so pretty. Her almond-shaped eyes turned on their corners, giving her an ever-inquisitive look that matched her personality. Her smooth, thick, black hair could have easily overshadowed her features if they weren't set against a backdrop of porcelain skin that illuminated her petite round face beneath the gorgeous mane.

"Ask away. Unless you're going to ask to borrow my red velvet mini dress. That's a definite no."

"No." She laughed in a way I imagined fairies would if they were real. "Nothing like that."

"Then what is it?"

"It's about Brian," she said, wringing the blankets in her hands like she was holding on for dear life.

"Yeah?"

"Gem. I really like him and he likes me and I just wanted

to know if it was okay with you if we started seeing each other. I told him not to break things off with Allison until I got your permission."

"Mimi, you don't need my permission to date my brother. He's my twin, not my husband."

"You sure act like an old married couple."

"Well, that has been years in the making. Look, I'm fine with you dating Brian, just don't come running to me when he does something monstrously idiotic."

"Thanks, Gemma."

I could see that she was still unsure about how this was going to affect our relationship as friends. So I did what I thought a good friend would do and drew her in for a hug.

"And next time, Mimi."

"Yeah?"

"Let someone else fold the blankets. You did an awful job."

"Better than you would have done." *She was laughing now and I could tell things were going to be fine.*

"I didn't say that someone else should be me."

We linked arms and headed to the car, blissfully unaware that it would be our last moments together.

The school bell brought me back to the room and I realized I hadn't completed the assignment. Not that I particularly cared.

"I'll meet you out front after school, Gem," Ian said, getting up from his seat.

"Yeah. Figure around five o'clock. Is that good?"

"Sure."

There is no way I'm missing out on this, no matter how pissed off Dad is.

I tried not to stare at his ass for too long. Between

my growing feelings for Ian and having no one to share my new or old experiences with, I was coming to a point where the floodgates were going to open and I was going to spill everything to Charlotte.

Charlotte's cool. I could tell her. Chances are she would be the only one to actually believe anything magic related.

She was convinced the key chain filled with lucky charms in her bag brought her specific types of good fortune. Her rabbit's foot was in tune with the universe's good shoe sales. Her green enamel rhinestone-covered four-leaf clover directs her to money she finds in the street. Even the plastic lucky Asian cat with the moveable tail got her free Chinese takeout. I kept telling her that one was a bit racist.

I finally caught up with her at lunch and was amused to see the look on her face when Ian joined us. "So, wow, Ian. I heard you're starting quarterback this season. That's so awesome," she started.

Both of them noticed the surprised look I had on my face as I scrunched my eyebrows in confusion.

"Yeah. Gemma. I didn't get a chance to tell you," Ian replied.

"Wow. That's great," I said and meant it.

"Yeah. Not too bad for a new guy," Charlotte said as she squirted a pack of ketchup onto the underside of her hamburger bun without getting it anywhere near her white belted blouse, which I'm sure wasn't meant to be worn like a dress. Charlotte, however, insisted that, at her height, everything was dress length.

"I'm really happy for you, Ian," I said.

"Let's see how happy everyone else is when we play the Knights next Friday," he replied.

"As long as you trash talk the other team, you'll be fine. No one expects anything out of our team since Brian isn't here. Not that you're probably not great, Ian, but Brian was super awesome. We even made it to the State Champions last year. I think I'll eat my food now," Charlotte said, diving into her burger.

With all of us silenced by our lunch, I realized that the sigil that had so far gone unnoticed was beginning to thrum beneath the soft leather cuff. I snuck a look. It looked the same as far as I could tell.

"What you got there?" Ian asked.

"Nothing." I let my arm drop to my side.

The tension was obvious from the lack of conversation. Charlotte eyed me from behind her last bite and gave me a knowing look. "I'm outie. Super nice talking to you, Ian."

As she walked away, I felt the sensation in my wrist begin to subside until she was out of the room then it faded to nothing.

"What's going on, Gem?"

"I'm not really sure."

"Sounds interesting." He grinned, his smile reaching his eyes.

I looked down at my hands, giving the leather cuff a turn and tried to come up with a good reason to tell him. And a good reason not to. I was pretty much on the fence until he said,

"Was that your brother's?"

I smiled, picturing Brian on his bed, playing the solo from *Comfortably Numb* for the millionth time, trying to get it perfect.

"Yeah. I always made fun of his geriatric taste in music."

"I got to hand it to him though. Pink Floyd could very well be the best rock band of all time."

"If I told you something important, do you promise not to act like I was crazy?"

"I'm pretty open-minded." He leaned in closer and I could make out the green flecks mixed in with the blue of his irises. "Remember, I'm the one with the freaky mode of transportation."

I unclipped the two buttons and showed him the tattoo.

"Nice ink. What does it mean?" he asked.

"Well, I've been doing a bit of magic and it turns out you can't get away with doing it for free. So here I am, left with a tattoo I have no way of explaining to anyone." I pursed my lips and blew out some air, sending the stray hairs out of my eyes.

"You sure you know what you're doing? That stuff can get complicated. And dangerous."

His concern warmed me more than I cared to admit.

"Yeah. I have help." I left out the part that our English teacher was also an expert in the demonic arts.

"Just be careful," he said clasping my hand in his.

"I will."

He didn't let go of me until it was time again for class. We confirmed our after-school plans and went our separate ways. Mine included another torturous session of gym and a chemistry class I was getting lost in.

I was happy to see that Allison hadn't made it to class and I could spend my time paying attention to Mr. Flynn's in-depth explanation of Hamlet's soliloquy. Ian, however, also wasn't there, which I should have expected from the way he kept verifying our non-date. Even though this was our third time spending time alone with one another, I wasn't jumping to any conclusions until he started using explicit terminology. *If he didn't use the word 'date' it didn't count as one. Even Mimi would agree with me on that one. At least, she would have.*

When it was just Thom and I in the room, he took his usual spot next to me as I pulled out the heavy grimoire from my bag.

"This thing is getting too heavy to lug around."

"I could lock it up here. You could copy certain pages or take photos with your mobile if you need to work on something specific."

"That might be a good idea. I don't like leaving it home either."

"So, have you given much thought to your demon of choice?" He was more at ease today, leaning back against the chair with his legs stretched before him.

"Can't say I have."

"Tsk. Tsk. Gemma. Get to work."

I skimmed through the texts as best as I could. At least the book was organized, each section catalogued according to the demon in charge and his or her underlings.

"How about him?" I pointed to a half man, half lion riding a bear with a serpent in hand.

"Meh."

"Alrighty, I'll keep looking."

I was getting antsy. In another hour, Ian would be waiting on the front steps of the building and if I didn't pick the right demon soon, I was going to be stuck here for a while.

Finally, I left my choice to instinct and settled on the page with a winged man, also holding a serpent named Ashtaroth. *What's with all the snakes?* His page held a complex drawing of a pentagram along with a short story describing his temptations of St. Bartholomew.

"How about this one? Duke Ashtaroth, says here he can answer any question posed to him. That sounds promising."

"Could work," Thom answered.

"You know, I can't tell if you're being sarcastic or not."

"Must be the accent. You Yanks seem to use so much energy deciphering the words, you lose much of the meaning."

"So, am I on the right track now?"

"I think we could give it a whirl."

I pulled out a piece of parchment, set on the task and with the last circular flourish, asked: "Am I going to find this somewhere on my body too?"

"You know it."

"How come I have to get them? Why am I the one who even needs to do this? You seem to know everything there is to know about this stuff."

He took a moment before answering. "Let's just put it this way. I don't really have what it takes. What does the old adage say? Whomever can't, teaches?"

I looked back down at the page. This sigil would not be as inconspicuous as the last. Ashtaroth, as the book indicated, needed the addition of a pentagram. I was going to look like a psycho demon worshipper.

"This blows," I said.

"Think of the greater good. You'll be doing your part."

"Fine."

Thom got up, checked the hallway, and closed the door to the classroom. On his way back to the desk, he picked up a large pillar candle and a small satchel. He placed the candle on his desk, took the paper with the sigil and placed it on the floor in front of me then proceeded to pace around our two desks while pouring a white substance from the small bag.

"No worries. Just salt," he said. "You always need to make a circle of protection for yourself."

"Doesn't sound like demons are all hunky dory."

"Well, you saw what it was like dealing with an angel. You get nowhere."

"I'm just saying."

"Keep your thoughts to yourself then, alright?" His voice was clipped. "We're here to work."

I rolled my eyes as he was tying the ends of the little cloth baggie.

"And I'd appreciate it if you didn't do that."

"Do what?" I replied, jutting my chin up in challenge.

"Be impudent." He was looking at me now and I could feel the blaze in his eyes. "This is important. More than you'll ever know. More than your little life. So just do as I say."

He lowered himself back to his seat and lit the candle. I took that as my cue to begin.

"By the power of three. I summon thee. Ashtaroth. By the power of black fire. Ashtaroth. By the power of black ice. Ashtaroth."

The sigil began to glow and expand until it had

tripled in size.

"Is it supposed to be doing that?" I asked.

"Just watch," Thom said, and gave me a quick pat of reassurance.

Smoke started to billow up in a slow, undulating pace. Then, in a flash of blinding light, the demon appeared before us. He wore a drab, mustard yellow suit with a mismatched purple silk shirt and green tie. He had one of those long twirly mustaches and small beady eyes that were too far apart on his face.

"I'm here. I'm here." He pulled out a pocket square and wiped away the sweat from his forehead. "You'd think I wasn't in the middle of something." He looked down at the summoning circle and grimaced. "And for future reference, can you please make these a little wider. It's no fun being funneled through a pipe that is two sizes too small for my Rubenesque figure."

Talk about two sizes too small. Those buttons look like they're ready to pop right off.

He adjusted his clothing a bit and continued.

"Oh yeah. Ashtaroth at your service." He bowed, bending from the waist like a concert pianist after giving the performance of his life.

"Hi, I'm-"

"No names," Thom interrupted.

"Oh I didn't see that anywhere," I said, looking back through the grimoire for any reference.

"It's a trade secret." Ashtaroth laughed, revealing rows of sharp overlapping teeth. "Do the powers that be know about your little plaything?" he asked, directing his question to Thom.

"Everything has had advance approval," Thom

answered.

"I see. Very well." He turned to me and began twirling the end of his mustache. "You're in luck, chicky. I'm running a back- to-school sale. My fee for today is one sigil. I'm not even gonna try to trick you since you've got your lawyer friend here."

"Whose?" Thom asked.

"Ah, ah, ah." He wagged his finger. "That's between me and the lady."

I looked to Thom for some guidance but found none. Instead, his face was drawn into a pensive frown.

"Tick tock," Ashtaroth continued. "How about it, chicky? You want me bad enough?"

I thought about the Dybbuk. We were supposed to be finding out the reason they were here. So far, though, other than Allison and Ms. Halle, I hadn't seen any more possessions. The thought that my dad could be under one now kept nagging at me. My head kept telling my heart that it was a coping mechanism to explain his shitty behavior.

Thom said that it was important.

"Sure," I said, reaching for his outstretched hand and giving it a solid shake. There was a sizzle followed by a jolt of pain and then the appearance of Ashtaroth's sigil, linking itself to Ambriel's. The blood in my face began to boil. I was seeing every shade of red.

"Can't anyone give fair warning before slapping me with their signature?"

"A small price to pay to be a sorceress." Ashtaroth's face gleamed. "You should be honored that I am forever plastered onto your skin."

I scowled and spoke to Thom through clenched teeth. "What are we going to ask him?"

He wiped the edges of his mouth with his hand and said, "Give me a minute. I need to phrase it just right."

The pentagram on my forearm was noticeably different from the other sigil. Instead of black lines and shaded areas, Ashtaroth's sigil was a bright orange red, the color of flames.

I'm going to be stuck in long sleeves for the rest of my life. I wonder if laser treatment can get these off. Hmm.

"Okay. Why are the Dybbuk here in Harrisport?" Thom paced his words.

"I'm disappointed. Someone like you should know that answer by now. To tie up loose ends. The soul needs to resolve any past sins in order to move ahead."

"That's not what I am referring to. Why are these Dybbuk specifically in Harrisport? There are more than usual."

I watched in silence as the two verbally jousted. Ashtaroth looked as though he was debating whether to answer.

"They are here fulfilling their end of a bargain with a certain someone whom I am not at liberty to mention. Word is something big is gonna go down here. They want in on the deal. Don't want to go through the regular steps to get back to the source. They've been promised something better."

"But it's the way things have worked for eons," Thom exclaimed. "Why now?"

"Sorry folks. Show's over."

"What do you mean?" I asked.

"One question per turn."

"You never said that."

"I didn't have to. It's your job to negotiate terms, chicky."

Before I could let loose my emotional tirade, Ashtaroth was gone with a poof, leaving in his wake the scrap of parchment that had once held his sigil but had now been replaced with three dreaded letters: I.O.U.

CHAPTER ELEVEN

"What the hell was that?" My shrill voice had Thom drawing back in obvious discomfort.

"I'd appreciate it if you watched your tone." He stood up from his seat and headed towards the closet, already halfway towards bailing on me.

"No. I don't think so." I jumped from my seat and cornered him. From this close, I could see the fear in his eyes. "Just tell me. I just need to know the truth. Is this something we can fix?"

"I think we're making a mistake. Well, I made the mistake. of involving you," he said as he pulled on his jacket and adjusted the strap of his bag to lie across his chest.

"You didn't. We're not. I can do this." The rejection stung.

"There is more going on than I first thought. It was wrong of me to force you into this."

"We'll figure it out. Please don't take this away from me. It's the only thing I have left that means anything." I couldn't let him go. This is what I had to look forward to. A time where I could forget about all the things that were going wrong because I knew somewhere in the recesses of my mind that I was meant for this. Somehow, when I worked on a sigil, I intuited its shape, I could picture what it should look like in my mind's eye and my hand automatically did the rest. He brushed his hand across his face.

"I don't know why I'm saying this," I continued. "Hopefully, there is some part of you that actually cares what I'm feeling. Maybe somehow you really do know what this means to me. Even if I ask too many questions."

He laughed. "You want the truth then?" he asked.

"Yes." The way he looked at me I felt like my soul was bare before him. The lines on his face smoothed and I took a step back, knowing now I had a fighting chance of getting some answers out of him.

"If what Ashtaroth says is the truth then the Dybbuk are the least of our worries. Someone has been making plans. The type of plans that change all the rules. And when the rules change, the game takes a dangerous turn."

"If it were possible to speak with a Dybbuk, maybe we could get some information from them?" I asked.

"It's worth a try."

"Then it's settled. We'll meet up tomorrow." I walked back to the grimoire and handed it to Thom. "And don't forget to lock this thing up."

"And what sort of plan might you be hatching?" He smiled.

"I like it when you smile," I said and felt my cheeks flush. "Um, yeah I have a Dybbuk who hangs outside my house. Maybe I can figure out a way to speak to it."

"Really?"

"Yeah, it's been sitting on my lawn since my accident."

"I meant about my smile." He leaned towards me and tucked a strand of loose hair behind my ear. I was tempted to touch his face but knew better than to interrupt the moment. "It's alright. I like yours too."

"Then does this mean I'm still on the case?"

"I'm afraid so." He sighed. "Gotta keep mum though. We don't know who's got eyes and ears about."

"Got it." I was relieved and about to turn to pack up when Thom brushed his face past mine and whispered in my ear.

"Have a good evening, Gemma." His breath was like fire against the tender skin of my ear and neck. The heat trickled down and warmed me from within, down to my bones.

"Bye," I whispered back, using all my energy to keep me from melting into the floor.

Ian was sitting on the concrete steps and playing a game on his phone that sent digitized beats out into the quiet cold air with every flick of his finger. I came up from behind and placed a hand on his shoulder. He turned and flashed me his baby blues.

"Sorry I'm late," I said.

He stood, shoving his hands in his pockets. "No worries. You ready?"

"More than ever."

"I don't have a car, though, or anything. Is it cool if

we walk?"

"Definitely." I laughed as we made our way down the stairs and onto the street.

He placed his arm around my shoulder and brought me closer to him. My arm went around his waist in an automatic response.

I enjoyed our walk back to the empty lot huddled against Ian's side and when we found ourselves back in front of the magical yew tree, I was a bit disappointed when he moved away from me. He placed his hand in the indentation that had been left in the ground and the tree responded as it did the previous time. Only this time, instead of a ram's horn, the handle was an intricately carved goat's foot, complete with cloven hoof made of solid gold.

"That's so cool."

"Maybe next time I'll teach you how to use it," Ian said.

"Really?"

"Sure."

He pushed on the handle and held the door open for me. I stepped through into the darkness and felt him lace his fingers with mine as the door shut behind us.

"Here we go," he said. With those words, I heard the whoosh of wind as the force snapped our bodies through the tunnels. The world continued to spin until we came to a jerking halt, sending my stomach to the ground.

"Is this a different room?" I asked, noticing the stark differences in the environment. Rolling dunes had been replaced by sheets of ice and jutting blue green crags of glaciers. The sky was whitewashed and dotted with thousands of blue stars that illuminated our surroundings.

"Amazing isn't it?" He set us down on a mound of snow that crunched beneath my feet. "This happens to be a different area. We took a different drift to get here. You've got to be careful though. Sometimes, someone decides to change up the scenery just for fun. You got to keep track of which door you call. Now, don't move."

Ian began counting his steps as he carefully paced across the frozen lake. At eighteen, he dropped to his knees and placed the palm of his hand on the ice. He then stood up and brushed his hand together, sending an explosion of new flakes to the ground.

"Okay, you can come down now," he called out.

I took caution with each step, stretching my arms to the side for balance. When I reached Ian, I saw the dark hole that was now in the ice.

"Trust me. It's not as bad as it looks but this portal doesn't have a cable. We need to jump."

"It looks pretty bad to me." My pulse sped up and my hands began to sweat.

"You think too much," he said, wrapping his arms around me and pulling us down through the abyss.

Electric beats and a deep thrumming bass line filled the large room. Bodies were packed end to end in a primal undulating dance as multicolored strobe lights flashed on and off over the crowd. The tempo kicked up, sending everyone into a frenzy, arms in the air and jumping to the rhythmic pulses. I felt the vibrations surrounding me and was awestruck.

Ian unzipped his jacket and I followed suit. He

grabbed our things and shoved them onto a booth in the corner. Then without further delay, we were on the dance floor.

He placed his hands firmly on my hips and we fell into the seductive rise and fall of the music. The last tendrils of confusion cleared and the constant weight dragging me down let up for the first time in months. I closed my eyes and reveled in the release. Ian moved to my back and rocked me back and forth until we moved as a single unit. I let my head lean back against him and looked up, taking notice of the catwalk full of observers looking down at us from their intimate perch.

I turned back to face Ian and placed my arms around his neck. I let the energy of the room soak into me, filling me with its power as I swayed closer and closer to his body. He leaned down, touching his forehead to mine and let his intense gaze capture my attention.

The world fell away and we were all that was left. He placed his lips on mine as I ran my fingers through his hair and squeezed, deepening the kiss. After what felt like hours, we broke apart. Ian led me past the growing throngs of people and up the staircase that led to the balconies overlooking the club.

"What do you think?" he said as the bass dropped, leaving a lull long enough to speak.

"This is beyond," I answered, leaning against the wall, away from the well-dressed people who mingled about, holding drinks and staring at the crowd below them.

The music picked right back up and Ian drew

closer. Time slipped away and we danced in slow motion in our own private world while the music around us throbbed.

Ian was the first to break the spell. "We should get going," he said.

"Why?" I groaned, relishing the haze I was caught up in and loathing the thought of going back to my life at home.

"You shouldn't stay here too long. It'll be night time soon." He rubbed the underside of my chin with his finger. "We can come back any time. Just say the word."

"Promise?"

"Promise." He smiled.

We went back down to grab our things and Ian ushered me through a pair of doors leading to a room, empty but for

a control panel filled with switches. He flicked one of them, turning the light beside it red.

I furrowed my brow in question.

"This is the elevator back home. Watch."

After a few more seconds, the light turned green and the doors slid open, revealing the dirt running path I used every day.

"Trippy," I said, walking out into the brisk gray evening.

Ian followed and the elevator closed behind him, leaving no trace of its existence. "Race you." He pulled at my sleeve and ran through the thicket of trees.

"Hey, no fair." Clutching my bag to my chest, I set off to catch him.

He wove through the trees at an impressive speed,

never once getting caught in the branches. When I got to my back yard, he was already leaning against the wooden beams of the patio, wearing a smirk.

"You going to catch me or what?"

"Count on it." I raced towards him. He feigned left and I followed. At the last moment, he switched to his right and whirled passed me. My foot slipped on the slick grass. I threw my bag down and used my hands to push myself back up.

"I'm waiting." Ian teased from ten feet away. I ran at him with all the force I could muster only this time he didn't move and we collided. Our bodies rolled down the hill until we finally came to a stop, with him on top of me. My breath was coming out in fast bursts and my heart was pounding out of my chest.

I don't think it's from the exercise.

I lay still, feeling Ian's chest against mine. He ran one hand down the side of my body and this time I let him. The flood lamps came on and I groaned. "That must be my dad. He has awful timing."

"Don't let him get to you."

"I don't but he's going to come out here and tear me a new one."

"Then we should go and get it over with." He smacked a quick kiss on my lips.

"You don't have to stay and witness the dysfunction that my family has become."

"Come on." He stood up and offered me his hand. We walked back up the lawn and onto the deck where my father was waiting and Ghosty was sitting in his usual spot.

"It's late," he barked.

"I know, Dad. Have you met Ian?"

Could I deflect or what?

"Pleasure to meet you, Mr. Pope." Ian offered his hand.

"Dr." My dad answered, leaving Ian's hand in the air and unwanted.

"I was just walking Gemma back home. She got stuck late at school and I didn't want her making the trip by herself."

"Thank you, Ian. I appreciate your concern, but I think it's time you left."

"Sure. See you tomorrow, Gemma." Ian took the hint and left but not without a wave to Ghosty.

"What is your problem?" I said to my dad when we were inside.

"I am tired of you breaking the rules, Gemma," he said, slamming the glass door behind him so hard I thought it was going to shatter.

"Relax, I'm fine. Ian walked me home."

"I saw you. You're a slut, just like your mother." Spittle lined the edges of his mouth and that's when I saw the blackness in his eyes. Panic filled my chest. I was living with one of these things now. With my coat still on, I headed to my room.

"What I do is my business," I yelled back at him, closing the door behind me and barring it with the pink upholstered lounge chair. I turned on the lights and dumped my stuff on top of my already junk-ridden desk.

There was a series of loud bangs on my door, followed by silence.

I listened as his dress shoes clicked against the hardwood floor towards the back of the house, where the master bedroom was. When I heard his door shut,

I let out a breath and began peeling away the layers of damp clothing. The dirty laundry on the floor was starting to form a nice pile. After rummaging through the remainder of my clean clothes, I settled on a white flannel nightshirt. I stood in front mirror and started from the top button. When I reached the last one, I looked at my legs. My scar had disappeared.

CHAPTER TWELVE

Holy cow. Holy cow. Holy cow.
Freaky. This can't be real.

I pulled up the hem of my shirt and lifted my leg up onto the dresser to get a closer look. The angry red lines and dents in the muscle were gone. G-O-N-E. Gone. I traced my trembling finger back and forth across my thigh and marveled at the smooth texture.

Like nothing had ever happened.

My head got fuzzy at the thought and I clutched the edge of the dresser, squeezing until my knuckles were white. I dropped to my knees as the breath went in and out of my lungs too quickly.

Then I waited, huddled between layers of pillows and down comforters, scared out of mind of both my father and what was happening to me. Rational Gemma chided delirious Gemma and said that there was a reasonable explanation for everything.

Different scenarios kept playing through my brain. Of my dad storming into my room with a butcher knife. Of the parasite within him leeching its way into my room through the cracks in the floorboards to choke the life out of me while I slept. My imagination got the best of me and kept my body frozen in place the entire night.

Finally, when the first hint of day splashed across the window above my bed, I crept down the hall and out for my run, in an attempt to avoid my father as much as possible until I figured out a way to cure everyone.

Remembering my idea to try to talk to a Dybbuk, I stopped on the patio. The spirit was stretched on the lounger and when I squinted, it almost looked like a person staring at the sky.

"Hey," I said.

The black smoke released it shape and reformed.

"Can you understand me?" I asked.

It evaporated and reappeared beside me in a poof.

"I'm going to take that as a yes. Want to join me?"

It didn't answer but as I jogged down the stairs, it followed.

On the brighter side of things, at least today I had a partner.

When I got back to the house, the sun was beginning its slow ascent over the trees. Ghosty had kept pace and I was hesitant to leave it when my run ended.

"I'll see you after school. I've got an idea," I said and went into the house.

My shower was quick but I couldn't help but linger a few extra minutes in front of the mirror, fascinated by the smooth skin that now covered both my legs.

Part of me wanted to cry at the loss. One more step pulling me away from the accident. No more physical reminders. If the scars are gone then what still connects me to Brian?

Stop it, Gem. It's probably temporary.

It was still early when I got to school so I opted to sit on a bench outside beneath an old maple tree instead of spending extra time trapped within the confines of the school. My view of the faculty parking lot wasn't much. There was a single car there, covered in dew.

Must have sat there all night.

A stray gray cat stuck its head out from behind the front tire, skittered across the pavement onto the lawn, and made its way around onto the granite base of the statue of James Madison that stood at the far end of campus. It then jumped onto the bike rack, padded across the entire length without skipping a beat, and jumped down, landing at the crosswalk. As I marveled at the little guy's agility, I heard the telltale sound of a car careening out of control. Tires screeched and a small green sedan slid into view, crashing right into the stop sign. The cat was nowhere to be seen. I got up and ran towards the accident, while pulling out my cellphone.

A scrawny tail twitched from beneath the front wheel.

Eww. Poor guy.

The windshield had shattered into a web of small pieces, still holding on to one another. The side window was fogged up and I couldn't make out if the driver was hurt. I opened the door, only to find the

125

vehicle empty. All the airbags had been deployed. I leaned over the seat to check the back row. Nothing.

I scrambled out and put a good distance between myself and the eerie scene. The preternatural feeling that I was being watched crawled up my neck and when I raised my eyes up the crest of the street, I saw all of them. Standing there, at the top, dozens of dark shadows. And in a blink of an eye, they dissolved into the air.

A deep rumble came from the other direction, breaking the thrall. A black motorcycle rolled into the parking lot and parked beneath the solar panel awnings. The rider was wearing white running shoes.

"Thom," I yelled and ran towards him, waving my arms in the air like a mad woman.

He pulled the full-faced helmet off and strapped it with a bungee onto the back. "Gemma." His voice was strong and clear, his eyes on me.

"The Dybbuk. They were there," I said, trying to catch my breath. "At the top of the hill. Then a car came crashing with no one inside. And the cat. He's dead. And my dad. He's off the handle and I think he's been possessed."

"Slow down. Let's go inside."

We went straight to our homeroom, passing several more Dybbuk lining the halls. "There's more of them. What's going on?" I whispered.

"Seems like someone has stepped up the timetable. Looks like it's become an infestation now."

"Is there anything we can do? These things aren't just dangerous, they're going to cause chaos. Did you see that empty car they rolled down the street? We need to resolve their 'issues,' isn't that what Ashtaroth said to do?"

"Even if we could figure out a way to communicate with them, there are too many now. We can't fix each soul's problem one by one. By the time we resolve a single soul's problem, ten more will crop up." He was pacing now and pulling at his hair.

"What other choice do we have?"

"We keep with the summonings. There is bound to be someone who'll tell us what's going on?"

"And you expect me to keep getting tatted up until then?"

"I told you this was important. I was willing to let you go back to your life. You're the one who begged to keep going. Remember that part?" Flames appeared in his eyes that scared me no end.

"Fine then. Let's go through the book and pick someone else. Should I close my eyes while you flip through the pages and we'll just summon whomever I land on? Or do you think you could, for one minute, give me some insight? You act like you know everything."

Thom stalked to the teacher's closet and pulled out his keys.

"Knock knock." The door swung open and Principal Kelly strode in, awash in a frilly, lavender blouse, a long, purple, tie-died tiered jersey skirt and purple cowboy boots.

"Good morning, Principal Kelly," I said, eyeing Thom, who continued to busy himself with an armful of books.

"Good morning," he said, placing a stack of paperbacks onto his desk.

"Just thought I'd check in on you. See how you

were handling things."

"We're having a jolly time, aren't we, Miss Pope?"

"Yup. Mr. Flynn is an awesome teacher."

"Good. Good." She kept staring at Thom and wringing her hands.

"Would you like to observe the class today?" Thom said.

"No, no. Just checking in." She began muttering something under her breath and left the room, never giving us her back.

"Do you think one of them got to her?"

"Don't think so. We'll continue our conversation later." He tugged on his ear and pointed to the door. I got the hint that now wouldn't be the best time to get involved in a satanic ritual.

I was disappointed that Ian was nowhere to be found for most of the day. Nor was Charlotte, until lunchtime. She was already seated at a table filled with some other members of the squad. "Gemma!" She waved me over.

"Hey." I stood there with my lunch tray, not making any move to join them.

"Sit," she said, tapping the empty space beside her.

I looked around at the faces of some of my former teammates, who were looking down at their food instead of at me.

"It's alright. I'll catch up with you later." I hightailed it out of there and kept going until I found an empty classroom.

"Gemma, wait up."

I turned to see Charlotte running after me in her ridiculously tall shoes. She tripped a bit but caught herself on me, sending the tray and half of my lunch to the floor. The other half was all over my clothing. I wiped the pea soup off the front of my jeans.

"Great. Thanks, Charlotte. As if my day wasn't shitty enough already." I could feel my marks ignite in awareness.

"Oh wow, Gemma. You can be a real bitch sometimes."

"I don't really need this right now. I didn't want to sit with you. What's the big deal?"

I have to get away from her before something happens with these sigils.

"The big deal is that you're my friend and you can't keep avoiding everyone."

"Morgan and Emma didn't seem too thrilled to have me there," I said, sounding more than snotty.

"Well, they're going to be there this weekend at my house. I thought now would be a good time to break the ice."

"I don't need your help, Charlotte. They haven't said a word to me since the accident. Maybe I just shouldn't come." I started to walk away.

Maybe I have some clean clothes in my gym locker.

"Gem, don't walk away from me."

I ignored her and kept going, the pain in my arm receding with every step, making it all the more easier to run away.

The locker room was humid as usual and the puke green walls added to the swampy feel. I rushed to my locker and managed to find a semi-clean t-shirt and a pair of sweats. After changing, I noticed how bare my arms were and hoped that the cuff would be enough to hide the growing marks on my arm.

When I turned to leave, Allison was blocking my way out of the aisle.

"Thought I forgot about you?" she asked.

"No, I thought maybe you'd have something better to do with your time." I shoved the dirty clothes into my gym bag and zipped it up.

I hope it doesn't start stinking.

"You're right. I am busy. Somehow I managed to carve out some time for you."

A shadow moved to the forefront, hovering just beyond her body. Allison mimicked every movement it made. First, taking two steps forward. Then curving her arms to the side of her body. Next, the skin and muscle on her hands fell away, revealing bone that elongated and sharpened into two scythe-like blades.

I stepped away, the backs of my knees bumping into the low bench, and toppled down to the ceramic tiled floor.

"That should be mine." She drew one blade towards me and I crab walked until my back slammed into the row of lockers. The sight of Allison's hideous form poised above me brought bile up my throat.

She slipped one sharp hand beneath the cuff and yanked. When the buttons gave, I felt the air on the bare skin of my wrist and watched as blood pooled on the surface of the shallow slit inflicted by Allison.

One hand reformed and snatched the leather cuff off the point of the blade.

"I'm the one that gave this to him. I'm the one who should have it," she said, shoving it into her pocket. "And what's this?" She grabbed my hand and examined the markings that were now visible.

"Leave me alone, Allison," I said, struggling to get

out of her grip.

"You're a freak now, aren't you?" She let out a cackle. "Wait until everyone finds out about this, you satanic whore."

Finally, distracted by her own glee, Allison released me and I ran straight for the door. Outside, crowds of students were waiting for the change of periods. With my head down, I walked past the row of administrative offices and the security desk.

"Gemma?" Principal Kelly stepped out into the hallway.

"Yes?"

"Where do you think you're going?"

"Out," I replied.

She looked down at my arm; the blood had coagulated and caked around my wrist.

"Is everything alright?"

"I'm fine. My lunch spilled all over me, I'm having a really bad day and I'm not feeling too well."

"Let's have the nurse look at that."

"It's okay. My father's a doctor. I just really want to go home," I pleaded.

"I'm going to let you leave now, Gemma, even though it's against school policy. But I expect a meeting with you tomorrow."

"I promise," I said, and ran as fast as my feet could take me.

Outside, I found Ian sitting on the stairs, like he had been the day before, engrossed in a video game. I sat next to him and leaned my head against his arm.

"Hey," he said. "What's going on?"

I placed my arm on his knee. "Allison has gone bat

shit crazy. I can't go back in there. Everyone will see my marks. I'm too tired of my dad to go back home. You know, regular teen drama."

"Come on. Let's go," he said, pulling me up. He took off his jacket and placed it over my shoulders.

"Can we go dancing?" I asked, looking up at his clear eyes and seeing the smile that grew at my request.

"Sure."

When we got to the tree, Ian sat cross-legged at the base of the trunk and I did the same.

"Let me show you how this works. This tree is special. It has the power to identify you whenever you come to access the Drifts. You gift it with a drop of your blood and it will know you for the rest of your life. Here, let me help." He drew my injured wrist towards him and pinched the wound. A fresh drop of blood beaded to the top.

"Ouch," I said.

"Relax. That's it. Now let it fall on the soil. It'll find its way to the roots."

I did as Ian said and the tree responded with a deep groan.

"Is that it?" I asked.

"Yup. Now for the real lesson." He placed my hand on the indentation I had seen him use before.

"I thought this was soil. It feels like stone." I marveled at the texture of the rock that had a botanical appearance.

"It is stone. A special stone that was quarried in a mine on the other side. That's how it works. This stone is a piece of the Drifts. It acts as a touchstone. Lets the tree know where you want to go."

"That's amazing."

"Now all you do is envision your destination and the tree sends the right door. The touchstone tells it that we're going to use the Drifts."

"What are the Drifts?"

"Think of it like Grand Central Station. A hub where all the tunnels converge."

"So I just think about yesterday?"

"Yup?"

"Ok, here we go." With my hand in place, I concentrated on the dancing, the mob of people moving in unison, the lights and the people watching from above.

The door with the golden goat leg appeared.

"One more thing before we go in," he continued. "Keep your thoughts on where you want to go at all times. This way the right drift picks you up. If your concentration wavers, I can't guarantee where we'll end up."

I stood up and took his hand. He raised one eyebrow, which gave him a mischievous aura, and we set off together into the darkness.

The trips through the Drifts were getting easier. Ian showed me his reference points when counting his steps on the frozen lake. Instead of free falling through the portal, we descended smoothly until our feet touched ground.

"Good work," he mouthed, cupping my cheek in his hand and placing a languorous kiss on my lips as the music engulfed us.

Either the DJ was better than before or I was in greater need of the release. I submitted to Ian and let him lead me to the precipice of ecstasy as our bodies moved to the tribal drum and bass. The energy that surrounded us was palpable and I could feel it soak into me. I watched as the slit on my wrist mended itself before my very eyes. Euphoria filled every cell in my body until I felt like I was going to burst.

"I could stay here forever," I told Ian, after we had made our way upstairs to an empty table.

"That could be arranged," he said.

Embarrassed, I turned my attention to the people below. At least, most of them were people. This time I noticed that not everyone here was human.

"Who are they?" I asked.

"Some of them are from Earth. Others are from a different place."

"And how does all this work?" I showed him the uniform skin of my once-injured arm.

"Good vibes. The energy here heals you. Heals your mind. Your body. That's why it feels so good down there. Come on. I want you to meet someone."

He took me around the catwalk and past the other tables of onlookers, some of whom had slitted eyes and a reptilian quality to their skin. One of the women wore a blood red velvet gown, a python around her neck. At her feet knelt a man on a leash.

We walked behind a bar to a door, framed with ornately cut wood, and guarded by a large shirtless giant covered in tattoos. They were sigils, like mine, but his undulated over his skin with power, even reaching his lips and eyelids.

My attention was caught by the sculpted figures behind him that acted out a grotesque scene of demons whipped into a state of agony by serene-faced angels.

"Ian." Mr. Muscle's voice was softer than I had expected. "Sister," he said, nodding in my direction.

"Sorry?" I asked.

"You are a practitioner. As I am. Or have I been mistaken?"

"Um. Yeah. I guess." I gave him a half smile.

"We are few and far between. Remember that. If you're ever in need of help." He bared his teeth, most of which were gold, and I couldn't help cringing.

"Let's get going," Ian said. He grabbed my hand and led me straight inside.

Plush black shag carpeting overpowered the entire area. The walls were lined with built-ins displaying various artifacts individually illuminated by the track lighting above. Behind a massive black onyx desk sat a middle-aged man with a bald head and good skin. He wore a black suit, a black collarless shirt and had a long silver chain around his neck bearing a large iron cross embedded with turquoise.

"Ian. What have you brought for me this time?" He steepled his finger before him and smiled.

"This is Gemma. The one I was telling you about."

"Ah, it's a pleasure to meet you, Gemma. I'm Sam. Please have a seat." Ian and I each sat in one of the cowhide upholstered chairs. "Are you enjoying your time here?" Sam asked.

"Yeah. It's amazing."

"I hear you have some experience in the arcane arts."

"Um. Just a little. I'm not an expert or anything."

"Don't sell yourself short, Gemma, darling. Someone with your talents, who can successfully summon anything, is truly rare. It takes the right kind of person with the right combination of talents to do what you're doing."

"Thanks," I said. *I think.*

"Show me your arm."

I hesitated.

"It's okay. He's cool. He owns this place," Ian said, with a smile of encouragement.

"This is beautiful work," Sam said.

"It is?"

"Yes. The manifestation of these marks is completely dependent on the skill of the practitioner. The better you are at creating sigils, the more intricate your tattoos will be."

I looked down at the marks and felt like I was seeing them for the very first time. Ambriel's had been a few lines and circles when I had made the sigil but on my arm it was surrounded by a series of creeping vines with tear-shaped leaves and flourishes. Ashtaroth's pentagram was now engulfed in flames that almost looked real.

"What does that mean?"

"It means you're very special, Gemma. You can harness the powers of these beings through the marks on your body. You don't need to cast circles and waste time with pen and paper. Their power is now yours."

"But I thought you can't draw power without summoning the being attached?"

"Can't or shouldn't? And I have a feeling that someone as powerful as you are doesn't need to bother with ritual. It's merely a formality at this point. Both beings have already conversed with you. They are the ones who left you their marks. You are free to use the power as you see fit."

Sam stood up from behind his throne of an office chair and walked along the walls of artifacts. He stopped in front of a small display case containing a beautiful bust of a woman, her hair wrapped in curls, crowning her head. He unclasped the pendant she wore, walked over to me and placed it around my neck.

"This is a talisman. Legend tells us it can magnify certain powers. My gift to you."

I looked down at the necklace. The delicate chain was an antique shade of gold and the stone was a roughly hewn rose- colored gem.

"I can't accept this. It's too much." I tried to hand back the ancient piece of jewelry.

"Relax, little one. This is me betting on the right horse."

"Sorry?"

Sam handed the necklace to Ian, who stood behind me and fastened it around my neck. Warmth coursed through my veins as the stone settled in the dip of my collarbone.

"Things are getting a bit out of control topside, wouldn't you say? I have a feeling you'll be the one to set things right. This trinket is my investment in you."

He leaned against the desk, exuding a confidence that was contagious.

"I guess I should say thank you," I answered, happy to oblige him if it meant I was going to have an advantage against the Dybbuk.

"It's my pleasure. And if you are ever in need of assistance, my door is always open."

"So what is it exactly you want me to do?" I asked, fidgeting in my seat, awkward at the realization that I was wheeling and dealing with an obviously loaded businessman in my gym clothes.

"Just keep doing what you do. And if I find something else that might be of any help to you, I'll let you know. Unfortunately, I can't leave this place so you'll have to make the trip down again."

"That's no biggie. I can't find music like this for at least a hundred miles from where I live."

"Good. Then it's a deal."

"Yeah."

We shook on it and I was thankful to see that I was walking away from this deal without any new bodywork.

I guess he's no demon. Or angel.

"You two go have some more fun."

Thrilled to get back to the dance floor, we said our goodbyes to Sam, I was happy to have met him. He was more than forthcoming about his intentions and it gave me a bit of peace to know I had some potential help if I needed it. But for some reason, as I spread my arms in the air reaching for the music around me, I couldn't stop worrying about what Thom would have to say about all of this.

Chapter Thirteen

It felt like we had been hours down in the Drifts but when my house came into view, it was still light out. I checked my watch. It was only five o clock. Too late to make it back to meet with Thom.

"I guess I'll leave you here," Ian said, walking me to the door.

"Do you think Sam's right?" I asked. "About me being able to end all this craziness?"

"That's why I took you to him, Gemma. I know you don't realize this. Maybe one day you will. But you are stronger than you think." He placed the pad of his thumb on his lips and then on mine. "I should go."

"You think you could walk me in? I know I sound a bit chicken but I'm pretty sure my dad is going to freak."

"Yeah, sure."

I turned the key and walked inside to the aroma of roast chicken and rosemary.

"Hi, pumpkin. I'm happy to see your home on time." He was already out of his work clothes and wearing jeans and a pullover beneath a French maid printed novelty apron. "Ian, looks like you're to thank for my daughter's punctuality. Care to join us for dinner?"

I looked from my dad to Ian and then back again. I could find no trace of the ghost that had inhabited his body. He was almost the same dad from B.A. - Before the Accident.

"I'd love to, Dr. Pope." Ian took my hand and squeezed as we made our way further in, stopping at the breakfast bar.

"It'll be another twenty minutes." My dad continued chopping vegetables. "You two go on outside. I think we could manage a meal al fresco with today's weather."

I leaned over the counter, pretending to get a closer look at the peppers when, in actuality, I was looking for evidence of the lurking spirit.

Nada.

Ian grabbed the stack of plates and silverware and we headed outside where the table had already been covered in a yellow floral oilskin cloth.

"He doesn't seem too bad, your dad."

"You missed out on all the good parts."

"Well, I'll stay as long as you want me to."

I started to set the table as Ian got comfortable in one of the chairs. When I was finished, I took a seat next to Ghosty on his favorite lounger and the three of us sat in comfortable silence.

"Do you have any idea who it might be?" Ian voice broke through the air, the timbre a bit deeper than usual. He was watching me, waiting for an answer, with sensuous eyes and the arrogant smirk I was now always associating with him.

"Nope. I was able to communicate with it a bit." I perked up, wanting to tell him but remembered that I needed to keep most of the magic hush hush because of Thom. "Not like it was able to reply but it definitely understands everything I say."

"That's pretty cool." He smiled. "You should try again now that you have the necklace." I fingered the jewel at my neck and watched as he ran his strong hands first along his thighs, then across the arms of his chair. Mesmerized by his movements, I couldn't help but imagine myself beneath him, continuing the seductive dance that we were carefully tiptoeing our way around.

"Dinner's ready." My dad chimed in, balancing the casserole dish atop the salad bowl.

We took our places at the table and I began serving out portions of crisp lettuce while my father sliced up the bird.

"White or dark meat, Ian?"

"White, please."

"Just like Gem here," my dad said, elbowing me, and my face flushed.

I felt a bit out of place. Like someone was going to walk up to me from behind the bushes and tell me that I had just been pranked.

Smile at the camera, Gem.

I watched the knife in my father's hand as it carved out thin pieces of chicken and kept my fingers crossed that he wouldn't start aiming the sharp blade at me. There was nothing in his demeanor that was off in any way.

That was the problem. Would I see it coming when he pulled a Miss Halle and went beserko?

"So, Ian, where are you from?"

"I'm an army brat so I've moved around a lot. I've been staying with my uncle to finish up high school. My parents are packing up for Germany."

Interesting. I continued to eat my food, not wanting to ruin whatever this was that was going on.

"What are your plans for college?"

"I've been thinking about NYU. They have a good study abroad program."

"Maybe you could convince Gemma to start getting on with those essays."

"Dad. I told you, I'll figure it out."

"There aren't any colleges within walking distance," my dad said, his tone more playful than it had been in the past.

"It's not a big deal," I said, taking out my fury on the last bits of food on my plate.

"Shotgun," I called, letting go of Mimi's arm and hustling into the front passenger seat.

"Relax, little sis. I got it covered."

"Didn't look like you got anything, yammering away with Jenny," I said, snapping the seatbelt into place.

"It was a stalling tactic," he said, smiling as he put the key in the ignition. The quiet engine of the hybrid didn't roar to life, which was always a letdown to me.

"At least put on some good music, Brian," Jenny said. "I can't listen to two hours of classic rock."

"Too bad," he replied, cranking up the volume. The melodic plucking of the guitar echoed the depressing lyrics in an

instrumental version of "Hotel California." The rest of us groaned.

"Okay. I have a great idea. We have a sing off. Whoever knows the most lyrics, wins." Classic Mimi. The peacemaker.

After Brian's rendition of "Baba O'Riley," where the three of us girls could only chime in for the Teenage Wasteland part, Jenny surprised us all with her singing of "Rapture." She even knew Debby Harry's rap verbatim.

"What is so important on your phone?" I asked Brian. "Could you please take a break from the endless checking of your messages?"

"I got it, one sec." He was scrolling through his texts while the other hand was on the steering wheel. The telltale ringtone he used for Allison had gone off.

"Dum, duh, dum, dum," Jenny sang.

"No kidding. I'm dead meat. We're supposed to be going out in an hour. I wonder if I could break up with her in between now and then."

"You're such an ass sometimes, Brian," I said. I leaned my head against the window and watched the other cars whizz past. The summer was already starting out hot. Many of the leaves were turning brown from drought and the earth looked parched.

Brian's phone buzzed again and I peeked at him from the corner of my eye. "Would you just pull over already? Your conversations are longer than War and Peace," I said.

"Let me just check what she said. Then the phone is all yours. You can hold on to it for the rest of the ride."

He reached over to pull the phone out of the small recess in the console.

"Brian!" Mimi yelled.

I looked up at the windshield, screamed, and braced my hands against the dashboard. The intimidating grill of a semi was accelerating in our direction.

Brian jerked the wheel to the left, attempting to avoid the collision but the truck, careening down the wrong side of the highway, was going too fast. With a loud crunch, it hammered into the side of the car. The screech of tires and twisting of metal was almost as loud as our screams. Then came the loud drone of horns honking. The impact took my breath away. I watched as the metal guardrail came into view and then the ravine below. In panic, I turned to Brian, whose bloodied face was limp against the airbag. The car tilted on its side, vacillating on the edge. For a moment, I had hope. I begged God not tip us over. But then all that was left was free fall.

"I could help you do some research, Gem," Ian offered.

"Sure," I said, pushing aside the potatoes that hadn't crisped up the way I liked them.

Beggars can't be choosers. Not like I ever got anything that wasn't out of a bag or box lately. Or a can.

"See, Gem. We'll figure things out," my dad said.

The rest of the meal was filled with small talk. I made up some story about the book club while Ian impressed my dad with his football stats.

After an hour, Ian was ready to leave.

"I promised to run some errands for my uncle," Ian said, as he helped bring the dishes to the kitchen.

"I'm glad you stayed," my dad said, filling the sink with hot sudsy water.

"Yeah, me too," I said, walking Ian to the door.

"You sure you'll be alright," he said in a hushed voice.

"I think so. Whatever is going on with him seems to have passed. At least for now. Anyway, where else would I go? It's not like I can leave."

As we stepped outside, I noticed how tall Ian was and how he filled up the space around me.

"Call me if you need me," he said, lowering his face to mine.

With his jacket open, I was able to place a tentative hand on his chest. I felt his heart beat beneath and the hard planes of his muscles. I looked up, drinking in his deep blue eyes and meeting him halfway for the kiss. His lips were warm, smooth and soft on mine. I felt his arms encircle me and I leaned in, taking him in deeper, opening up that bit of my heart that I had been keeping shut since Brian died. We clumsily side stepped until my back was up against the hard brick, his body pressing against mine. He trailed kisses along my neck as he held my hands in place at my side, sending shivers down my spine. With my eyes closed, I pulled my hands away from him and reached for his face.

The slight stubble scraped against my palms and I brought him back to my lips. I ran one hand through his hair and inhaled his scent, crisp and clean like the pine that watched us in the distance. He grabbed me by the waist and as he eased one hand under my shirt, my eyes flew open.

"I should get back in. My dad will wonder what's taking so long," I said, panting from a mixture of lust and sudden shyness.

"Like he doesn't know," he said, nipping at my ear.

"Really. I don't need him going all Jekyll and Hyde on me. I'll sleep better."

"Alright." He groaned, easing away from me. "But I intend to pick up where we left off." With an impish smile, he waved and was gone.

The next morning, as I stared at my body in the hazy light of the morning, I tried to find any evidence of the injuries I had sustained only months before. The angry, raised, red lines of thick skin were still gone.

I pointed my foot to the side and checked my leg from all angles.

I guess it's gone.

With the enthusiasm of a kid on Christmas morning, I opened my closet and pulled on a navy silk dress with billowy sleeves, stand-up collar and decorative pearl buttons. The ruffled hem ended mid-thigh and I twirled in front of the mirror with glee before lacing up my boots.

When I walked into the kitchen, my father was already seated, eating his breakfast. The place next to him was already set with a plate of scrambled eggs and toast waiting.

"Morning, Gem. Not going for your run?"

"Not today," I said, pouring myself a mug of coffee and settling down to enjoy my meal. "Thanks for cooking, Dad."

"My pleasure, pumpkin." He leaned away from his newspaper and placed a kiss on my forehead.

Maybe he's coming around. Maybe he needed to lose it a bit before putting himself back together.

He looked down at my leg. "What happened to your leg?"

"It's great, isn't it? Looks like it was never sliced open." When I saw the confusion on his face, I added, "I've been using this new cream for scars."

"Wow. Maybe Moab is in the wrong sector. We should be making beauty creams."

"Dad, trying to cure diabetes is way more important," I said, shoveling the eggs in my mouth to quiet the growling in my stomach, and get my dad off topic.

"I've got to get in early today," he said, wiping his mouth on a napkin. "Can you take care of the dishes before you leave?"

"Sure thing. You cook, I'll clean." I smiled.

"You think you can manage to get home again on time?"

"Oh yeah, I forgot to tell you. Charlotte is having a bunch of girls over for a sleepover. It's her birthday tomorrow."

"That's fine. Make sure you call me when you get to her house if I'm not here. I'll try to get home before you leave." He stood up and kissed me again before going.

Alone in the house, I took the opportunity to do a bit of snooping. I rinsed the dishes and loaded the washer before scurrying down the hallway to my father's room. Everything was in order.

Clean and tidy. Normal. A little too normal?

I sat on the peach silk comforter of his king-sized bed and opened the drawer of his side table. The room always gave me a strange feeling. He hadn't changed much in the room since Mom left and insisted that she was going to come back some day. I leafed through the stack of papers and couldn't find anything significant. Most of them looked like reports he had brought home with the Moab Labs' letterhead. There was a stack of old photos, mostly of Brian and me as children.

On the bottom, I found a faded yearbook picture of my mother. People always said we looked so much alike. Her hair stood two inches above her head, teased into its own orbit, and dangling from her ears were large pearl cluster clip-ons, which now had a home at the bottom of my jewelry box.

I stared at the picture, waiting for some kind of answers. Instead, all I was left with was more questions as I caught sight of the same necklace that now lay tucked beneath the fabric of my dress.

Having some newfound confidence, I was intent on making things right with Charlotte. I found her chatting with Morgan and Emma at the lockers, already dressed in their uniforms, as the squad usually did on practice days. Standing tall, I headed straight for them.

"Hey Charlotte. Morgan," I said, ignoring the buzzing I was feeling at my wrist. "I'm really sorry about how I acted yesterday. And I'm saying this to both of you. I don't want to be stuck in that place where all I have is myself."

"Oh Gemma," Charlotte started, "I'm so happy. You're really starting to look like you again." We joined in a quick embrace.

"Does that mean you're back on the team?" Morgan hesitated a bit.

"If you'll have me?" I looked at the two of them.

"Wow, Gem. I'm so proud of you," Charlotte said.

"What a relief." Morgan laughed. "You can't land a back flip but you are so much better coordinated than any of the new girls."

"Is that a backhanded compliment?"

"Oops." The color drained from her face. "I didn't mean it that way."

"Practice is during lunch today. We moved it so Charlotte could get home and set up," Emma said, not seeming all that impressed by my recent change of heart.

"It's alright, Morgan," I said, ignoring Emma's blasé attitude and reminding myself not to let anyone else's opinion get the best of me. "Am I still invited tonight?" I asked.

"Wow, silly. Of course," Charlotte answered. "And I have a big surprise for everyone," she squealed.

"Charlotte. You always amaze me," I said.

"Word is you're a freak, Gemma. Allison's been telling everyone about your tats. How'd you even get them?" Emma said, with a knowing look in her eyes. I turned to see Allison already making her way towards us.

"Hey freak," she said. "Gonna get a tramp stamp tonight to add to your collection?"

"No one was talking to you, Allison," Morgan said. Her quick defense surprised me.

"Free country and all that," Allison replied. "Just warning you girls that sluttiness is contagious."

I saw Matt looking around as if he were looking for something very important up in the ceiling. "What have you been telling her, Matt?" I asked. His lying about our relationship stabbed deeper than any blade Allison could use against me.

"He told me all the juicy details," Allison interjected before he could answer.

"There are no juicy details, bimbo," Charlotte said.

"Gemma's a virgin."

"I'm pretty sure the entire school heard that," I muttered.

"That's not what he said. And it would be even more pathetic if you were."

I felt the hopelessness sinking into me. A small crowd had already gathered around us, holding on to every bit of gossip. Allison stepped closer and I watched as the shadow filled her eyes. Smoke crept up from behind her and enveloped us. Around us, everyone had frozen mid-action. Emma was sneering from behind Morgan. Charlotte had her hand up in the air, finger pointed at Matt, her mouth ready to give him a beat down. The rest of them were frozen in various states of amusement. A blanket of silence coated them all.

"I'm supposed to get you, Gemma. For them."

"Allison?"

"No. But does it matter who I am? I find it more important who you are."

"I'm just Gemma."

"And they want you. But I'm going to have a little fun first."

My emotions ran from furious to scared silly. Finally, though, anger won out. I found myself wanting to fight back. I was just beginning to piece my life back together.

I felt the pulse of the sigils at my wrist. I touched my hand to the place where my necklace lay beneath the thin layer of clothing and I coiled all the energy I was feeling through me. I tugged at the invisible strands of electricity that started at my wrist and pulled them through my body until they fluttered beneath the gemstone. I let the energy grow and expand until it reached the point where I could no longer contain it. With one final thought, I let it go.

The force exploded through me into Allison, shoving her to the far wall and drawing all the surrounding blackness back into her. Then, as if someone had pressed play, the sound came back on and everyone came back to life.

"Just for the record," I said, as all eyes were on us wondering when exactly Allison had gotten kicked to the ground. I pulled at my sleeve exposing the marks. "Consider this a tribute to Brian. And Mimi. And Jenny. Not like you could even fathom what it means to care about someone more than yourself."

I turned to Matt who was probably seeing the real me for the first time and said, "And you should be ashamed. I hope your meat and two veg fall off."

"What the hell is that supposed to mean?" he asked, helping Allison up to her feet.

"Ask Mr. Flynn. It's British."

After the whoots and the whistles died down, I waved to Charlotte and Morgan. I even managed half of a nod to Emma, who smiled back, undoubtedly switching her eggs to my basket. Then I made my way to homeroom, trying to figure out who exactly wanted me and why.

CHAPTER FOURTEEN

The look on Thom's face, as I sat in homeroom, pained me. I tried my best to pretend that disappointment didn't weigh heavily on his already deep black eyes. It was harder knowing that he had turned up the setting on his ignore-o-meter to nonexistent. I felt despondent and alone in a crowd of dozens of people.

Ian walked in twenty minutes late and took the seat behind me.

"Mr. McQueen. You're tardy."

"I had something," Ian replied, hanging his backpack on my chair.

"Something?"

"Yeah, something."

"Care to explain, in private?" Mr. Flynn said standing from his chair and motioning to the door.

"Not really," Ian said. I could feel him rustling through his bag. When I turned, he smiled and winked. I smiled back but it felt empty, knowing the time we spent the day before was all at Thom's expense.

"Mr. McQueen. I am the teacher here. Outside. Now."

"Well, you're not really a teacher. We all heard you begging Principal Kelly for your job," Ian said with a snicker.

Thom stepped forward and placed his hands on Ian's desk.

"Insubordination will not be tolerated." He was looking at Ian but I knew he was really talking to me. I could feel his words pinning me to my seat and I was angry that he had a way of making me feel so small. "I cannot mark your attendance if you cannot provide a reasonable explanation as to your whereabouts."

"I guess I'll take the day off then. Long weekend." He grabbed his bag and stood up. "Catch you later, Gemma."

"Bye, Ian," I whispered.

As he walked passed me, Ian brushed his hands across my shoulder and I grabbed at them, realizing that he was really going to leave.

"If you're going to be leaving, do so now. I will not have you disrupting the rest of the class," Thom said. His voice was commanding yet remained in check. He folded his arms across the plain black cotton tee he wore, giving him an intimidating appearance.

"Sure," Ian said, and with one last wave to me, he was gone.

Not ten minutes went by before the bell rang and I sighed in relief that I was going to escape Thom's heavy aura of dissatisfaction.

"Miss Pope." He called after me when I was mere steps away from liberation. Ninja stealth couldn't have helped me escape Thom's notice.

"Yes, Mr. Flynn?" I said, backtracking my way to his desk.

He waited for the last of the students to leave and then resumed. "Do you think I'm running a bloody day care here?"

"I'm really sorry I never showed up yesterday. I was having a bad day. I sliced my arm by accident and Principal Kelly gave me permission to go home."

I started to pull up my sleeve. *It's not there anymore, genius.*

"I was under the impression that I had already explained the gravity of the situation we are in." He stood up, his body imposing. I rocked on my heels and looked down, avoiding his brutal gaze. "You saw what they did to that car. Do you think all the craziness going on in the world right now isn't more of the same? The rules are changing and we need to figure out why before it's too late. Can you manage that, love?"

I wasn't sure how to respond. If I even should. It seemed juvenile to even try on any of the excuses I had come up with, so I answered from the heart.

"I'm sorry. It won't happen again."

"That's better," he said, and heaved the grimoire onto the desk. "We try again after school. Today. You mentioned a Dyybuk living near your home. We'll try there. The next step is to summon a demon who can get these things to talk."

"Got it." It felt safe enough to look up and when I

did, I caught Thom's turbulent gaze. Nothing compared to how pissed off he was now and I could only imagine that it could get much worse.

"Meet me outside at two-thirty."

I didn't argue.

"Gemma, awesome. I'm glad I caught you." Charlotte was walking towards me in her cheerleading uniform and, for once, a pair of comfortable white Keds.

"Your shoes aren't up to code, Char. They are at least three inches too low." I laughed, shoving my books in the locker.

"Wow. So the girls are outside already. You in?"

"Sure. Let me go change."

I was extra cautious in the girls' locker room, keeping my senses on high alert. I didn't want Allison catching me by surprise again and nearly broke my nose trying to get my sweats on without taking my eyes off the door.

Outside, the rest of the squad was warming up on the field. Emma, still a junior, was showing the new recruits some of the basics while Charlotte and Morgan were on the bleachers.

The air was clean and crisp. The sun was just reaching its apex in the sky and, for once, I felt normal again; my only care in the world being not dropping anyone at the bottom of the pyramid. Then I saw the line of Dybbuk huddled behind the row of billboards at the far end of the field. I used my hand to shield my eyes from the sun and counted six of them. *Goddamnit.*

"Hey, I'm here."

Charlotte and Morgan looked up from the Harrisport Cheer Bible, a binder that's been passed from captain to captain, each one adding their new routines.

"Cool. You can just sit here with us. I don't want to push you in the fitness department."

"I can handle it, Charlotte," I said.

"Yeah, but we're not even sure what we're doing this year. Everything is so stale. Besides, you know all the stuff Emma's working on now."

"Fine. But next time, we're all getting our butts up."

"Yeah. For sure."

"Have you seen the stuff the Knights have been posting on their site? Hot stuff. I wish we could come up with a routine like that."

"Why don't we work on it tonight?" Morgan suggested. "We'll crank up the music in your basement. I'm sure it'll click. It always does."

"Yeah but this year the stress is all on me," Charlotte said. "If I don't come up with something to impress, I'm toast. And I know we're all besties, but Emma's going to be the first one to kick my ass about it."

"Just ignore her. She's got her panties in a bunch about something," I said to reassure Charlotte.

"Oh and I totally forgot," Charlotte said. "You guys have to come watch me in the revue. I'll die of embarrassment if I get on that stage and the seats are empty."

"Sure. When is it?" I asked.

"Not for another two weeks but apparently ticket sales haven't exactly been stellar in the past."

"I'm in," Morgan and I said. "Jinx," we said again

and joined in a fit of laughter.

I let my eyes stray across the grass. The Dybbuk hadn't moved. *At least that means they haven't gotten closer.*

"So am I going to be the one to ask you what are you and Ian about?" Charlotte said, tucking her legs beneath her, ready to take in all the dish I had to offer.

"What's his story? I hardly see him. He like comes and goes as he pleases," Morgan said. "So mysterious in a tall, dark and handsome kind of way."

"He's different. I can't explain it. He has a way of making me feel calm and excited at the same time. He makes everything else fall away and keeps me wondering what's next. He makes me care about what I'll be doing next week and even next month," I said, looking out onto the field, thinking of Brian's last home game.

After a very undemanding hour of gossiping, I rushed back into school, excited to finish up my classes and have the day come to an end. Before I could get to Mr. Flynn's class, Principal Kelly stopped me in the hallway. "Gemma. Just the person I was looking for."

"Hi, Principal Kelly. Nice boots." She was wearing a loose yellow overcoat embroidered with multicolored feathers, paired with a brown fringe skirt and light blue cowboy boots.

"I was hoping we could have that meeting now. I'm concerned about your plans. You haven't even met with the guidance counselor about which colleges you'll be applying to. If you have any interest in early admission, the deadline is sooner than you think."

"Well, you see, I have English now and Mr. Flynn is super strict about attendance."

"That's good to hear. I was worried his inexperience would show and that you kids would prey on him like carrion in the African bush. No worries. I'll write you a pass." She started walking to her office and then looked back. "It shouldn't take long," she said, waiting on me.

In her office, Principal Kelly liked to play a soundtrack of healing Tibetan singing bowl music. She told everyone that it helps clear the mind and heal the body and soul. I wasn't too sure if it worked but she seemed to look good for her age.

"Have a seat, Gemma."

I dropped into a blue canvas upholstered chair that reminded me of the kind they bolted down in rows in hospital waiting rooms. The fabric was itchy and wore easily in spots that were high use, like the center of the seat and arms.

"I'm glad to see you joined the squad again."

"How did you know?"

She pointed to the window behind her that overlooked the football field.

"Charlotte's been a big help," I said. "And Morgan."
No shame in taking the time to brownnose for my friends.

"That's good to hear," she said, leaning back in her chair. She didn't say anything else and the silence was beginning to grate on me.

"So," I started. "About college. I'm not too sure what I'll be doing. I promise I'll set aside some time this weekend to do some research. I don't really want to go too far."

"I understand."

Yeah right.

"Can I go back to class?" I asked.

"Gemma," she said, "I didn't really ask you here to talk about college. Knowing your father, he's probably already planned out that part." I noticed the slight derision in her voice. "I'm not sure if you know this but I was very close to your mother."

"No, I didn't. But then again, I don't know much about her. She kind of picked up and left." *Now it was my turn to make snide remarks about my own parent.* "And my dad tries his best."

"I'm concerned about you." She leaned in closer and reached for my hands, which were clasped on the table. "I'm concerned about this," she said, pulling back my sleeve and revealing the sigils.

"I don't think my body is much of your concern," I said, yanking my arm out of her grasp.

"Your mother and I practiced together. We were part of a coven of witches. I know better than anyone what those markings are. You are playing with fire." Her voice was strained and I could see the petrified look in her eyes.

"I'm fine, Principal Kelly," I said. "Is that it?"

"Gemma, I am begging you to stop. Whatever it is, it's not worth the risk."

"Like I said, I'm fine. Can I have that pass now?"

She took out a pink slip of paper, checked the time and signed. "For you mother's sake, I am pleading with you to stop whatever dark magic it is you're doing." She held out the slip and I snatched it out of her hand and headed straight for the door.

"I owe my mother nothing," I said. My blood boiling at Principal Kelly's presumptuousness, I stormed right out of there and straight into Thom's chest.

"Where were you, Miss Pope?" he asked. The sleek leather jacket suited him well. *Was anyone ever going to tell him how god-awful his shoes were?*

"Here," I blurted, shoving the pass into his hand. "Can we go now?"

He unfolded the crumpled slip of paper and nodded. "Yeah. Let's go."

We walked in silence side by side until we reached the parking lot, where he unlatched the helmet from his bike and tossed it to me.

"Put that on."

I caught it in my two hands against my stomach and then dangled it away from me by the strap like a dead animal. "Uh-uh. No way. Not happening."

"Come on. It's safe." He straddled the large leather seat and patted the small cushion behind him. He turned the ignition and kicked the bike into gear, sending out a plume of smoke that soon evaporated as the bike warmed up.

"You don't understand."

My eyes are open. I can't hear a thing. There is a sharp pain coming from my leg and I see bone jutting out from my thigh, tearing through flesh and fabric. I take a deep breath.

I turn my head and Brian is still out. I frantically search for the door handle amidst the layers of ballooned nylon and take a deep breath to keep back the wave of nausea that is threatening to drown me in terror.

I hobble out of the car, keeping pressure off my injured leg. Using the car as a crutch, I hop my way around to the driver's side. I look up and at the top of the cliff, there are people jumping up and down, waving in panic. None of them are looking at me. I tear at the door until it gives and Brian's arm slinks out. There is blood caking his shirt and pouring down his shoulder. I grab his head and send my fingers dancing around his neck for a pulse. I can't find one. I pull on his arms until his upper body is dangling out the side. I drag the rest of him out. His cellphone lights are blinking and I stare at the texts. I bash it against the rocks until it dies and toss it as far as I can.

I can't let Brian die like this. I open his mouth and breathe in. I beg him to open his eyes and I punch his chest. I look up again and see no one. I still can't hear. With a burst of adrenaline coursing through my veins, I start pulling Brian out and drag his limp body to the passenger side of the car. I don't stop until he is sitting in my seat and I hear the clink of the seatbelt. I rest my head against the pebbles on the floor and pass out.

"Gemma. Gemma?" Thom's voice was loud, breaking through my panic.

"I can't get on that."

"Tell me."

"I just can't. I can't. I can't."

I fell to the ground and curled up in a ball, shutting my eyes tight against the memories that were flooding back and the deluge of blood that plunged me into my worst nightmares.

"Tell me, Gemma." His voice held a mixture of authority and compassion.

I wiped my eyes free of tears. He was sitting beside me, cross-legged and waiting.

"It comes back every night. The blood."

"What blood?"

"Brian's. The accident. It was so awful." As hard as I tried not to cry, I couldn't stop the heaving.

"Relax." He put a hand on my back and I was filled with warmth. It soothed every muscle in my body and just as it was starting to burn, he took it away.

I looked at him, trying to find a sign of what he truly was but whatever mask he wore was firmly in place, and I didn't see a hint of him sharing that part of himself.

Maybe if I opened up, he would too?

"It was the beginning of summer. It was me, Brian, Jenny, and Mimi. I forgot whose idea it was but in the end, we headed to Jenny's lake house. It couldn't have been any lazier. We did nothing but lie in the sun and eat junk. On the way back, it all went to shit. The truck came out of nowhere and we were tossed over the side of the highway like a tin can."

"Your brother. He was your twin."

"Yeah. He was my best friend. I know that sounds weird. We fought like cats and dogs but it was all a joke to us."

"Sounds nice. To have had a brother like that."

"Had. That's the operative word. He's gone. I'm alone. And can't seem to get myself back on the horse," I said motioning to the bike. "Can't get in a car, bus. Train. When I try, the blood fills me until all I see is red and I think I'm going to choke on it."

"Do you trust me, Gemma?" he asked.

"I'm not sure."

"Smart girl." He smiled. "But I'm telling you that in this case, you can."

"Yeah?"

"If I told you that you are going to put on that

helmet and get on the bike with me and that I will protect you, would you believe me?" All the humor had left his face, leaving an intensity that made him seem wise beyond his years.

"Do I have much of a choice?" I asked.

"If I gave you one, would you do it?"

"Probably not."

"Then I won't." He stood, bringing me up with him, and placed the helmet over my head. He pushed open the visor and stared. "Your job is to get on the bike and hold tight. I'll protect you. I give you my word."

He turned the ignition back on and I took my place behind him, wrapping my arms around his strong back and resting my head against his shoulder blade. I felt the power of his muscles as he put the motorcycle into gear. Then, with a turn of his wrist, we were off.

CHAPTER FIFTEEN

We started off slow. I could tell that he didn't want to jump the gate and scare me. As I loosened my vise-like grip on him, he went a bit faster. I alternated watching the blur of trees go past and squeezing my eyes shut so that I couldn't see a thing. Before I knew it, we were in front of my house and Thom was rolling the bike up the driveway. When we came to a stop, he jumped off, helped me down and gently removed the helmet.

"We made it."

"We did." I smiled, proud of myself that I had taken the chance.

"Now, take me to your spirit." He took the grimoire out of the black leather saddlebag, tucked it under his arm and handed me a plastic bag. "I brought the candles just in case you hadn't any."

"This way," I said and led him to the back of the house.

We set up all our supplies on the patio table.

Ghosty moved from his spot on the lounger to hover behind us as we flipped through the pages of the grimoire.

"How are we going to find the right demon?" I asked. "All their powers overlap and on top of that, not everyone is cooperative."

"Do not despair. We will find him or her soon enough."

The leaves rustled in the background and I watched a squirrel race across the ledge onto an overhanging branch. Ghosty was starting to sway back and forth in the breeze, something I had never seen it do before. When it caught me watching, it darted to the stairs and began its descent then paused halfway. I stood up and looked down. It continued down to the grass and headed towards my running trail.

"Not now," I yelled back at it. "I'm busy."

"You've been talking to it, I see." Thom crept up behind me. We watched as Ghosty waited by the first tree of the dirt path.

"Should we follow it?" I asked.

"Might be a good idea."

"Might be a bad one," I said. "But it hasn't bothered me yet."

"Then let's go."

We dashed across the yard and as we reached Ghosty, he darted away into the woods. When we got to the fork in the trail, Ghosty went left.

"I usually go right," I said through heavy breathing.

"It wants us to follow." He leaned against a pine.

"No. I don't think so."

"Why the hell not?" he asked.

"That place gives me a bad feeling. Always has.

Forget it."

"Oh come now. You're an all-powerful summoner in training. Scared of the dark, are you?" He laughed.

"Fine. Come on. Before we lose it."

At the end of the densely-shaded path, there was a clearing where we found Ghosty hovering in the center of a ring of boulders. The ground was mostly mulch that smelled like fresh organic decay and the recent rain. The canopy of branches that extended overhead had dimmed whatever sunlight was left to the day. The large rocks, however, shimmered with a blue incandescent glow.

"What is this place?"

"It's the shit hitting the fan," Thom answered. He walked over to the boulder closest to him, knelt beside it and brushed away a layer of moss.

"You see, I was right. This place is bad news. Wait," I said, seeing a familiar arrangement of lines and circles. "Isn't that a sigil?"

"Unfortunately, yes," he said.

"Care to elaborate?" I said in my best fake British accent.

When he looked at me, his eyes were stone cold.

"This is no joke, Gemma. This is a chamber."

"And a chamber is?"

He frog leaped from stone to stone, revealing each one's markings.

"It's bad news. It means that Harrisport is in danger. A chamber is the only way for demons to get back onto this plain without being summoned. If they know about this, they can have someone open the chamber, releasing whatever demons are tied to it."

"So it's like a portal."

"What do you know about portals?" he said with a chill in his voice.

Proceed with caution, Gem.

"Suppose, hypothetically, that I had traveled through one."

"Then I would, hypothetically, kick your arse and tell you to stay the hell away from them."

"Then it's a good thing this conversation is all theoretical." I turned away and pretended to examine one of the etchings. *The sooner I shut up, the better.*

"It better be." He kept his eyes on me and it took all my energy to resist the urge to tell him about Ian, the club, and the new necklace.

"Does that mean there's more than one chamber?" I asked.

"There are seven, each one closing off a different sect of the Otherworld. Open all of them and you're basically creating a hell on Earth."

"Maybe it's a coincidence. I'm sure no one knows about it. I've been living here all my life and it's the first time I'm seeing this."

"And your Dybbuk over there got us here in a matter of minutes."

"I see your point."

"I'm hoping that means no more arm-twisting when it comes to the summonings. I need you on board. Fully committed."

"You got it." I walked to the center of the ring. The ground felt no different from the surrounding area. "So how do you get one of these chambers open?"

"That's a mystery in itself. I doubt many know."

"So we stay on course," I said. "We summon the right demon and get rid of the Dybbuk. Whatever this chamber needs seems to stem from them. No Dybbuk, no problems."

"I hope you're right," he said brushing the loose soil from his knees.

Me too.

Thom left soon after, assuring me that he would ask around and find the demon we needed. I told him I was staying at Charlotte's that night but that I was free the rest of the weekend to work whenever he needed me.

Back in the house, I packed a bag with toiletries, what I liked to call public-pajamas (the kind you could answer the front door in) and a change of clothes.

When I was finished showering and had changed into what I referred to as fancy-sweats (the kind you never exercised in), I heard a commotion in the kitchen.

"Hey Dad," I said, unsure of which father would be greeting me today.

"Hey, pumpkin," he said, looking normal but weary, scouring through the junk drawer. "I thought I would throw on some steaks."

"I'm on my way to Charlotte's house. Remember, the sleepover."

"Right. I forgot. I'm sorry. Can I offer you a ride without fearing for my life?"

I looked out the window and it was already dark. Charlotte's house was more than a mile away. I could have managed on my own but I couldn't risk seeing my dad's other face, especially after having gotten on a motorcycle with Thom.

"Sure. Yeah that would be great."

He smiled and grabbed his keys off the small tray he emptied his pockets into every day.

"Come on," he said, and I braved myself for the second trip of the day.

When we drove up to Charlotte's house, along the neat pattern of pavers and passed the elaborate bronze fountain and birdbath, the moon was already heavy in the dark night sky.

"See you tomorrow," I said, planted a kiss on my dad's cheek and bolted up the stairs. He waited until the front door opened and I stepped in before he waved and drove away.

"Gem, did you just do what I think you did?" Charlotte asked. She was wearing a baby pink cashmere slouch sweater and gray crop leggings.

"What?"

"Like get in a car." She shut the large wooden door behind me.

"Oh yeah. Figured it was about time to give it a try."

"I'm so proud of you."

"I didn't think anyone noticed."

"I'm not anyone." She squeezed her cheek to my arm and led me passed the formal dining room and kitchen to the casual, yet professionally decorated, den. It was the kind of room that was meant to be cozy and inviting but was way too put together to give it the real lived-in feel. I knew that the Senator usually locked himself in his library with a tumbler full of scotch in one hand and the whole carafe in the other. Charlotte's mother, Patricia, was either at a fund-raising meeting or shopping, drifting from one champagne glass to the next until she came home and blacked out on her bed, surrounded by bags filled with her designer purchases that would probably end up with the tags still on, never to be used.

"True," I replied. "So where are your parents?"

"I kicked them out for the night," she answered. "Here, make a plate." She passed a square of white porcelain and I filled it with the bite-sized sandwiches and appetizers that had been thoughtfully arranged on the large, wrought-iron coffee table.

Charlotte flipped through the channels while we waited for Emma and Morgan to show up. "I wanted tonight to be intimate," Charlotte said, explaining the short guest list.

"I hope you didn't do that for me?" I said, biting into a miniature-sized burger.

"Nah. It's because of the surprise I have planned. Super exclusive and hard to get. I couldn't have more than three other people."

We were halfway into a juicy episode of *True Life* "I hate my plastic surgery" when the doorbell rang. Charlotte brought Morgan and Emma through and we all vegged out while debating who was the most underrated celebrity.

The next time the bell rang, all of us, except Charlotte, was caught by surprise. "Oh wow. That must be our surprise."

"How is it your surprise if you know what it is?" Morgan asked, tossing a piece of caramel kettle corn at Charlotte's head.

"Is it a stripper?" Emma asked in a tired voice. I could tell though that she wouldn't complain if her night involved a lap dance by a hot, built, topless, preferably Italian, guy in a G-string.

"Nope. This is even better." Charlotte ran back to the front of the house and returned with a woman who looked like she could be any one of our mothers.

"Um, hi." I waved.

"I'm going to let you introduce yourself," Charlotte said to the petite woman with spiky bleached hair.

"Hello, girls. My name is Sylvia Nicks and I am a psychic and medium." Charlotte pulled a chair for her and she sat down between the two overstuffed love seats that Emma, Morgan and I had divided ourselves amongst.

"I've seen you on TV, right?" Morgan asked.

"Yes. I'm asked to share my gift sometimes." She smiled.

Charlotte took the empty spot beside me and whispered,

"This part was for you."

"Let me pull some tarot cards out first while we wait for any spirits to come forward. Sometimes it takes a little time. Who would like to go first?"

"Birthday girl," Morgan squealed.

"Yeah, Charlotte. You should go first," Emma seconded.

"Oh wow. This is too cool."

"Please cut the deck and focus in your mind's eye the question you are putting out to the universe." Sylvia handed her the large deck of cards. They were double the size of playing cards and decorated in an ornate curlicue pattern of deep red, blues and silvers. I noticed that her manicured nails were done up in the same colors as the cards.

After a short silence, Sylvia drew ten cards, placing some in a cross-shaped pattern to one side and the remainder in a straight line on the other. One by one she turned each card over, displaying their pictures and positions on the coffee table.

"This is the three of swords and it is the heart of the matter. You are unable to reconcile certain new parts of your life."

"Ohmygod. That is so true," Charlotte said, leaning in closer to the table and the cards she thought would hold all the answers to her life.

"The next card is the hanged man. You are trying too hard to please others and work to their benefit instead of your own. You need to focus more on yourself and what you want."

The rest of us crowded in on the reading. It was starting to get good.

"This is the Queen of Pentacles and it is a practical woman in your life that is getting in the way of true success."

"That's totally your mom," Morgan whispered.

"Shush," Emma blurted, edging closer to Sylvia's chair.

"The five of discs shows that you recently tested this new you and have had measurable success. And this," Sylvia tapped on the card with a beautiful woman seated on a throne holding a sword in one hand and a scale in the other, "is Justice. Your future is filled with a balancing act. It is up to you to keep both sides equal."

"What's that supposed to mean?" Emma asked.

"Wait a minute. Someone is coming through the veil." Sylvia placed three fingers to her temple and looked off to the side as if she were listening to someone speak. "Yes, I understand. Does anyone know of a girl with a J name? A Jennifer, Joanie?"

"Jenny?" I asked. I didn't want to be too forthcoming and make her job at snowing people over too easy but I couldn't resist giving her that bit of information with the hopes that she could actually commune with the dead.

"Yes. Jenny has a message for all of you. She said that she is at peace and didn't feel a thing. That she passed on quickly and that her grandmother was there to bring her over to the other side."

We all looked at one another and I found my surprise reflected on everyone else's face. I remained quiet, not wanting to sever whatever connection Sylvia had with our friend.

"She also wants you all to know that it wasn't Gemma's fault and that you should stop letting her take the blame for it."

I nearly choked on the cracker I had mindlessly put in my mouth. I grabbed a can of soda and washed down the dry flakes that had coated my throat.

"What does she mean by that?"

Sylvia continued to listen and nod her head. "She says that Gemma will tell the rest of you when its time. Whew. That was a doozy." Sylvia took a napkin and wiped the sweat form her brow. "She was a strong one. Now where were we?"

Sylvia continued her vague predictions of Charlotte's future and then Emma's. Morgan passed, claiming that she didn't really want to know her future.

"Ditto," I said. My mind was reeling with the message that had come through from Jenny. The fact that Sylvia was even able to get that detail proved to me that she had a gift of some sorts.

How come it wasn't Brian?

"Okay, so how about we move on to something different?" Sylvia asked and we all nodded our heads in unison. "Let's start with you, Morgan. Since you didn't want to see into your future, how about we pick through your past lives."

Morgan perked up. "Sure."

"I'm going to need a little more space for this."

Charlotte, Emma and I all squished onto one couch while Morgan lay on the other, her head close to Sylvia's chair.

"Have you ever gone under hypnosis before?"

"Nope," Morgan answered.

Sylvia lowered her voice and began soothing her with words, reassuring Morgan that she'd be sliding deep within her psyche to reconnect with her past selves. I watched as Morgan's eyes grew heavy and shut. Her hands, palms up, relaxed into the pale green paisley cushions.

"Morgan? Tell me where you are."

"It's beautiful. A field of wildflowers."

"What do see?"

"Pinks and yellows and blues. The sun is shining."

There was a flicker of activity beneath her eyelids.

"There is laundry. It's white and smells fresh. The house is small. It's made from wood. There's a daisy chain in my hand."

Morgan was mumbling and jerking now.

"No. No. They're coming. The house is too far. It's so loud. The ground shakes from them. I grab my mommy's apron. She's carrying the baby. I can't hold on. She's on the porch, waving her hands. Mommy is screaming and I'm running. I see them now. The buffalo. No!" Morgan was screaming now.

"Morgan, I am snapping my fingers," Sylvia said, unperturbed by the distress she was showing. The snap of her fingers cracked like a whip. "Wake up."

Morgan opened her eyes. "Was it good? Was I like Nefertiti or something?"

"No, Morgan. You were a little girl who got stampeded by a herd of buffalo," Emma said.

"Wow, Emma. Be cool," Charlotte said in a warning tone that I rarely heard her use.

"Fine. Now it's Gemma's turn," Emma said.

"Okay." I switched spots with Morgan. "Let me know what kind of awful life I had."

Sylvia went through the same charade and I had to admit I was feeling a bit loose and tired. Time had suspended. Everything had fallen away into a spiral of blackness where there was no light or sound. Before I knew it, everything was dark. Then there was a snap.

"So was I Marie Antoinette and had my head chopped off?" I joked, bringing myself to a seated position. When I looked up, everyone else was quiet, jaws open. "Are you guys okay?"

"Gemma, honey-" Charlotte started.

"You came up blank," Morgan continued.

"And sounded like the kid in the Exorcist," Emma added.

"What do you mean?"

"I know what you are." Sylvia pointed a long nail at my face and stood up. "I'm sorry, Charlotte. Happy Birthday but I've got to leave. There's no charge."

Sylvia left like the house was on fire and I was the one holding the matches.

Chapter Sixteen

After Psychic Sylvia's departure, we went on to watch the entire season of a recent paranormal activity show from start to finish as we super-analyzed all the relationships in school, including the strange one between Allison and her new lap dog, Matt.

"I heard he was hoping to make QB," Morgan said.

"Didn't take him long to start riding the bitch train," Emma muttered as she dipped a stalk of celery into the homemade ranch dressing. "I kind of wanted him." She grinned shyly from behind the tall plate of crudités.

"Guys. A bit of sensitivity here," Charlotte said nodding her head in my direction.

"For me? Don't bother. I don't know why I wasted my time with him. I never even really liked him. He was just friends with Brian since we were all in diapers." I swirled the swizzle stick in my lemonade and stabbed at a piece of fresh strawberry. It was Charlotte's idea of a mocktail. "Now that I think of it, Brian probably orchestrated the whole thing."

"I wish my brother would hook me up with some guys." Emma sighed.

"Your brother is twelve!" Morgan cried.

"You know what I mean," Emma replied, throwing a fancy silk pillow to get back at her, knocking a drink to the floor.

"Emma, look what you did," Morgan shrieked, jumping up from her seat and letting a pool of the pink sticky drink run off her lap and onto the oriental rug.

"I'll get the paper towels," I said, zig-zagging between the furniture through the sliding pocket door and into the gray and white marble kitchen. I found a roll of paper towels hanging beneath one of the cupboards and wadded a long stream of it into my hand. As I ripped it, there was a flash from outside the kitchen window.

Floodlights automatically flicked on, one at a time, down the length of the long narrow French-style garden. Walls of neatly manicured hedges surrounding the path were now illuminated in a harsh yellow green light. And at each lamp stood a thick black shadow.

I grabbed the edge of the counter to steady myself. One of the sigil's on my arm flickered with life.

What does that mean?

I wanted to check which one but there was no way I was taking my eyes off the stalker type ghosts that were waiting for me. If I knew what my soul felt like, I could swear on a stack of Bibles that they were trying to draw mine to them.

There was a loud crash behind me and I jumped.

"Hey, chicky."

"Ashtaroth?" I asked in confusion.

"Call me Ash," he said, walking down the length of the granite-topped island until he was beside me and sat down. "Looks like you got yourself a problem." He pulled a silver case out of the breast pocket of his electric blue overcoat and pulled out a thin white cigarette.

"Gross," I said, sticking out my tongue.

"Just for show, chicky. I've been trying to quit."

"Can I ask what you're doing here?"

"I'm here for my prize."

"Right, the sigil." I said, wondering how I was going to do it without any outside help.

"Yup. You're not so dumb for a …"

"A girl?"

"Those wouldn't be my choice of words." He shrugged his shoulders. "You ready to pay up?"

"Can I say no?"

"Not if you want to sleep tonight." His smile was more grotesque than I remembered and the odor coming out of his mouth was foul.

"But seriously, why do you need me? Can't you just do this stuff on your own?" I said, while rummaging through the drawers for paper and a pen.

"Tsk tsk. Your teacher has been censoring your lessons. Angels and demons can't touch that stuff. Burns and shit like that if we try. We don't do magic. Our gifts are part of nature. Something the Big Guy gave us," he said, pointing upwards.

"Okay, I'm ready," I said, when I found what I needed.

"Abbadon is the name. Death is his game."

"Ooo scary," I sang. "Not."

"You should be scared, chicky. You've got no idea what mess you've dropped yourself into."

I closed my eyes to block Ash's annoying face out of my sight and to picture the sigil wheel. With a few strokes and flourishes, I was done.

"Here." I shoved the scrap of paper into his hand. "Now can you leave?"

"Aw. I'm hurt." He gently folded the paper, tucked it into his pocket, and then stuck the unlit cancer stick in my face. "You'll be crying for my help soon enough. Don't forget it."

With a sudden rush of energy, Ash was sucked back in to the Otherworld and I was once again alone with my thoughts, and a dozen or so evil spooks waiting for me.

It wasn't a surprise to me that I was the last one to wake. I had waited for the others to fall asleep and checked multiple times to see if Dybbuk still littered the half-acre long expanse of backyard. They were still there. All of them. Waiting. Standing motionless as the smoke within their core roiled. Sleep finally overtook me as the first rays of dawn approached and drifted through the gauzy white curtains of Charlotte's bedroom.

I took a quick shower, made my way downstairs and followed the sounds of clinking cutlery to the breakfast room, where I found everyone just about to sit down to breakfast and the large bay window framing a pair of Dybbuk like something out of *American Gothic*.

"Sit down, Gem," Charlotte said, tapping the empty

spot beside her on the built-in.

I tried my best not to look too awkward but I couldn't help staring at the two ghosts that were peering at us through the thin pane of glass.

"You see something, Gemma?" Morgan asked.

"Nah, just the herd of buffalo coming to get you." I laughed, piling the french toast and sausage onto my plate.

"Stop it. I really think that happened to me. It must explain my unnatural aversion to animals," Morgan said matter-of-factly as she attempted to section a grapefruit without squirting juice in her face.

"I just wanted to thank the three of you for coming over. I know I usually get ridiculous on my birthday but it didn't feel right this year." Charlotte voice trailed as she took my hand and I knew that I wasn't the only one who had lost something. Everyone around me had lost someone. A friend. A crush. A classmate. A teammate. I was starting to realize that for the last few months, I had been internalizing my grief while those around me were losing one more person. Me.

"Thanks Charlotte. You're the perfect hostess. Martha Stewart style," I said.

We then all belted out an off-key version of "Happy Birthday" while Morgan pulled out a dark chocolate cake from the fridge and lit a sparkler. And for once I let myself enjoy the moment.

I followed Morgan and Emma out onto the porch after saying a big goodbye and thank you to Charlotte. Her mother's Mercedes was just pulling into the two-car garage.

"Thank God." Emma laughed.

"I know, right?" Morgan said. "She is like the hardest person ever to make small talk with."

"Give her a break. She's married to the Senator," I replied.

They both cringed and Emma wrapped a fake noose around her neck.

"Need a ride?" Morgan asked.

"No, it's alright. It's nice enough to walk. Need to keep the leg moving." I smiled, knowing full well that for days, my bones had never felt better and that my skin was still smooth as a baby's behind but I had reached my fill of socializing and was anxious to hear back from Thom.

With my duffel at my back, I started the trip back home and as Morgan's car drove past me, two Dybbuk slipped in through the partially open window.

Just great. Maybe I should try to stop them. And then what? Tell them two evil souls are about to take possession of their bodies?

I continued on my own, thinking about what I could have possibly said last night to freak Sylvia out. The others seemed to think that I had put them on. About half way through my walk, my cellphone buzzed from my jacket pocket.

Ian: Hey.

Me: Hey. What's up?

Ian: What are you doing tonight?

Me: No plans. On my way home from Charlotte's.

Ian: Had fun?

Me: Yeah.

Ian: Want to go out with me later?

Me: Sure.

Ian: K.Is seven a good time?
Me: Yeah. What did you have in mind?
Ian: You ;)
Me: No really. Where are we going?"
Ian: My favorite place. Wear something special.

My smile was still plastered on my face when I walked through the front door and greeted my father. "Hey Dad."

He grunted in response from amidst a mountain of papers. Usually, he worked through reams of lab results and testing questionnaires. Today, the Moab Lab stationary had been pushed aside and replaced by large maps and land surveys.

"What's that?" I asked.

"Quiet," he barked. I took note of the word Harrisport in the legend and the smattering of color-coded stickers in various positions. Not wanting the shadow inside him to rear its ugly head, I withdrew to the security of my bedroom. *Bad cop is back.*

As I dumped my dirty laundry in the hamper, a familiar rumbling out on the street had me rushing to the window and seeing if it was possible. Thom had parked his motorcycle behind a tree and was striding up the driveway. *A man on a mission.*

Instead of heading towards the door, I watched as he got closer to my bedroom window. He waved and then headed to the side of the house, which sent me scrambling to put on my sneakers. I gave my hair a quick check in the mirror and stuck my tongue out at the piece in the back that refused to lie back.

"I'm going for my run," I said to my dad in passing. The kitchen, living, and dining rooms were now a full-blown mess. He looked up from his work and I saw the darkness had returned. I didn't wait for him to respond and jogged to the forest trail, hoping that when I returned, his mood had passed.

As I turned the bend, it caught me by surprise that Ghosty had joined Thom in the center of the chamber circle.

"Hey, what are you two chatting about?"

"Very funny," Thom answered. "I brought the grimoire. Turns out our best bet is to summon Ronwe. He is the studious type so may be more inclined to share knowledge. We should move elsewhere." He picked up his satchel and handed me the bag of goodies that had gone unused the previous day.

"There's a place about ten minutes away. I go there sometimes to think. It's secluded enough."

"Lead the way."

We continued passed the dirt path and into the forest itself. I knew the way in the dark. We passed a denser thicket of trees, the branches reaching out like the limbs of old ladies, until the earth beneath us became rockier and more and more sky appeared overhead. When we passed the last of the tall pines and spruce, we walked single file along the rock face of one of Mohonk's larger peaks until, at last, we reached my cave.

"Haven't been here in a while," I said.

"Quite a bit of firsts we're sharing, huh?" His response was so innocent but the words sent my mind racing into fantasies that I needed to hold back.

Think of Ian. He's hot. He's my age. He's not a pain in the ass.

"I usually keep a lantern in here. Let me check." I took a few steps into the cave and blindly reached down for the LED camping light. When my toe kicked at something and it rang metallic, I knew I had found it and groped for the handle. I pulled it up and turned the knob, filling the small den with a dim white light.

Shadows danced across the wall, playing along the rise and fall of crevices along the ancient limestone. Evidence of interlopers was strewn across the floor in the form of empty water bottles and cigarette butts.

"I'll set up. You stay put," Thom said, arranging five red pillar candles around me in a circle.

"Shouldn't I be working on the sigil?"

"Not yet. I'm taking some extra precautions. Let me finish the protection circle first. Then we'll give it a go."

Just then my phone buzzed. Thinking it might be Ian, I checked my texts. What I found instead was a message from the local emergency broadcasting system.

NYSYS: Tornado watch in effect for Orange, Sullivan, and Ulster counties 2 p.m.

The current time glowed at the top of the screen. 12:30.

"Thom, we should probably hurry up." I passed him my phone and he replied with a harrumph. "Nope. Doesn't faze you? Not a bit?"

"You'll be back in your jimjams and under the covers before it hits," he replied while pouring a barrier of salt just beyond the flickering candles.

When did he light those?

The cave was bathed in a subtle warm glow and I looked around, trying to remember my last visit here.

It was for sure B.A. File it under the same category, as I can't remember the last time I was alone with Brian.

"There," Thom said and handed me a photocopied sheet of Ronwe's page in the grimoire.

"Where's the book?" I asked.

"Didn't want to be seen lugging it about," he replied and passed me a pen and leaf of parchment.

"But I need the sigil key."

"Pish posh. You can do it on your own now." It didn't sound like there was any room for arguments.

"Alright." I groaned and placed the tip of the pen to the paper. Before starting any of the markings, I closed my eyes and tried to search for the pattern in my mind. Slowly, the black fuzz cleared away, bringing into focus the flickering memory I had of the rosette until the pattern was as solid as could be. With my eyes still shut, I circled the letters. R.O.N.W.E. Then, with a flourish, I connected the power bearing letters to one another. When I surveyed my work, I was proud to see that my lines were no longer rough and jagged with inexperience.

"Good work," Thom said from his perch atop a smooth natural outcrop of stone that made the perfect bench. "Continue."

"I'm confused." I turned to him. The shadows were playing across the rugged planes of his face, casting a sinister glow. "Why the solo act?"

"You need to learn. I won't always be here."

"Are you leaving or something?"

"Don't worry. Not yet. But it would be reckless of me to leave you with only a hint of what's needed.

You must get a feel for the entire process. Next time I expect you to prepare the circle," he replied.

I checked the parchment once again and, trusting my instincts, added two small crescents before tossing it into the salt-lined indentation before me. Having trouble making out the incantation, I lifted the page closer to my face and recited the prayer.

"I call upon you, Ronwe. I summon you, Ronwe."

What appeared before us was no larger than a garden gnome with a torso covered in green and black scales. Instead of hair, flexible black quills protruded from his scalp and settled in a dark heavy mass beneath his shoulders, framing his red-skinned face. He wore a sleeveless shirt of mail, edged by a mass of long turkey feathers that stopped at his knees. When he pulled one leg behind him in a deep bow, I noticed that his legs were made of pure bone. His foot scratched against the floor like the talons of a predator.

"How may I serve?" Sarcasm dripped from his mouth, which I didn't think would make for an auspicious encounter. When he straightened, he caught sight of Thom and froze. "*Yip!* What are you doing here?"

"Please address your mistress," Thom said in return.

"Duly noted. But I do require payment."

"Naturally," Thom said, his smile anything but natural.

"So what will it be?" I asked.

"Parchment and quills." He rubbed his two bony hands together in anticipation

"That's pretty ordinary. Can't you go to the demon

supermarket for that stuff?"

"Do not mock me. I seek nothing save knowledge."

"Sure, you got it. Put 'er there." I extended my hand and we shook on it. "I hope you have another stash of parchment I can borrow, Thom."

Ronwe's sigil settled besides Ash's.

I must be getting used to this. Didn't feel a thing.

"You have five minutes," Ronwe chirped.

At this point, I was expecting Thom to interject but he didn't. Fearing that the time would pass before getting any real answers, I started the questioning.

"Who is sending the Dybbuk to Harrisport?"

"Ah, so this is what you humans are concerned with. Ba'al always has his sights on ruling this world."

"So it's him, then?" I asked.

"I never said it was. But if you are looking for clues about any demon who is remotely interested in this plain then you turn to those under Ba'al's dominion. The other rulers forbid meddling."

"But why come to Harrisport?"

"You know why, little lady." There was a wayward twinkle in his eye. "You found it out there. In the forest."

"The chamber?"

"Gemma," Thom said in warning.

"He obviously knows about it," I protested. "You can't keep something a secret if it's common knowledge."

"Not too common," Ronwe interrupted. "Those of us who sacrifice our existence in order to preserve our knowledge have been aware of the Seven Chambers for eons. Interesting to know who's been going through the logs."

"How are the Dybbuk involved?" Thom stepped down and closed in on us.

"Bah. A diversion tactic, no doubt. The real issue is the chamber and the means with which one opens it. Ah, but look," he said, displaying the face of his Kermit watch. "Time is up."

"I shall deliver your payment," Thom said.

"But wait. If we can figure out how they're going to get it open, we can stop them," I said.

"Another day. Another favor," Ronwe said and blinked out of sight.

With the pressure of surviving the summoning gone, I noticed the rain flooding and the hail popping in from outside.

"Come on," I said to Thom as I put out the candles and dumped the contents of our supplies back into the plastic bag.

"Keep it here," he said. "It will slow you down."

I chucked the bag onto the ledge as Thom took me by the hand. When we reached the mouth of the cave, I snatched my hand back.

"Ouch. Why can't I touch you? What are you?"

We stood there, pelted by gob-sized drops of freezing water. When they hit his skin, they sizzled and evaporated into puffs of steam that plumed behind his ears and off into the distance.

"I can't explain right now." He lightly caressed my cheek with the back of his hand and my nerve endings came alive. "You have to trust me."

I wiped the sections of drenched hair away from my face, looked him straight in the eyes and licked my lips, despite the moisture already coating my face. I briefly let myself imagine myself in his arms, safe from everything that threatened to hurt me, knowing deep down that he was probably the only person with the ability to do so. I brushed the thought away like cobwebs.

"Okay," I said.

A bolt of lightning forked through turbulent slate-colored clouds, followed by a thunderous rumble that shook both heaven and Earth. We gave each other a final glance and launched into a sprint through the shadows ahead.

Chapter Seventeen

Thom was a true gent, as I would imagine he would put it, and held his waxed canvas jacket over my head right up until we reached the front door. A frantic twist twist of the doorknob had us barreling into the house, making full body contact with a   disturbed father, pacing and mumbling up and down the foyer.

"Who's this?" he hissed. His eyes were solid black and shiny, like marbles of hematite set into the sockets.

"Pleased to meet your acquaintance. I'm Mr. Flynn, Gemma's English teacher."

My father stood and stared. "What happened to the other boy? Have you been whoring again? Just like your mother," he spat.

"Dad!" I yelled. "You should go, Thom."

"I didn't get a chance to tell dear old dad about your performance. She is quite the student." Thom didn't wait for my father to shake hands. He put out both of his palms and lowered the finger that was still sticking in my face. "Leave her be."

Fascinated, I watched as Thom gripped my father's hands. As he muttered beneath his breath, the shadow of the Dybbuk began to recede slowly, revealing the clear blues and whites of my dad's eyes.

"I'm sorry, Gem. I think I'm coming down with something. My head is killing me. It's a pleasure to meet you, Mr. Flynn. You're a bit young to be a teacher." My father was back to normal.

Whatever that meant nowadays.

"Just finished uni. Had my heart set on teaching." Thom gave his most impressive grin and I took notice of the small dimple that formed in the crease of his cheek.

"And what brings you here on a Sunday?" Taking notice of the disaster area around us, my father began securing the maps and piling his papers into neat stacks.

"Dad," I started, completely annoyed that he decided to go all parental at the worst possible times.

"Gemma is a member of the book club I host after school. I was trying to get her some copies of the piece we're reading." Thom held up some pages running with ink and soaked through by the rain. "Unfortunately, I ride a motorbike and these didn't fair too well."

"Well, thank you for the extra help. I'm sorry you came all this way." My dad headed for the door and held it open. "I think I'll lay down for a bit."

Thom took the hint and walked out. The weather had settled down.

"I guess there was no tornado after all," I said, seeing the usual autumn leaves that had migrated from branch to floor.

"I'm not so sure," Thom continued and pointed to the right. "Get a look at that."

Both my father and I poked our heads out, curious to see what could have happened. Down the road, trees had collapsed onto each other, flattening cars in a path heading south. Whatever it was had destroyed everything in its path. In the distance, sirens rang out.

"I hope no one's hurt," my dad said as he patted me on the back and returned to his work. I couldn't bear to think of someone leaving this life in such a senseless disaster.

Waiting until I was sure he was out of ear's reach, I tugged Thom's sleeve. "What was that in there? How did you get rid of it?" I said in my quietest voice.

"It's not gone yet. Once they get their hooks in, it's hell trying to get them out," Thom whispered. "Just be careful."

Leaving me with that idea in the forefront of my mind, he walked back to his bike and was gone.

Twelve reported missing as rescue teams begin to scour the area after an unknown weather pattern rips through the Greater New York area…

A large crane suspended above a Manhattan apartment building collapsed today, killing six and injuring twenty. Five are in critical condition…

Passengers swim for their lives in frigid waters after an Alaskan cruise liner crashed into a glacier…

Dad was watching the news again and I didn't want to provoke him by closing my bedroom door. Before the accident, those were the types of things that would set him off on a lecture about not wallowing in teenage angst. Now I was scared he'd just rip the door down in a rabid tantrum if the Dybbuk should rear its ugly head.

So I listened to every awful thing that was happening while I filled my notebook with doodles that resembled sigils. The list of apocalyptic phenomena seemed to be growing so long that there were no more sensational filler stories about "deadly diet pills" or "killer bird flu."

It was hard concentrating on any of my homework. My thoughts kept getting jumbled up between my alleged strange behavior while under Sylvia's hypnosis, her supposed contact with Jenny, and Thom's mysterious identity. All the entities I had summoned thus far had either feared him or been surprised to see him.

What did I really know about him?

Aside from him being a pretty cute substitute teacher, the rest of my evidence all pointed to doubt. He showed up out of nowhere. His skin didn't bear any marks and he was warm to the touch. Not to mention the weird voodoo he did on the parasitic spirit using my dad's body as its personal robot.

I slammed my chemistry textbook closed and collapsed onto my bed. The feeling of cool sheets relaxed me and I let my mind wander away from all the thoughts that were begging for my attention as I stared at the small cracks fissuring their way across the white ceiling.

The one thing I couldn't ignore though was the way Thom was helping me. I had never felt this type of control over my life and it felt really good. He even got me to get on his bike. And no matter what, he had always kept me safe. Even from myself.

I tried picturing his face again. The way he looked right into that deeper part of me. Before I knew it, I dozed off.

Gemma!

Who's that? The space felt vast by the way my words echoed and bounced. I tried to move but my feet felt like they were firmly planted in thick sludge.

Gemma, it's me.

This is a dream.

Part dream. Part something else.

Who are you?

You don't know?

Sorry, but I can't see a thing.

Lil sis. I'm offended. Forgot me already?

Brian? Where are you?

This was one of those stupid dreams where you just hear everything happening and your brain just decides to forgo logic, nonchalantly telling you to just play along while everything remains dark and sketchy.

You can't trust him.

Brian. I can't move.

You can't trust him. You've got to stay away.

Trust who?

Promise me you'll stop.

Stop what, Brian?

I can't stay.

Tell me, who?

My question kept floating on and on. When it was finally gone, there was no reply. Brian had disappeared.

194

I woke up with a start. When I turned my head to the side, I found my dad hovering above my prostrate form, phone in hand.

"It's been buzzing. A lot," he said, handing it to me.

"Sorry. I didn't hear it."

"Are you going out tonight?" he asked. The mattress dipped as he sat beside me.

I sat straight up. "Have you been reading my texts?"

"And if I were?" He furrowed his brow. "You're still under my roof."

"I'm going out with Ian," I said.

"That's okay, pumpkin." He kissed the top of my head. "It's the other one I don't like. Your teacher. There's something about him that I can't quite put my finger on."

"He's cool, Dad," I replied. "So, can I go out tonight?"

"Yeah. I've got some research to finish."

"You work too hard," I said. I stared at the indentation he left as he stood.

"I have my reasons, honey." His posture was hunched and I could see the sadness in his face. There were more wrinkles smattering the corners of his eyes than I had noticed before.

"You think she'll come back if she finds out Brian's dead?" I asked.

"Your mother was the stubborn type." He laughed. "Once she dug herself into a hole, there was no convincing her to get out. If she did come home, it would mean she had truly changed."

"Do you think people can really change?"

"Not really, pumpkin. But then again, I'm a bit jaded at my age. You shouldn't stop hoping. That would be a sad day for me."

As soon as he left, I remembered the phone in my hand and started scrolling through my texts. I had two new conversations highlighted. I went to Charlotte's first.

Charlotte: Hey. Just checking in.

Me: Hey. You alright?

Charlotte: Wow. Freaky storm.

Me: I know. Weird. Where were you?

Charlotte: I was gonna meet Emma at the Commons. Then Sylvia called and told me not to leave the house.

Me: Seriously? Psychic Sylvia?

Charlotte: Swear to God. All the trees down Old Country Road are down. I would have totally been crushed.

Me: Wow. Glad you're safe. So was I totally possessed last night?

Charlotte: Nah. You were just muttering. Kind of sounded like pig Latin. Emma was blowing the whole thing out of proportion.

Me: That's a relief.

Charlotte: Oh btw, I snagged those free manis you wanted. Let me know if you can go. Figured we could do lunch together.

Me: Sounds perfect.

I had saved the best for last and went on to check what Ian had written.

Ian: We still on?

Me: Sorry just saw this. Dozed off.

Ian: Crazy night at Charlotte's?

Me: Kind of.

Ian: If I were a fly on that wall.

Me: Not that kind of crazy. I'll tell you about it later.

Ian: Make sure to wear a bathing suit.

Me: Huh?

Ian: I've got something special planned.

Those last words had my belly doing flip flops. I had never been nervous around Ian before but knowing that he had planned our next outing took our relationship (whatever that was) to the next level. I had been so focused on solving the mystery of Thom's identity and tiptoeing around my dad that I hadn't had time to pick out my clothes.

Was this a date?

I was in a panic. When summoning demons, I keep my cool. Getting dressed for a night with Ian, I completely fall apart.

Good going, Gemma. Way to set back the feminist movement back a few decades.

I had never had a mother's help putting myself together. I didn't even know if I would have wanted her help if she were around. I'd like to think that we would have been close enough that I would value her opinion.

Or she could have totally been like Charlotte's mom. Not such a farfetched assumption considering the fact she picked up and left her kids.

I jumped from my bed to my closet and thumbed through the hangers, unhappy at every option.

What goes with a bikini in the middle of September?

There were plenty of hoodies, denim and flowery

shirts. The slinky silver dress from last year's junior prom.

Yikes. I need help.

Me: Problem.

Charlotte: What's up?

Me: I'm seeing Ian tonight.

Charlotte: Go you.

Me: What do I wear?

Charlotte: Skin-tight jeans. The kind that show off your ass.

Me: He told me to wear a bathing suit.

Charlotte: Hot. Slouchy sweater. And those suede moccasins you have.

Me: Thanks.

Charlotte: I want to hear all the details tomorrow.

Me: You got it.

I fluttered around for another hour. Showering. Ironing my hair. Mussing it back up when I thought I looked like a sad puppy. Trying on three different swimsuits until I settled on a black and white polka dot bandeau bikini that contrasted with the gold metallic slouchy knit sweater. I slipped on my favorite waxed-denim jeans over freshly shaven legs and slid on the supple, turquoise-beaded, brown moccasins.

Finally, after swiping on and wiping off the pink lipstick from Charlotte's hand-me-down pile, I opted for a black leather necklace instead of fussing with any makeup.

Not too shabby.

I twirled in front of the mirror, checking and then double checking. I was petrified when the doorbell rang at seven o'clock on the dot. My nerves were simulating a roller coaster with a genuine stomach-dropping feel.

As I headed to the front door, I passed my father who had tidied up in his usual anal fashion but was now seated at the head of the dining room table, engrossed in a telephone conversation. I waved and mouthed goodbye, which got a nod in return and a tap of his wrist watch, his way of saying 'you better not be home late.'

I took my windbreaker out of the closet before opening the front door. There Ian stood, with one hand rubbing the back of his neck, wearing a charcoal gray blazer, black crewneck tee and a narrow tie around his neck that made me want to pull him in for a kiss. Resisting temptation, I took him by the hand and we headed out into the night.

CHAPTER EIGHTEEN

It was like a drug. The Drifts. My palms got sweaty and my heart sped up as I watched Ian conjure a door I hadn't seen yet. The sight of the bright blue lapis and patina aged bronze wave handle had me itching to lose myself in the timelessness of this other place.

"You ready?" His smiles now had me shivering down to my toes. Ian had gone from hot daydream to me shamelessly willing to rip my clothes off for him.

"Yeah," I replied with a smile of my own.

His grip was firm against my hand while he pushed the door open. I was getting used to the feeling of getting sucked through the air and was no longer caught off guard by the power that funneled us through to the other side. As we sailed through the ether, I tried to take in the surroundings before I blinked and it was all be gone. Shapes and colors spiraled together to form streaks and clouds that looked like galaxies pinned together by jeweled stars.

When we came to a complete stop, Ian had one

arm around my waist and one hand cradling the base of my head, his fingers tangled within the messy strands of fine hair. He gave me a rough squeeze before pulling me down to the ground onto a wooden slatted walkway.

Snow-covered peaks surrounded a pool of aqua blue water as breathtaking plumes of steam lifted off the lake's surface and into the sky, where it communed with the clouds above. An arctic chill brushed along my skin, raising goose bumps that had me shivering from the cold.

"This is amazing," I said. My voice came out annoyingly breathy and I mentally kicked myself.

"We could've done Paris or the beach. I hoped you'd like this more." There was a hint of uncertainty in his voice.

"I do." I was still avoiding the telltale look of desire in his eyes.

There is no way this could be real. What does he see in me?

He led me down the walkway and around a small hill to a small cabin that stood like a gem amongst the black rock and mist. The glass-mirrored exterior reflected the landscape and amplified the light and gray white colors of the sky. Each mirror was framed by beams of dark oak and the pitched roof melted seamlessly into the sides.

I freed myself from Ian's hold and ran up to the structure, amazed at its sheer beauty. I was met with my own reflections and didn't recognize the person who looked back at me. She had flawless porcelain skin and bright, wild eyes. I turned my head to the side and she followed without delay. I picked up one hand and moved to meet hers but all that was there was the cold slick material of the house's exterior.

"You're beautiful." Ian walked up behind me and leaned his body over me, wrapping his strong arms around my body.

"At least you think so," I answered, meeting his reflection.

"And you're special." He turned his head to me and gently sucked on the thin layer of skin on my neck. The sensation sent pulsating feelings through my body. "Let's go inside. You're shivering."

"I'm not cold. It's you."

He lifted me off my feet and scooped me into his arms as he backed into the wall, pushing open a hinged door to reveal the candle-lit interior. The room was sparse yet luxurious. Minimalist. What little furniture decorated the space had clean lines and monochromatic tones. Two gray leather club chairs sat in front of a long narrow table that held two large silver candelabra and was spattered with dozens of tea lights. A well- made mattress rested atop a low gray stained wooden platform. The headboard nearly reached the ceiling and was the only thing blocking the view of outside. The sheets were bluish in hue and the comforter was black, echoing the scenery.

"This is home," he said, setting me down on the plush rug at the base of his bed.

"Really? In the Drifts?"

"Yeah. I may not get to come here that often anymore but it'll always be the only place I can relax. I've moved around so much this is the only constant I have."

I hugged my knees as he sat down beside me. He took my hand and placed a kiss on my wrist.

"This one's new," he said.

"Yeah." I pulled my hand back and tucked it behind me.

"Gemma. You really need to stop." His words brought back to me my brother's warning.

Is that what he meant? Stop the magic?

"I can't."

"Why not?" he said.

I winced at the realization that I wasn't going to be able to keep it from Ian much longer. "He needs my help. He says he can't do it without me."

"It's dangerous. One day you're going to summon a monster and you won't be able to control it."

"I can't stop. The Dybbuk. They're everywhere now if you haven't noticed. I know we go about our day like nothing is really happening but my dad is slowly going crazy and Allison is stalking me. There are ones floating out there that follow me wherever I go and I feel like they're just biding their time before they all decide to attack."

He cupped my cheeks with his warm hands. My breath hitched by the concern that lined his face.

"Gemma, you…"

"Thom thinks I'm right. He thinks if we can figure out who sent the Dybbuk to Harrisport then we have a good chance of kicking them out."

"Mr. Flynn?" he asked.

"Yeah. He has a grimoire. He's been teaching me about demons. How to summon them. Negotiate with them." There was a measure of relief that followed my confession. I didn't feel like I was hiding a part of me from Ian anymore.

"Then we need to go see Sam. He needs to know

what Mr. Flynn is making you do. He'll tell you what to do to protect yourself."

"He's not making me do anything. I'm good at it and it feels right. For some reason, I can't put my finger on it, when I let my mind grow quiet and draw the sigils, I feel like myself. The real me. Not the Gemma that goes to school every day and puts on a normal face." I turned my head, unable to face him as I let the last words spill out. "It's like the way I feel when I'm with you."

"Gem. Promise me you'll see Sam with me."

I knew that Thom wouldn't want me divulging any of his secrets but it's not like I was sharing any details. Besides, I couldn't lie to Ian, and the amount of concern he was showing made me tingle.

He cares about me.

"Fine," I replied. "I promise."

"I guess I killed the mood, huh?" Ian said, nodding towards the bed.

"It's alright. I don't think I'm as ready as I thought I was." I smiled, bracing myself for some sort of rejection or smooth-talking convincing.

"It's okay. I'll wait as long as you want."

That's when I decided that maybe I didn't know when I would feel ready to give up my last shred of innocence but it was for sure going to be with Ian.

CHAPTER NINETEEN

The blaring noise of a car horn woke me. My body was still warm and relaxed after my night in the ethereal lagoon Ian had called his home. I stretched my arms over my head and languished in the after effects of a restful sleep. After Ian had brought me back home, I had gone out like a light. I hadn't even gotten up for water.

Whiiiiine.

There it was again. Like the driver was leaning against the entire steering wheel, letting out one long stretch of a drone. I sat up and peeked out the window. Charlotte's car was running in the driveway. I looked at my clock and saw the time.

Shit. I forgot about today.

I practically jumped into my sweats and gave a quick stroke of deodorant after doing a fast rendition of the ABCs as I brushed my teeth. I doubt it took the two minutes recommended by dentists nationwide.

When I ran out the door, I rammed right into Charlotte, sending the two of us onto the wet grass.

"I'm so sorry, Char. I was rushing to get out. I kind of overslept. Do you think the roads will be open?"

She took great care getting back up on her black platform wedge booties.

"Wow. You must have had some night. Let's get in the car and you can tell me all about it. The highway is clear and I think I can swing back around the way I came. I called the salon before I left the house. They said they'll be open but might be a few minutes late in case of traffic." She giggled and ran to the driver's side of the car.

I was about to get in when I realized what it was I was about to do. I had woken up to the sight of her car and completely expected to get right in and go off with her, as if I did that sort of thing every day. I stood by the door as Charlotte gave me a questioning look.

Can I do it?

I hopped from one foot to the next as I tried to decide whether or not I could get in the car again. I had read about treating phobias with something called exposure therapy. If the person with the phobia is slowly introduced to the thing they are most afraid of, they can start to control their biological reactions and avoid freaking out.

Just think of this as a continuation of the ride on Thom's bike. I can get through this.

I heard Charlotte's Bluetooth pick up a phone call. It was her mother.

Good. Now I can think without any pressure.

Thom's voice echoed through my thoughts, telling

me that I was stronger than anything. I imagined myself once again clutching to his body and relishing the road and the freedom of the ride.

I opened the passenger door, sat down and clicked my seatbelt shut. Charlotte put the car into drive and we pulled away from my house, listening to the esteemed Mrs. Harris yap away about dresses for the upcoming fundraiser while I tried very hard to ignore the throbbing sigils at my wrist.

Charlotte bombarded me with questions as soon as my fingers were soaking in a tiny bowl of lemon-scented water.

"Tell me everything," she said as she pulled off the stacks of rings she wore on her right hand. More good luck charms, she claimed.

"He took me to his house." Just fudging a little bit.

"So does he have an indoor pool or what?"

I tried to think of a real world equivalent to the lagoon.

"Nah. Outdoor jacuzzi."

"Wow, Gem. That's like *Bachelorette* behavior."

"You should have seen him. I'm still drooling."

"So did you do it?"

"Shush," I said, eyeballing the manicurists who were filing away at our nails. "No. But I really wanted to," I whispered.

"Squee!"

"Char, quiet."

"Yeah but it's a good thing you're holding off. Makes it better."

"You think?"

"Totally. Did he care?"

"He was pretty cool about waiting."

"Which of course made you want him even more," she answered.

"Too true." I sighed.

"Oh I forgot. I got you a ticket for Saturday. It's opening night of the revue. And I want to squeeze in another practice tomorrow during gym. There's a pep rally Thursday night and Friday is the game so we don't really have much time."

"I'm so excited for you. Will the Senator be making an appearance?"

"We'll see. If he can find a way to make it worth his while, I'm sure he'll be there."

"This is nice. I'm happy we're normal again."

"Yeah it is," Charlotte said and leaned her face against my arm.

After a quick bite at McCloone's, Charlotte dropped me back home. I was surprised to see Ian sitting on the couch with my father, who seemed more relaxed than I had seen in him in a long time. The two of them were laughing.

"Hey pumpkin," my dad said as he saw me coming from the coat closet.

"Hey. What's going on?" I asked.

"Ian here was just filling me in on the Knights. Thought maybe I'd come to the game this week. You're cheering again, right?"

"Yeah." I was dumbfounded but excited to see that someone was getting through to him. Thom might have been able to settle the Dybbuk down a bit but Ian was the one who was drawing him out of whatever downward spiral the accident had set him off on.

"Thought we could go out," Ian said. He was

looking even yummier in a soft blue shirt. He grabbed his leather jacket from the armchair and headed straight towards me, not even giving me the option of answering. "I'll bring her home soon, Dr. Pope."

"You kids have fun," he said and raised the volume back on the television.

Ian ushered me out the door and thrust his jacket at me.

"Put that on. We need to be quick."

"What's going on?" I said, pulling on the jacket that held the distinct smell of Ian that had me almost begging to go somewhere alone.

"Sam. He said he has some news. I told him about Thom. He said it's not good."

"What is it?"

"He wouldn't say. Said we needed to head back to the club now."

"He didn't give you any hints?"

"Nope. If he needs to tell us in person that means it's big. It means he can't trust outsiders hearing what he has to say."

Our pace went from speed walking to a brisk jog. I expected some kind of post-storm clean-up effort by the city but there were no woodchoppers or garbage trucks to be found. Lots of people were milling about, looking lost and bored, until we reached the knee-high grass of the abandoned lot. When the gold handle came up, I shivered with excitement.

Traveling through the Drifts was feeling like second nature now. There was where I started and within a few heartbeats, I was in the familiar frozen lake. It was as if I had always been here. We trekked together, side by side, dropping into the ice and coming out into the pulsating room.

The room was even more crowded than usual, both on the dance floor and the balcony above us. All the tables were filled and whatever the capacity was for, it was definitely maxed out.

I couldn't resist the pull in the room, grabbed Ian by the waist of his jeans and dragged him into the undulating mass of people.

"We don't have time."

I gave him puppy dog eyes and a big pout. "Just one dance," I yelled over the thrumming bass.

He stood still amidst the throngs of people.

"Please," I begged.

He held up his index finger and replied, "Just one." He smirked and rocked his hips to the music until he was firmly planted up against my body. He spun me around and set me on his thigh.

Power filled every cell in my body. The pulsating music filled my mind as my chest swelled, taking in more of the energy that lay thick in the air. Our bodies moved as one and I could feel the heat of desire rushing up like a deluge, threatening to drown me.

I was reluctant to meet with Sam just yet. I didn't want to know what he had to tell me. I wanted to stay clutched within Ian's strong hold until I lost myself but when he stopped on a dime at the transition of the next song, it was hard to ignore what had now become my responsibility.

We walked past the bar towards Sam's office. Mr. Muscle, as I now referred to him, was guarding the door again. His sigils had now crept up his neck and if the strobe lights hadn't been flicking on and off, I could have sworn the tattoos were moving across his skin like they had a life of their own.

"Good. You're here," Sam said when we walked in. "You. Sit."

As Ian and I sat down, Sam walked around us and closed the door, shutting out the noise. When he came back, he sat on the desk in front of my chair and placed his hand on my shoulder.

"I need to know that whatever I tell you stays between us."

"Um. Sure." I gulped.

"I'm serious. No one can find out about this. I'm in hot water just asking around about it."

"Yeah. I get it." I shifted, trying to loosen his hold on me but he stayed firm.

He brought his face closer to mine and looked into my eyes, checking for something. When he appeared satisfied by what he saw, he let go.

"I did a little background check on your Mr. Flynn. Seems he's not what he appears."

"I figured that much." I scoffed at the lack of credit I was getting in the intelligence department.

"There is much subterfuge about who he actually is so my hands are tied for now."

"That doesn't help me much."

"True. But patience is a virtue. Is it not?"

"What now?" Ian interjected.

"I'll keep digging. But Gemma, you need to keep going along with whatever Mr. Flynn wants. We don't want him thinking you don't trust him anymore."

But I do trust him. I think.

"So you want me to keep going along with Thom's ideas and really just listen to you."

"That's the idea, sugar."

"And why should I do that? I barely know you."

"I'm trying to look out for you."

"Why?"

"It's complicated."

"I'm sure but that's not getting me to jump onto your bandwagon."

"The necklace. Have you tried it?" he asked.

I put my finger to the stone.

"Yes," I answered.

"Feels good, right?" His smile revealed a pair of super sharp canines. "Coming here also helps."

"It does?"

"Sure. You think all that energy out there is just for show? People pay good money to sit up on the rafters and indulge in a bit of soul sucking. Literally."

"Is that safe?" I thought about all those people dancing their hearts out to no end.

"Don't worry about them. They belong here. They chose it. It was better than any other alternative they had. They get to stay here under my protection and, in exchange, they provide rejuvenating energy for the paying clientele you saw out there."

It sounded awful and I had to ignore my conscious at the knowledge of how much I enjoyed feeding on the masses myself.

"Is that how my scar went away?"

He nodded.

"So when you find out more about Thom, you'll let me know, right?" I asked.

"You have my word. And do me a small favor, will you?"

"What's that?"

"Try using your powers. Practice makes perfect and all that jazz. You might surprise yourself and see how much Thom has been withholding from you." Sam's parting words left me more confused than ever.

When we left Sam, I had a newfound appreciation for the club. I saw everything now with new eyes and watched the interplay between the two factions of people.

"Wanna stay longer?" Ian asked.

"No. I think we should head back."

"Sure."

We rode the elevator back up.

"Are you going to try them? Like Sam said?" Ian said, tracing his finger along Ronwe's curlicued sigil.

"What do you think?" I asked.

"I think you should. You need to watch out for yourself. Don't ever rely on anyone else to keep you safe."

When the doors opened up onto my front lawn, Ghosty was waiting for me at the front door.

"What about him?" I asked.

"You'll figure it out."

"You think so?"

"Yeah. You're the smartest person I know." Ian brushed his lips against mine and I could feel his smile widen. I thought I could feel Ghosty's tendrils sweeping in between us.

"See you tomorrow," I said, uncomfortable at the thought that we had an audience.

"Yeah," Ian said. "Call me if you need me."

I watched Ian walk away until his silhouette turned

the corner and I could no longer follow him. Ghosty still hovered on the top stair like a faithful guard dog as the trees rustled in the strong wind that brought in the cooler autumn air. The rumbling in my stomach had me throwing an egg and cheese on a biscuit into the toaster oven. When the timer dinged, I coaxed the sandwich out with the tips of my fingers onto a paper towel. I sat down on one of the breakfast stools and flipped through the pages of the paper already laid out in a haphazard mess.

More and more bad news kept piling up. Ms. Halle was arraigned and charged with multiple counts of attempted murder and child endangerment. They even threw in kidnapping for good measure. The prosecutor wasn't letting her slide off without a super long jail sentence. Rescue teams were still trying to find several people reported missing during the tornado.

Freaky weather. This stuff is going to make me paranoid as hell.

Everything was happening around me and I had no control. That wouldn't last for long. I was going to try to fix things now. Thom wasn't helping at all. We were wasting time trying to find out whatever it was he wanted to know. No one was going to help us rid the town of the Dybbuk. I was going to have to take matters into my own hands. Next time I was provoked by one of them, they were going to wish they had never been born. Or died. Or whatever they were.

I trudged through enough homework where I felt comfortable that I wasn't going to piss off any one particular teacher. I pulled out my uniform from the back of the closet and hung it back up on the top of my door. Maybe tomorrow I would try it on. Make sure it fit before Friday. It was just terribly cruel how my personal life was just starting to come back together while the rest of the world was going to hell in a hand basket.

CHAPTER TWENTY

I flicked the play button on my new pepped-up morning routine playlist. The abrasives tones of Crystal Castles pumped through the small dock speaker and I jumped to the beat as I picked out my clothes - leggings and a flowery tunic.

"Morning, Dad," I sang as I passed my father in the hallway on my way to the shower.

"Good morning, pumpkin," he said, raising his mug of steaming coffee as he walked back into his bedroom.

I finished my morning routine in a flash and was back in my room having missed only two songs.

New record for me. I usually find a lot more to fuss about.

After getting dressed, I went through my books, trying to lighten the load for school and carefully folded the cheerleading uniform into my bag with the plastic still on.

"Hey, Dad?" I said, as I peeked into his room. He was standing at the large window, staring out onto the porch where Ghosty was still hovering.

"Hmm?" he asked before taking another sip of his drink.

"Can you give me a ride?"

That got his attention. "Sure. Yeah. Just give me a minute." He pulled his briefcase out of the closet and arranged some of the files that were sitting on his nightstand into the accordion folder in the side pocket.

I walked back to my room to get my own things, checking myself in the mirror one last time. I fingered the necklace underneath my blouse in a solemn promise that I figure out its potential and maybe a way to get rid of the Dybbuk. I opted for a chunky sweater instead of my jacket, hoping that the nice weather would hold up and my ride to school would do the rest.

"Ready?" My dad said, jingling his car keys. The collar of his trench coat was mildly askew and although he looked like he was working way too hard, he still managed to be in good spirits.

"I think so," I said, realizing that no matter how much time passed I would think of the crash every time I got into a car.

When we reached his navy blue sedan, I waited for him to get in first. My breath was getting ragged and forced. I was starting to panic.

This isn't Charlotte. This is Dad. I'm the reason his life is so awful right now.

Then an idea dawned on me that might help the situation. I looked at Ash's sigil and focused my attention at the gem at my neck. I felt a strand of power. It was like spider silk held taut between me and the other side of the veil. I could feel the tug between this world and the Otherworld. Then, without warning, the energy came pouring through like waves from whatever was holding the other end.

I let the power wash over me and I relaxed into my own body. The panic had disappeared with the tide and I settled into the passenger side of the BMW.

"I'm proud of you, Gem."

"Thanks." I smiled and looked out the window. He was driving ten miles below the speed limit and I appreciated the gesture.

The lyrics of the Nine Inch Nails song that came on as I left my room were looping through my head.

Nothing can stop me. Nothing can stop me now.

When I walked into homeroom, I could feel the solid tension in the room. Ian was eying Thom. Thom was eying Ian. Neither of them breaking away from their private staring contest.

I sat next to Ian.

"Good morning, Miss Pope," Mr. Flynn called out in a loud clear voice.

"Good morning," I replied and turned my attention to Ian after making sure I was marked down as present. "Hey," I said, breaking whatever spell had taken over the two.

"I feel a little silly," Ian started.

"Why?" I said, finding it hard to believe that someone so sure of himself as Ian was could ever feel anything but confident.

"I never got to ask you something and I really wanted to do it in person. I think it would have sounded a little lame in a text."

"So, ask me now," I replied.

"Okay. Here it goes." He cleared his throat. "I was wondering if you wanted to be my girlfriend. Okay, that was really lame. I'm sorry." He went back to his dog-eared copy of Hamlet.

"No, it's not. It's sweet. Yeah. I'd love you. I mean, I'd love to."

Nice Freudian slip there, Gem. Smooth.

We spent the rest of the period huddled together. All the while, I could feel Thom's eyes on me but whenever I turned to check, he was deeply engrossed in writing in a thin black soft- covered journal. When the bell rang, Ian and I parted ways with shy affirmations of seeing each other in English class.

When I reached the girl's locker room, I hesitated.

I'm sure I can find an empty classroom where I could change quickly. But what if someone walks in. I don't need to add to the list of things that make Gemma strange.

That's when I remembered my new strategy. My Gemma's gonna kick ass instead of stand there like a loser while everyone else messed her up. I slammed the door open, ready to brawl, but there were only a few people inside who looked right at me and then away again. I pulled my uniform out, figuring now would be the best time to try it on and see how it feels during a routine.

A chill brushed my ankles as I fastened the hook eye closure of the blue and gold pleated skirt, letting lose a wave of goose flesh that ran up my bare legs up to my shoulder and turned down my arms. The energy proceeded to raise the fine hairs on the back of my neck. I turned and found the room had emptied out. Allison was standing ramrod at the end of the line of dark green lockers.

"What do you want, Allison? I'm really not in the mood." I jerked the matching long-sleeved, cropped jersey shirt over my white tank.

"It's time, Gemma."

"Yeah, yeah. Time for you to lay down the law. For a total smack down. I get it. You're going to show me who's boss." I shoved the rest of my clothing into the locker along with my backpack. I tucked my cellphone into the waistband of my skirt and started to head down to the emergency exit door that led to straight to the field. The alarm was forever out of order, leaving it one of the prime short cuts to get onto the field or for slackers who liked to sneak off and cut class.

I didn't make it two feet before Allison was lunging for my bag. The two of us were on the floor and the side of my cheek made contact with the cold tile. I tried to push myself back up but she forced my shoulders down to the ground. The coppery taste of blood filled my mouth.

"Time to go, Gemma," she snarled.

That was when I noticed the additional set of shoes in front of me. I looked up and saw Matt blocking the exit, with his arms crossed in front of him.

"Matt," I managed to eek out before Allison shoved her elbow between my shoulders, knocking the wind out of me. The room began to spin. My thoughts grew panicked when I felt Allison binding my wrists behind my back. I rested my forehead to the floor to stop the waves of nausea when I caught a glimpse of the rose-colored stone swaying back and forth away from my neck as if it were begging to be noticed.

Rage filled my every pore. I was letting things happen to me all over again. I wanted to be the one in control. I wriggled my fingers and pulled at the bindings.

"Let me go," I said.

"Don't worry. I'm not the one who'll be having all the fun with you." Allison stood, her heels clicking against the hard floor. She pulled me upright in one swoop. Matt was there in an instant, holding me steady as my knees began to wobble.

As they began to argue over the logistics of getting me out of the school without anyone else noticing, I focused on Ashtaroth's sigil. He was the most bad-assed out of all the one's I'd met so far. If anyone was going to pack my punch, it would be him. I focused on channeling the energy from the sigil to the stone. I felt the tug at my neck, tethered to the Otherworld. I tried to imagine what that place looked like. Was it all fire and brimstone like we were all taught?

The power coursed through my veins until the excess began pooling into my hands. When I could no longer hold on to it, I let out a deafening scream and spun on my heels, releasing the orbs that weighed heavy in my palms. A blinding white light filled the room, pulsing like the strobe lights in Sam's club. I kept the stream going as I heard thrashing against the hard metal of the lockers. The longer I held my ground, the easier it was to channel the power out at Allison and Matt.

I turned to check on them. They lay writhing on the ground, convulsing, their eyes rolling to the backs of their heads. Allison's blonde hair stood on end as if she had stuck her finger in an electric socket while the skinny blue veins in her face began to zig zag across her pale white face.

I watched them as they convulsed across the floor, going this way and that. Part of me was appalled at the smile that was on my face but I couldn't help reveling in proactive Gemma.

"Gemma!" A strong voice boomed through the ionic haze that engulfed the three of us.

I looked up from the two sickly forms at my feet. I couldn't make out who this intruder was. The silhouette burst at me with such speed that I could have sworn it had flown straight at me. Thom's face pierced the thick cloud that was being continually expelled from that bit of Otherworld I had tapped into.

His presence didn't faze me. I kept all my cylinders going until I could see the black inky tendrils of Dybbuk begin to withdraw from my peers.

"Stop it. This instant," he yelled at me, over the whooshing tunnel of energy that erupted into a larger force, headed straight for Allison and Matt. It encased them in a brilliant green light that began to squeeze the Dybbuk out of their forms.

"Now," he mouthed over the rushing noise. His eyes turned from the trusting warm brown to a hideous blood red. The sight had my concentration tripping over itself. I felt the connection tumble out of my hands and watched as the Dybbuk eased their way back into Allison and Matt's bodies, curling as a snake would curl back into their dens.

The power was sucked back through me, back to where it had come from. God only knew where.

When my eyes and ears began to readjust to the dank and humid room, I saw Thom kneeling beside the two limp forms on the floor. He had his fingers on their necks, checking for pulse.

"Are they alright?" I asked, not quite sure about which answer would have relieved me more. There was a definite silver lining to not having Allison wake up for a while.

"Yes. But I reckon we get you outside and into a crowd before they decide to wake up." He ushered me through the door and out into the brisk light of late morning. He placed his body between myself and the squad that was still mulling about. I'm sure they were waiting on me.

"Why did you stop me?" I asked, extremely peeved at the way he had rudely interrupted my Jackie Chan, Kung Fu, kick ass styling.

"We will not discuss this here." His eyes had not changed back to their trusting warm orbs. They remained on the verge of implosion. Red helixes of fire churned where his pupils should have been.

"Why not? I don't have the right to defend myself? I guess it's okay for Allison to keep torturing me."

"You will do as I say or you will perish."

"Is that a threat?"

"No, but it's a warning. You could have gotten yourself killed like that."

"I can handle it." I looked away, ashamed to think that I would crumble in front of this man.

He came round to face me while blocking my view of my friends. "I am trying to protect you, Gemma. Can't you see that? It's not right to use your power like that. For every action there isn't an equal reaction.

It's much bigger, and will come back looking for you for payment."

"I said I've got it. I don't think I can stand around doing nothing for much longer."

"We'll get to the bottom of this. You just have to trust me on that one," he said. "But you can't go letting loose willy nilly. It'll only end badly for you."

"But they were about to…"

"Then you need to find a way out. Violence isn't the answer."

I looked over the field and saw the line of Dybbuk that had congregated around us. That was when Morgan looked up at me. I could see the shadow blackening her soul from a distance. It was rooted deep into her heart. It wasn't coming out to play just yet.

"What about them?" I asked. "They have no problems terrorizing everyone."

"Come after class. We'll figure it out. I think I've got something."

"I hope you're right because I don't know how much more of this I can take," I said. "What about Matt and Allison?"

He briefly took my arm and checked the sigils. As he turned my wrist and examined the markings, I felt the heat envelop my hand.

"I'll take care of them," he said, already heading back into the locker room. His face, half in the light, half in the dark, appeared restless as he surveyed the field once more before letting the door slam behind him.

I let another minute pass, wracking my brain about

the excuse I would make up about my swollen cheek, and how to handle Morgan now that I glimpsed the Dybbuk within her body. Then I headed over the short sparse grass, equally perturbed by Thom's nick-of-time appearance.

CHAPTER TWENTY-ONE

Principal Kelly caught me once again as I was headed to chemistry. "Just the person I was looking for." She wasn't smiling this time. Her hair was pulled into a severe bun atop her head and her clothing was of a darker palette than usual. Her blouse reminded me of a Picasso and the navy pencil skirt polished off her look. She was even wearing pumps.

"Me?" I asked, looking behind me for someone else she may have been talking to.

"Yes, Gemma," she said. "Please join me in my office. I'd like to continue our conversation from the other day."

"I'd love to but I have chemistry. I really don't know what's flying in that class. I shouldn't really miss it."

"Gemma." She looked over the purple frames of her glasses. "I doubt chemistry is your biggest problem right now."

There was an intelligent twinkle in her eye. If she

knew more than she was letting on, I guess I had to find out. I needed every bit of information I could get my hands on.

Today her office was sunny. The ferns on her windowsill languished in their pots as flakes of dust danced in the air.

I heard the door close behind me as I sat down. I hugged my bag closer to my chest and wrapped one arm around the other so that the sleeve wouldn't pull and call attention to the tattoos. I didn't want her revisiting that lecture if that wasn't first on her mind.

"Gemma," she started as she sat behind her desk, "I'm sorry if I might be overstepping my boundaries but I think I owe it to your mother."

"Principal Kelly. This may come out sounding really snotty but my mom's gone and I don't really care."

"You shouldn't be practicing. It isn't what she would have wanted for you."

"If that were the case then she would have stuck around and made sure I did whatever she wanted."

"Life doesn't always work the way we want it to." Her eyes drifted away to some other place or time. "She had her reasons for what she did."

"Whatever," I said. "Is there anything else?" I stood up, ready to bolt right out of there.

"Please, Gemma." She no longer sounded like the same person. Her skin paled and she placed both hands on her desk. There were two pieces of paper tucked into each fist. "Don't make me do this."

"What?"

"I'm going to have to bind you. It's for your own good."

She began chanting as she placed a photo of me in front of her. It was my second birthday. I was wearing a frilly pink dress and white patent mary janes. My mother's half-turned face was beside me, looking right at a younger Principal Kelly in the background.

"What the hell!" I jumped out of my chair like I had just been electrocuted. The sky outside had turned from blue to gray to pitch black. The wind had picked up, whipping through the trees. The Dybbuk that up until now had stayed on the fringes of the campus were now pressed up against the window.

Thump. Thump.

There was no way of telling if the howling was coming from the wind or the spirits as they thudded up against the glass, trying to break in.

"Gemma, I bind you." She started to fold the paper. Again and then another time. That's when I noticed the stack of pins on the desktop calendar.

Thump.

"Holy shit. This is turning into a cheesy Goth Emo movie." I lunged for the doorknob and started to jiggle but it wouldn't give.

"Power of the witches rise. I call upon the elements." She took a pin and stuck the paper.

"Open up." I banged on the door, screaming until my throat burned.

"I bind you in fire," she said, producing a long red taper from her shirtsleeve. "Guardian of the ancient towers, I call upon your powers."

The dozen or so spirits outside began to huddle closer together, their translucent edges converging until they formed one large bulbous entity that churned with speaks of electricity at its core.

"Look, I know you're trying some voodoo crap on me but I think we've got some bigger fish to fry."

She didn't break from her concentration. The wick of the candle ignited on its own and she placed the paper in the flame while continuing her chant without pause.

I tried the door once more for good measure but the effort was futile. The mass of blackness bled across the edges of the window until it obstructed the view of the outside completely.

"Principal Kelly, please!" I felt like a hamster on a wheel, running circles around my chair with no end in sight. I rolled up my sleeves and caught the sigils on my arms giving off a deep amber glow.

Should I try?

Thom said not to.

All I wanted to do was go back to that place where I was the one in control but I was too scared to try after Thom's heated warnings.

"Great Mother. By the powers of three by three. I bind thee." The candle exploded in a spray of melted wax that sprayed the room and splattered across my shirt.

"Okay great. You're done. Can we get the hell out of here?" I yelled, pointing to the cloud of evil that had sprouted garish red eyes. Branches of current began to splice across the window in a web.

"It didn't work," she said.

"You'll try again next time. Can you please get us out of here?"

"It didn't work," she repeated, running a hand through her hair, messing up her updo, forming a messy halo around her face.

I stomped to the other side of the desk and dragged the stunned principal to the door.

"Let's go," I said, keeping my eye on the fireworks spectacular going on mere steps away.

She did a little more chanting and the door swung open. It was no better out in the hallway. The metal doors of the lockers were all being rattled open by an unseen force while students trampled one another on their way out the exit doors in a mass exodus.

Thom came barreling down the hallway towards us.

"Gemma!" he shouted over the screams and ringing fire alarm. The sprinkler heads shot out with a pop that had me jumping out of my skin. In moments, we were caught under a deluge of ice water.

"Thom, we need to do something." I pointed to the dark window. The Dybbuk were seeping in through the cracks at a steady pace. We had only minutes before they were inside.

"We need to get out." He grabbed my bicep and with my hand still clutching Principal Kelly's sleeve, the three of us made a run for it down the slick hallway.

That's when the feeling of shame struck me. Running away from this was killing me. I needed to do something to help the hundreds of students who were now under attack. I was the only one who could. I doubted Principal Kelly's pansy-assed fake magic would do anything help.

"Stop. Thom." I dug my heels into the ground.

"Don't do this, Gem," he said.

"We can't leave. This is just the beginning. They're taking over," I yelled over the noise.

"Not now. We've got to keep moving. Away."

"Just let me take a look in the grimoire. I'm sure I can find something to stall them. We can't run from this. It'll just keep coming." I knew I was grasping at straws but if I just got a peek, something would jump out at me. By no means was I expecting total success. Just hoping that I could buy some more time.

"No. Absolutely not. They're out for blood." His answer sounded pretty final.

"Please trust me. Just this once. I know I can find something useful."

We stood there. Thom and I. Principal Kelly was still caught in her daze, muttering nonsense to herself although I couldn't give two farts about how she was handling everything. Finding out what she had planned on doing with me in her office was now tacked on my to-do list.

"We have to leave." He wasn't budging, which got my blood really boiling now.

"Why won't you ever listen to me?"

"It's not that, Gemma. You just don't see the bigger picture."

"Oh and you do, Mr. High and Mighty? I don't remember you flashing your know-it-all badge."

"Gemma, now is not the time for this."

"You're right." I got up really close to his face. His smell was intoxicating, stronger than it had ever been.

"I know I am." The gleam in his eye displayed a confidence that raked at me.

"But this is it. Things are getting out of control," I said.

"That's why we need to retreat and regroup."

"This isn't a game. Or a puzzle. This is our lives." I

pointed to the kids down the hall who were crawling on their knees to get away from the deluge of spirits attempting to find hosts.

"I'm trying to protect you," he said but I wasn't satisfied with that answer. "Especially after what you pulled earlier."

"That's it." I turned the other way and ran down the hall to homeroom. Every room I passed had windows seeping the black mist and the building groaned at the intrusion.

When I reached the office, I watched as the remaining wisps of smoke snapped into place. Morgan was there. Her eyes were on me. She jumped on top of the desk and lunged, her arms outstretched, clawing my shoulder on her way down.

I let out a scream and kicked her in the stomach, putting some distance between us. I tried to make a run for it but she grabbed me by the hair. Before I knew it, I was on the floor, thrashing in a defensive posture against the repeated onslaught of her claw-like hands. My shoulder was wet and sticky. I could smell the metallic taint of blood.

God, how I hate blood.

There was a loud crash and Morgan was pulled off my curled- up form. Thom stood above me, hurtled my friend back inside the office and slammed the door. He helped me scramble back up to my feet.

"Are you alright, luv?" he asked.

"Fine," I said, not forgetting his reluctance to help me, and kept going until I reached his classroom.

Thom was right behind me, dragging Principal Kelly in before slamming the door shut. He pulled the desk over to barricade the entrance. "Are you mad?"

Thom yelled.

"Maybe I am. Where's the book?" I asked.

"I don't know."

"This is really exhausting. I don't think we have time for this. Just tell me where the goddamn book is," I screamed.

"I'm telling ya the truth. I don't know where it is."

"Is this about before?"

"Whaddya mean?" He looked honestly perplexed.

"Are you keeping it from me?" My mind started chasing after its own tail. I couldn't get the idea out of my head that Thom might have been sabotaging everything from the beginning. That's why no one wanted to help out. I looked at the shell of Miss Kelly, huddled in the corner, rocking herself back and forth. All she kept muttering about was how her stupid spell hadn't worked.

"You are out of your mind. Why on earth would I do that?"

"Then open it." I pointed to his closet.

"Alrighty, but this behavior of yours is only proving my point that you shouldn't be handling any of this on your own. Without adult supervision." He pulled the ring of keys out of his pants pocket.

"Spare me. Please. You're, what, four years older than I am?"

"What difference does it make?" He turned the lock and I sprang for the book. Only it wasn't there. Most of the closet was emptied out. Stacks of old papers were on the top shelf and a pair of white running shoes were on the floor.

"You got to get new shoes," I growled.

"What's wrong with these?"

Before I could explain to him how a nice leather boot would suit him much better, the desk began to rattle, sending Principal Kelly into a fit of hysterics.

The cloud of smoke had seeped beneath the crack below the door and was now enveloping her. A loud cackle came from behind.

"Thom, now would be a good time to be straight with me." I said, looking around for any means of escape. The windows were tall but could only be cracked open. Not large enough for a person to fit through.

"I am. The grimoire is missing. I don't know where it is."

I could feel the flood of emotion threatening to come out. I hadn't felt this helpless since after the accident.

"Please stop lying to me."

"Gemma, will you get it through your thick head already? I'm not lying."

That was when Principal Kelly began to thrash wildly on the floor. I was about to run over to her when Thom shouted, "Don't get too close."

I ignored him and slid on my knees to her fragile body. A fraction of the cloud had broken off and entered her body. I tried touching her and was met by an invisible wall that knocked me back against the desks.

Thom was at my side and the two us stumbled across the room to the windows, putting as much distance as we could between ourselves and the bulging body of Principal Kelly. She was yanked upright like a marionette on strings, swaying back and forth as if the puppeteer was getting the hang of things.

Thom starting cranking the window open which only confirmed our trapped situation.

"I'm not fitting through that."

"Neither am I." He looked me up and down as though he were calculating a way to squeeze me out.

"Now would be a good time for some magic. I can do it," I said.

"No fucking way." It was the first I had heard him curse and I had to stop myself from cracking up.

I looked back to Principal Kelly. Her body had sprouted bulbous pustules filled with blackness that expanded until her skin was paper thin and threatened to burst.

"Too bad. I'm doing this." I closed my eyes despite my fear and concentrated on the space between myself and the Otherworld. I felt his hand tighten on my wrist. It was beginning to burn through my skin and threatened to go down to the muscle.

Fat chance stopping me.

I kept focusing on Ash's sigil. I knew this would be the second time in a single day but I was hedging my bets that two favors for him would be less painful.

Plus, he liked me.

I think.

He could tack everything on to my tab. I kept the tears of pain that were leaking out the corners of my eyes at bay and opened myself up to the shot of power that thrust through me like a bullet train. I sucked in a deep breath and tried to funnel it through my body in a conduit, letting it course through my cells in a natural flow.

My eyes flew open when the venomous bubbles

riddling her skin popped. The smoke whipped out of her, leaving her skin and flesh hanging off her limbs. It swirled around her body and reentered her through the mouth, unhinging her jaw in a grotesque scream.

I let out the energy bit by bit, hesitating when the thought of damaging Principal Kelly started tickling at my conscience. I ignored Thom's hand still heating through my skin and let the power rush through.

"Get out," I yelled, staring down the menacing eyes that were hiding in the shell of my principal.

It cackled through her.

I set my sights on the chairs to the left and then back at her. They all rose up into the air and collided with her frail body but the power within her kept her rooted to the spot.

That's when I had an idea. I began to push at the spirit mentally. It may appear on this plain but it didn't belong here. If I tried to find it behind the veil, I might be able to punch its lights out. I sifted through the layers of this world until I found the Dybbuk's root.

A loud crash sent my mind reeling back. A shower of glass came down on our heads and a large object went whizzing past my ear and into Principal Kelly's abdomen, knocking her and her evil eyes down to the ground.

With my mind fully in the moment, I grabbed my arm out of Thom's hold and looked out the empty space that was once a window. I carefully brushed off pieces of glass from my shoulder and peered over the ledge.

That's when I saw Ian standing with a baseball bat in hand, waving at me. "Come on," he said.

There was no one else in sight. I looked down at the drop. The way the building was situated and the ground sloped, it was more than a two story fall. I brought one hand up to grip the frame while I clutched the other to my chest. Layers of skin had burned away, leaving a grisly maroon mark in the shape of his hand.

"Hold on," Thom said. He took off his blazer, wrapped it around his fist and dragged the gray fabric along the perimeter, knocking away the ugly shards of glass sticking out.

"Do me a favor, Thom. Stay away from me."

"I was trying to look out for you. Give me your arm, I can heal it."

"It's not just that. You don't trust me. You haven't this whole time. And I'm not sure I can trust you anymore either."

"If this is about the grimoire…"

"Goodbye, Thom," I said, hoisting myself up to the ledge and letting myself drop.

CHAPTER TWENTY-TWO

Ian's body was right there to break my fall. He didn't catch me like I kind of expected him to but I don't think it works that way. Jumping out of a building into someone's arms. You can blame Superman for those delusions.

It was nicer, though, crashing into his chest than making out with the hard soil.

"What happened to you?" he asked.

When I pulled my hair out of my face, he turned from stunned to a dark shade of pissed.

"I'll explain later," I said. "We need to get out of here." I looked back up at the building one more time and met Thom's eyes.

"Did you do this?" Ian was buzzing with anger now.

Thom never replied. He gave me one more disappointed glance before turning back in to the school.

"Let's leave," I said, dragging my bag behind me

while I headed towards the street.

"Give that to me," Ian said, taking my tote and throwing it across his shoulder. "What the hell did he do to you? I'm going to beat the crap out of him."

"Drop it, Ian. Let's go to my house. Then we can plot our next move."

I turned to look back at Thom one more time. Needed to see the look on his face when he saw the one of betrayal on mine. But all that was left was the mass of Dybbuk that had enveloped the building and their army of human puppets racing towards us, Morgan and Emma in the forefront.

We hightailed it towards my house. Only it wasn't a romantic leisurely walk, it was more of a 'run for your life keep checking your back' kind of thing. Main street was overrun with looters, breaking through storefront displays and taking with them as much as they could carry. Grown women were vandalizing cars and street signs while stroller-napping toddlers were wheeled away by the crowds.

"I think I can find something online. It's worth trying. Am I wrong?"

"Didn't you say there was a book?" Ian asked.

"'Was' is the operative word," I said, shoving my way through a horde of burly men fighting over six packs of cheap beer.

Our breath came in and out in short rough wheezes as we picked up our pace. The brand on my arm, courtesy of Thom, was starting to ache. The skin was beginning to contract and pull tight, amplifying the burning sensation.

By the time we reached the familiar tree-lined block of my house, all my energy had been depleted. My foot got caught on a tree root, sending me skidding on the concrete.

"Ow. Shit," I cried out.

"You alright?" Ian said, catching my elbows and lifting me up. He looked down at my palms, raw and riddled with tiny pebbles and dirt. "Let's get you cleaned up."

I leaned on him for support until we got inside. Ghosty's absence on the front porch had me worrying.

Et tu Ghoste? Did you go bananas, too?

Before I could peek out the back to make sure, Ian dragged me to the bathroom and sat me on the countertop.

"Peroxide?" he asked.

"Under the sink."

He crouched down and rummaged through the contents.

Eek, my pads are in there.

He stood back up with a handful of cotton and a brown bottle, the sight of which always made me wince.

"I hate that stuff."

"Don't worry." He turned my palms up and began to clean away the debris.

My eyes drifted down the curve of his neck. The thought of his skin sent shivers of longing through me. Visions of his body flooded my mind and I tried my best to sit still as he gently swiped the cotton across my palms.

"All done," he said. "Now, let me look at this."

He pushed up my sleeve and let out a fierce rumble.

"It's not as bad as it looks," I said.

"Oh, yes it is. And I'm going to seriously kick his ass next time I see him. You can count on it."

After rubbing some antibiotic cream in, Ian wrapped my arms with gauze, tying it closed with the frayed ends.

"Thanks," I said when there was nothing left of me to fix.

He didn't respond. Only sent a sly smile my way, which didn't progress any further as the sound of a slamming door interrupted the moment.

"Gemma!" My father's voice boomed through the thin walls.

"In here," I called.

As soon as he filled the doorway, I knew something was wrong. The blackness in his eyes had seeped its way down his face. Tiny veins dragged down his cheeks and swelled, throbbing and pulsing while his tongue stuck out the side of his mouth.

I jumped off the counter and slipped on the bathmat, the toilet breaking my fall.

"Dr. Pope. Are you feeling alright?" Ian took a step, blocking my dad's path towards me. I was at a loss for words at the sight of him.

"Gemma," he replied, stretching his arms past Ian's shoulders to get to me. Ian pushed back, sending my father back into the hallway.

Then he turned to me. "Get your things. Whatever you need for a few days. Meet me at the tree." He closed the door behind him, which was followed by MME-worthy slams that vibrated through the walls.

When the sounds of grappling moved far enough away to the other side of the house, I used the time to jump straight into my room. I pulled a small duffle from the top shelf of my closet and began packing up my laptop and a change of clothes as well as the notebook of sigils with all my copies and parchment.

I was hesitant to leave. My father's behavior might have been unstable but he always managed to pull through and turn back to his old self.

It'll only be for the night. Tomorrow he'll be better and I'll come back.

I walked away from the grunts and sounds of wood splintering to the master bedroom. There was a picture of Brian I had to take with me.

The generally immaculate room was in shambles. The bed was unmade, sheets and blankets were strewn all over the floor. Hangers and clothing covered every other inch of the room. The closet doors had been torn off their hinges and were leaning against the thick damask drapes that were now torn to shreds. With my fists in front of me, I walked to the large vanity where the words *Get Gemma* were scrawled in red liquid that had caked dry only after it had oozed down and collected into a pool on top of the mahogany table.

I really hope that's not what I think it is.

Not willing to risk myself any longer and find out what exactly *Get Gemma* meant, I grabbed my favorite framed photo of my brother and jumped out through the bedroom window.

It was cold and dark at the base of the tree. My senses were on high alert, still fueled by the adrenaline it had taken to get here past the flying Dybbuk that had cloaked the town in search of their next host, and hordes of possessed people looking for more violence.

At night the overgrown grass looked menacing and the pile of junk was the perfect hiding places for boogey men. The damp earth filled my mind with exaggerated visions of enormous killer centipedes crawling up my legs. I made sure to stomp my boots every few seconds just in case.

When a figure began to move towards me, I jumped from my spot on the low-lying log.

"Thank goodness you're here. How is he?" I asked, hoping my dad was okay.

"Didn't reckon you'd be so glad to see me." There was only one person around Harrisport with that accent.

"Thom."

He stepped closer until we were inches apart. The only light coming from the nearby gas station was enough to highlight more than a days' worth of five o'clock shadow. And somehow, even amidst the chilling night, he was able to exude warmth.

"What are you doing here?" I tried to come off strong but I only sounded petty and obnoxious.

"Could ask you the same thing. Hope you know what you're doing."

"I'm fine. Actually, I'm better than fine. Even after the stunt you pulled earlier."

"I'm trying to protect you, Gemma. When will you realize that?"

"When you start trusting me back and telling me what the hell is really going on," I said.

"You're driving me mad, girl."

"You hurt me," I said, tucking my bandaged arm

into my jacket.

The cicadas turned up the volume and the chittering was surrounding us.

"I'm truly sorry for that. That's why I'm here." He drew something out of his jacket. It was the leather journal I had seen with him the last few days. "Couldn't get everything in there. Only bits and pieces that I could remember. Maybe you can find something in there to sort out this mess. I can't interfere anymore."

I took the book and shoved it into my duffle. "I'm not an idiot, you know. I can kind of figure out who you are. I just don't know which side you're playing for."

"For your sake, I hope you don't find out." He placed a gloved hand on my cheek. I drew back, expecting only pain but he held my cheek steady, showing me that I was safe. His face hovered above mine and I caught the sweet scent of cinnamon once again. "Sweet Gemma. Don't ever change."

My heart was racing.

"Is this goodbye?" I asked.

"Something like it."

"How will I know what to do?"

"You seem to have it covered. My hands are tied from here on in, however this story may play out." He perked his head up and looked around. "Gotta run," he said.

"Wait. What if.."

He was gone before I could finish my question. Before I could call back out to him, I heard a crunch from behind.

"Hey." It was Ian. "Who were you talking to?"

I stuck my hand in my bag, feeling the smooth leather of the book Thom had entrusted to me.

"No one," I said. "Just was freaking out a bit."

"I would have been here sooner."

"Is he alright?"

"Let's just say he's taking a nap."

We headed off into the Drifts and I didn't look back.

When we got to Ian's house on the hill, it was daytime.

"Strange," I said.

"What is?"

"This place stays gray. It doesn't change."

"Don't expect things to follow the same rules in the Drifts. Let's get in." Ian stopped at the lake to pull his sweater over his head, revealing a smooth expanse of taut skin over well-formed muscle.

Gulp.

"It's freezing." I rubbed the sides of my arms as he continued to undress, unbuckling the thick black leather belt at his waist. "And I'm tired."

"Just go with it. I promise you'll love it," he said as he tucked his thumbs into the waistline of his fitted jeans and stepped out of them.

"I don't have a suit," I said.

He didn't seem to care and showed no signs of stopping. I followed his lead and began peeling away the layers of clothing until we were both standing in the frigid wind in just our undies. I wrapped my arms around my soft stomach that running couldn't seem to get rid of, embarrassed at how I must look in front of such a perfect guy like Ian. His yellow octopus print boxers hung precariously past the edge of his pelvic bone, revealing the deep vee of his oblique muscles and I followed the line all the way down his legs.

He even has nice feet.

If I hadn't been standing near naked in the freezing cold, I would have jumped into a cold shower to calm my raging hormones. As he gracefully slipped into the water, I took note of the large skeletal wings tattooed across the entire expanse of Ian's back. He beckoned me to follow. Mesmerized by the way his eyes reflected the intense blues around him, I sat on the wooden boardwalk that ran alongside the water and slid my feet into the soothing hot water, eventually lowering myself beside him, happy to obscure the rest of my body from his heated gaze.

I never had the chance to even fumble or hesitate or babble because Ian was beside me in seconds. His face leaned closer to mine. I was giddy and nervous at the chance for another kiss. And more. He took me in his arms and placed them on his shoulders. Instinct had me wrapping my legs around his waist and he swam us towards a bevy of volcanic rock that was coated in white chalky silica.

I tucked my face into the dip of his shoulder and watched the water glow, painting a picture for myself in my mind so that I could remember this moment. Ian swam wide circles around the small island while I held on and tried to steady the frenzied beat of my heart. I took a strong deep breath. The smell of him and the minerals was heady.

When I finally got the courage to look up, Ian was there with his all-knowing smirk and devilishly arched brows. He lowered his face until our noses touched and brought one hand up my ribs until it rested just below my breast. I remained frozen as his soft lips touched mine. He ran his index finger under the elastic of my bra and I sucked in the cold air as he pulled me deeper into the water and his embrace.

I ran my hands across his jaw and pulled him deeper into the kiss letting my hands travel along his spine. That's when his face turned serious and he pressed my back up against the chalk rocks, crumbling them beneath me. He planted a trail of desire along my neck, collarbone, breastbone, all the way down my abdomen and back up again.

We lay there, his body on top of mine on the small white island while he twisted strands of my hair into coils. Our eyes met once more. He peeled a wet strand of hair away from my eyes and brushed the back of his hand up and down my cheek. He did the same on the other side and I recoiled, having forgotten about the bruise Allison had inflicted. It felt like years had gone by since then.

"Shh. I'll make it better," he said and he left his kisses on every part of me that felt battered and bruised. After unwrapping the wet gauze, I caught the wicked purple handprint on my forearm. He didn't balk at the sight. Instead, I felt the whisper of his breath as energy left his voice and infused my skin.

When he was finished weaving whatever magic he used, I gasped. The skin had mended. No hand in sight.

"Thank you," I said, my voice hushed. And with that gesture, I let Ian take me to yet another place.

CHAPTER TWENTY-THREE

My mind felt foggy. It reminded me of being a kid when you weren't too sure of what was going on around you or what was going to happen next. All you really knew was going on in the bubble around your head, floating right within your grasp while everything else faded out into fuzz.

I licked my dry lips and looked around me. Ian, whose sleeping form was face down, sprawled across the bed, appeared to be at war with the blankets.

There was a deep thrumming sound coming from somewhere outside that kept intruding behind my skull. My bare feet hit the wood floor without a sound. I let the sheets drop away and pulled on yesterday's sweater.

Today, the world here was gray. Dark and light played off each other in a dramatic contrast. Rain cascaded down the sides of the house, warping the view of the surrounding hillside.

I rested my cheek against the glass and let the cold

sink in while looking at myself up close in the reflection, checking my eyes for any differences.

No one would probably notice except me.

The clouds were blacker now, spreading their wings across the sky as they dumped bucket loads of rain. Only when landing in the lagoon did the raindrops dive into a colorful existence of aquas.

It was sad and beautiful. I could understand why Ian sought refuge here. It was the sort of bleak beauty that caressed you and made you feel comfortable with your own depression. No expectations of happiness. Just serene passivity.

The urge to feel the fresh air overtook me. I slid the heavy, barn-style wooden door to the side. The thrumming got louder and discordant, scraping against my insides. It was not a language known to man, yet somehow I knew it to be words. Screeches and clicks. I pulled at my hair, trying to relieve my scalp of the throbbing pressure. That's when the snickering began tunneling its way to my eardrum. My hands came up to cover my ears and I stepped out and let the rain beat against me.

Then the noise stopped and when I saw him at the top of a cliff, I dropped to the ground.

Brian.

I scrambled up, clawing my way up the through the mud. My hands and feet were sinking into the ground, releasing with a wet slurping pop as I struggled for an even hold with each step. I reached the top, panting and choking on the wind. He gave me his hand and I took it.

Gemma. Don't speak.

His words pierced my mind.

They can hear us in the Drifts.

I tried to press my thoughts to him to see if I could do the same.

It only works one way.

He was wearing the same shirt as the day of the accident - a vintage Zoso concert tee I had found in the sale bin at Past and Presents.

You can't trust him.

"Who?" I said.

He brought his finger up to his lips.

Shh. They'll hear you and find you. They're all looking for you.

I watched a dark damp circle the size of a quarter appear on his chest. It bloomed larger and larger. A bloody flower unfurling its petals.

He knows. They'll follow you.

His clothing was drenched but the more the rain washed over him, the more blood spilled out of his body, pooling at our feet. The ground beneath us began to give way. My feet sank in up until my knees and the rain and the blood rushed in. Panic set in. I frantically started to dig out my legs but the mud was stronger. It held me in place as I watched Brian's eyes go black. He opened his mouth and a flock of crows exploded around us. Their wings flapped against my skin. I brought my arms up to protect my face and screamed.

"Are you okay?"

I bolted up, surrounded by warm flannel sheets and Ian's embrace. I turned to the window, my heart still trying to beat its way out of my chest. There were no signs of birds or rain. Or Brian.

The question hung heavy in the air and held more

weight than mere concern about my nightmare.

"I think so." The air was chilly and I drew the blankets up to my neck. Ian looked wounded at the retreat and I quickly tried to smooth things over. "I'm great. Last night was great."

He inched his body closer to mine and planted a kiss on my bare shoulder.

"I'm glad."

Suddenly, with Ian so close to me, I became aware of my own need for basic hygiene.

"Bathroom?"

"There's a pocket door hiding past the table there."

I turned my back towards him and put on my shirt, knowing that I was being shy for no reason, considering we were naked together all night. In the harsh light of the morning, though, I needed to feign modesty for my own comfort.

Once in the privacy of the small room, I tried my best to rinse out the morning breath and tame the wild nest of bed head while sneaking a peek at the medicine cabinet. It was empty.

Back in the room, Ian was sitting on the bed, watching the sky, giving me another glimpse of the intricate artwork that graced his body. The shading on the bones and wings made the tattoo appear lifelike. I sat behind him and traced my finger along the lines. "When did you get this?"

He laughed. Not in a funny, haha way. It was bitter.

"It's been there a while."

"Is it from some sort of magic? Like mine?" I leaned in and rested my head on him.

"Yes." He exhaled. "And no."

I didn't press him for any more details. It would be

a pretty easy way to ruin the moment and I figured if he wanted to tell me about it, he would in time.

We sat there until darkness descended once again. "It's not night time already, is it?" I asked.

"It can't be." He put on his shirt, stood up and headed for the door. It slid open with ease. Ian stood in the doorway, turned and then looked up. "Get your stuff."

"What's wrong?" I asked, searching for my jeans on the floor.

"They found us," he said as he struggled to get the door closed again. It groaned and squeaked at his attempts but didn't budge. "The door's stuck. Hurry up!"

I zipped my jeans closed and grabbed my duffle. He took me by the arm and led me to the door.

"Wait," I said, stopping us in our tracks. All I saw were heavy clouds rolling in, blotting out the sky. "What exactly is out there? I don't see anything."

"You don't want to know." His eyes were feverish with fear. "Just keep your eyes to the ground and don't let go. I'll get us out of here."

I let him lead me outside and kept my head down as we traversed the hills, heading in the opposite direction of the lagoon.

"Where are we going?"

"We need to get back to the club. There's a porthole a few miles away. Don't stop."

The ground was rocky and coated in slick green lichen. I was glad of my Doc's that seemed better suited for gripping while on the run. Curiosity got the best of me when I heard noises coming from behind us. It was the same chittering that I had heard in my dream.

I looked back to find hundreds of black birds flying towards us. My foot stubbed a rock and I tripped but Ian was there to keep me on pace. When the birds got closer, I could see they weren't birds at all. They were the size and shape of a small monkey but the similarities ended there. Their small round heads were all eyes and teeth atop a body that was slick and black. The fur around their necks plumed out like a crown while the skin beneath it was hairless and taut, enhancing their emaciated forms. Their taloned wings were leathery and spanned five feet across.

"Ian, what the..?"

"Just run."

And that's what we did. Across the plain, exposed to our predators without any cover. Finally, we ran passed brushes of knee-high grass to a stagnant pool of brown water. An odor of decay wafted up to my nose and I sneezed.

"The porthole is at the bottom of the lake."

"'Scuse me?"

"I'll navigate down there. You just need to make sure not to let go of my hand."

"No way. I'm not getting in there."

"You have to. It's the only way out. And you do not want them catching up."

"What are they?"

"They're the Dybbuk. On this side of the veil that's what they look like."

I turned again to see them rolling in like a wave towards us. The screeching was vibrating the ground beneath us and sounded very much like echoes of my name.

"Let's go then," I said and braved myself for the lesser of two evils.

Ian took my hand and said, "Remember, don't let go." He gave me a smile that had me thinking of our night together, which, now amidst the hoard of mutant flying monkeys, seemed so long ago.

I slid my arms through both handles of my duffle so that it rested on my back, took his hand and smiled back.

The water was a shock to my system. I had expected it to be at least as warm as the lagoon. It was cold, shooting its icy tendrils down to my nerves. After the initial splash, we dove right in. I squeezed my eyes shut, afraid not only of the dirty water but of what could be lurking in a place like this. We swam deeper into the abyss until the pressure began to press against my lungs, setting me into a panic. I opened my eyes to get an idea of how much longer we would be descending. I couldn't see much through the haze so I gripped Ian's hand a bit tighter and tried to swim a little stronger.

Suddenly, we were bombarded. Projectiles whizzed past us, splashing their wake at us. One of them had unfurled beside me and flashed his milky yellow eyes at me. I opened my mouth in fright and sucked in a mouthful of putrid water. I shook Ian's arm and frantically motioned to the Dybbuk, which was about to pounce on me. I pushed the water out of my mouth but it was too late. I had lost whatever air I had been holding.

The Dybbuk landed on my chest and dug its sharp nails into my shoulders, piercing through skin and muscle. My hands gave way from the pain and Ian was gone. I thrashed against my enemy and kicked, trying to break it away. Another one had jumped on my duffle, weighing me down. With no more fight inside me, I relaxed into the sinking feeling while my mind tried to float away. I closed my eyes and left.

My lashes fluttered. Strong hands rolled my body to the side and I felt a gush of water pour out the side of my mouth, followed by a deep, wrenching, hacking cough. I inhaled deeply, cherishing the sweet taste of oxygen on my tongue. My teeth chattered and I tried lifting my head but the throbbing made me put it back down.

"Relax there, sweetie."

"Where am I?" My nose and throat were raw.

"You're in my office. I'm gonna need to have the carpets cleaned. No worries. You're here and safe. Ian told me you had a scare."

"A scare." I laughed but kept my cheek on the floor, curling my body up for comfort. Salty tears burned their way down my cheeks and I let out an agonizing cry.

"There, there. Let's get you on the couch."

I let them lift my limp body and set me on the cool leather couch. Someone placed a heavy wool blanket around me and the telltale sound of a fire crackled nearby.

I must have fallen asleep because when I sat back up, the room was empty and all that remained in the fireplace were glowing embers. I wrapped the blanket around me and moved to the armchair that had my duffle. The dark green canvas was soaked right through. Inside, my clothes were rank and the journal was ruined. I flipped through the pages, aching at the sight of ink running down most of them. There was one page that looked salvageable and I rushed to tear it out.

After setting the parchment on the warm floor by the mantelpiece to dry, I walked around the room, taking a closer look at all of Sam's treasures.

If this is the stuff he keeps out, I wonder what's in his safe?

When I felt that the parchment had had enough time to dry, I looked it over and folded it into my bra, not having recognized the symbol at all.

"How are you feeling?" I heard Sam's voice behind me.

"I think I'm alright."

"I told Max to get you some clothes. He should be back soon."

"Max?"

"He usually stands guard there."

"Oh, Mr. Muscle."

Sam laughed at the moniker and then let his gaze fall to the floor. "Gemma, I think I've found someone who can help with your problem topside."

"Really? That's good, right?" I said. The two of them didn't seem as excited at the prospect.

"There are some issues," Sam continued. "You're going to have to summon him and then perform a banishing ritual."

"Is that hard?"

"I'm not going to lie to you. It's not hard but it can leave you with a hell of a debt."

"That's fine. Everyone up there needs our help. You don't know what it's like up there."

"I can imagine," Sam replied. "Then I'll give you the true name and this." He pulled a round metal disc from the pocket of his black blazer. The cross around his neck shone in the light as he placed the warm amulet in my hand.

It was engraved with letters and looked vaguely familiar. I tried to rack my brain on whether I had ever seen a symbol like this before. Then it hit me.

"This is the symbol on the cover of the grimoire."

"Which one is that?" Sam asked.

"Just the one Thom was using with her," Ian interjected.

"Do you have it?"

"No." Heat began to flood my face as the anger coursed once again through my veins. "It's gone."

"Isn't that convenient," Sam said. "In the middle of a crisis and everything. You keep that in mind lest you forget."

"So if I summon this demon and perform this spell, the Dybbuk will go away?"

"In essence. There are a few minor details. You must perform the spell by a chamber. That can make your task a bit more difficult. The location of these chambers are a heavily guarded secret. But I'm sure, with your wiles, you can coerce another one to tell you."

"In the woods near my house. I can't believe this."
My luck was finally turning.

"And you must wait until his sigil has bonded into your skin before you can perform the banishment."

"Okay then. I'm game."

"It's good to have you, Gemma," Sam said. Those words sounded heavy in the air, like I had no idea how far it went.

CHAPTER TWENTY-FOUR

It was nice to see that Tat Man, or Max, had reliable, yet classic, taste in clothing.

"Here," he said, closing the door behind him and tossing me the garments.

I feared he would come back with something with more spandex and a lot more revealing so I was thrilled to put on the black jeans and a wife beater. The sweater was a bit grungy but it was the kind people paid lots of money for in the hopes of replicating a street trend.

"Can I get some privacy?"

"Sorry. Boss said I either leave the door open or get in here with you. Don't know yet what could have followed you back so I can't leave you locked in here on your own. I thought you might prefer one set of averted eyes to a crowd full of onlookers." He gave his back to me and I jumped at the chance to put on the clothing.

"Alright. I'm done," I said.

"Good." He turned back to me. "Because I wanted to let you know that I knew your mother. She would have been proud to see you here with Sam."

I didn't know how to take that comment so I asked a question instead. "Do you know where she is?"

"Not exactly. But we used to spell cast with each other and having that type of relationship gives me the ability to sense her presence. She is close. Always has been."

"Well, isn't that just great?" I gave him my most sinister smile. "But I don't really care. In fact, I'm more pissed than ever. She leaves, and was right here all along. Not dead somewhere in a ditch or off in Maui with a boyfriend."

"I'm trying to help. Focus on your work and you will surpass both her and I in power. That ominous day will come soon. Just know that I will be here then." He left me with my own thoughts and anger. I stormed out right after him, ready to tell him off but found a smiling Ian instead.

While Sam worked the crowd of patrons, Ian led me to the dance floor.

"Do it," he said. "I can see it in your face. You're pale and need the energy."

"I don't think it's right," I said.

"But they do. You can't imagine what torture waits for them beyond these walls. They're the lucky ones with enough soul energy left for Sam to take in."

I took his advice and leeched a bit of energy off the senseless people around me. I even went ahead and made physical contact with one to see what would happen, and was rewarded with a double shot that buzzed through my fingers. The guy looked at me and gave me a brief smile before the muscles of his face caved into his cheekbones. The process continued, hollowing out his eyes until he collapsed in a pile of boneless flesh.

"What was that?" I screamed.

"His time was up." Ian replied.

Before I could react, Sam found us and led us to the elevator. "Good luck," he shouted over the music as he handed me a small book. There was a scrap of paper sticking out. "I marked the page for you and the name is on the paper."

Ian and I held hands as the doors closed onto the club.

"I'm not so sure about this anymore," I said.

"I'll be there the whole time if you need me."

When we reached the front of my house, I was shocked at what I saw.

The sky looked like it had been blacked out, a starless expanse that held an artificial quality. The entity the Dybbuk had become had cloaked itself over the entire city. It didn't look like anything could pierce the bubble.

The air within the town was cloying catching in my throat and sending me into a coughing fit. Smoke rose up to the air as a fire blazed within the forest while shadows zoomed and whipped all around me.

We didn't say a word to each other on our way to the chamber. I led the way and used all my effort to remain undetected. An occasional howl pierced the silence beyond the roaring inferno that seemed to be contained in the east. My legs knew the way and we arrived without any problems. Ian helped me brush away the leaves and moss that had covered the indentation where the chamber gate lay. The place still made me feel sick.

"I don't have any salt or anything. I guess if I use the chamber as the circle, I can kill two birds with one stone and hope the demon doesn't get a chance to kill me."

"I told you I'm here." Ian rubbed my shoulders and I looked down at the small black book. The scrap of paper curled up when I opened to the page. It was the sigil I had prepared for Ash that night at Charlotte's house.

WTF?

The spell in the book was handwritten in a sweeping cursive that echoed from a time long past that included hoop skirts, corsets and bloody wars.

"It says here that I just need to place the amulet in the lock. Do you see a lock?" I asked.

Ian investigated along the perimeter. It wasn't until he reached the center that he called me. "Over here. I think this is it."

My heart dropped when I realized that I would need to be steps away from the demon when I summoned him. "Alright. Here goes nothing. You should get on the grass. It won't do me any good if you get eaten by it while I'm doing the spell."

"You're stronger than you think, Gemma." Ian leaned in and kissed me on the lips before taking his place against a nearby tree. He saluted me and I took that as my cue to start. I sat on the cold hard gate and pulled out a pen. I checked to see if I had the spelling down.

"Gemma!"

I whipped my head around only to find Charlotte

in her platform silver sandals struggling to keep her balance on the dirt path. She was wearing a red strapless chiffon dress. The beading started on the edge of her sweetheart neckline and cascaded down the side.

"What's going on?" I asked.

"There's one more detail I neglected to mention." Sam appeared from the darkness as he pushed Charlotte forward. "You need a sacrificial lamb."

"Are you nuts?"

"I'm sorry, sweetie, but it's not going to work without her."

"Can't we find someone else?" I was surprised at my willingness to offer up another human life but there was no way I was putting my best friend in the middle of this mess.

"Afraid we can't. This one's special. She's lucky."

"Wow. I promise you it's my charms. Look." Charlotte pulled her key ring from the small silver clutch that coordinated with her shoes. Leave it to Charlotte to look perfect. I, on the other hand, still smelled of rotten fish. "I've got a rabbit's foot, a horseshoe, my leprechaun."

Sam didn't let her finish and took a swing at her head. Charlotte dropped like a sack of potatoes.

"What do you think you're doing?"

"I thought I was helping you. Go on," Sam's sneer rubbed me the wrong way.

My eyes met Ian's and he nodded at my questioning look. Around me the shadows of the Dybbuk were creeping in through the trees and converging around us. My heart was tearing into pieces; it's shards piercing me from the inside out.

"I can't do this," I said, shaking my head.

"You have to," Ian's voice was concerned but unyielding. The rich timbre evoked the deep emotions I had developed for him. He had become the constant in my life that I could rely on.

"But Charlotte," I heard the quiver in my own voice.

"Everything will be okay but you have to do it soon," He pointed to the approaching flames.

"That's enough chit chat," Sam said. "Do it or I'll make sure Charlotte's soul finds its way to my club. She's got plenty of juice to power everyone up for a few millennia."

The threat to my friend's soul was all that I needed to make up my mind after seeing the bitter remains of the man whose soul I had leeched to its very end. This was how I was going to make things right; by saving Harrisport.

Reluctant to waste any more time, I set on my task and created the sigil. I unfolded the crisp paper only to find my own handwriting. I had forgotten how interesting Abbadon's shape was; tall and narrow with a curve at the top. I cleared my throat and began the summoning. I didn't have any real texts with me but I went with my gut and spoke from the power that was seated inside of me.

"I summon thee, Abbadon the destroyer." My voice was clear and the Dybbuk were melding into one entity of infinite darkness. "I call you by the fire that consumes us. I call you from the bottomless pit."

At first, I thought it hadn't worked so I pushed away all my thoughts and focused on my surroundings. The great mass of shadows was beginning to obstruct my view of Ian and Sam as it thickened like a wall around me. I prayed that, if anything, Ian would try his best to save Charlotte. When I was about to give up, I felt a faint tendril of power and latched right on. It was unwilling to come, something that I had learned in theory but had yet to experience. I drew the power towards me and started reeling it in until it slammed right into me, knocking me ass over to the ground.

"Oomph," I said as my back connected to the floor. "Some manners would be nice."

I brushed the hair out of my eyes, hoping I wouldn't have to shave it all to get the smell out and looked up, only to have my heart sink like a punch in the gut.

"Thom?"

CHAPTER TWENTY-FIVE

"Thom, what are you doing here?" I stood up and brushed myself off, cranky at the prospect of having to redo the summoning.

Just then, Sam parted the wall of Dybbuk. "So the Great Destroyer has finally been wrangled in by a girl."

Thom stood there in a flannel shirt, his arms crossed in front of him. He seemed larger than usual.

"Sweetie, this is Abbadon himself. In the flesh."

My eyes grew wide and then wider when Thom said nothing to discount the accusation. "What?"

Sam circled around the two of us, stopping when he reached my back. He spoke right into my ear but I knew that Thom could hear every word he was saying.

"Abbadon here is the Reaper. He is the taker of souls. Neither angel nor demon. He doesn't take sides. But he also doesn't interfere. Usually. Then again, he took your dear brother from you."

I shook my head violently back and forth, thinking

that my memories would be wiped clean like an etch-a-sketch and I could start my whole life over again. I pushed back the rush of tears that wanted to burst from my eyes and all I could do was mewl. Sam put his hand on my shoulder, steadying me.

"Sammael. Who gave you leave to part from your den of inequity?" Thom's voice reverberated with power.

"This is all part of the new order." Sam stretched his arms out towards the air, sending the shadows into a frenzied dance around him then towards the sky where they reinforced the cage holding Harrisport hostage. "Gemma. Time's ticking."

I took a step closer to Thom and searched his face for anything that would change my mind. "Is it true? Did you kill my brother?" I asked.

"It doesn't work like that." He looked at the floor and twisted the toe of his combat boot on a sod of earth.

I couldn't help but let out a nervous giggle, the kind of laugh that you hear when a person is losing their mind. "I see you don't have such awful taste in shoes as I thought."

"I reckon you don't know a lot about me. But that's not the point. Whatever you do now is your choice. Like he said. I don't interfere."

"You took my brother," I screamed and pounded on his chest with every ounce of energy I had left. "He was all I had left in this place."

He grabbed me by the wrists and shoved his face up against mine until we were nose to nose. "I didn't have a choice. I do as I'm told."

"Why not me? They were all gone. Who told you to

take them and not me?"

"And the plot thickens." Sam chuckled. His foot was now on Charlotte's back, keeping her in place. "Tick tock goes the clock."

I dropped my hands to my side and inhaled until my entire body coursed with energy. I drew power from everyone around me. I was charged with a push that I knew had originated from Charlotte's soul. I wove it around me like armor until something clicked open inside my brain. Visions flooded my mind of red caves filled with molten lava and never-ending screams; a black sun that burned across a desert landscape and a power that fueled it like nothing on this Earth.

Somewhere deep inside me the words came out. A lesson in rote that I had learned somewhere in the womb. "Omni bentidoct inversio thundora emperoct. Voidus pyro. Voidus cyro. Voidus animus."

Thom's eyes flashed with disappointment but he did nothing to fight me. The Dybbuk began to converge around him and I placed the amulet in the lock, sending hidden gears into motion.

"Why not me?" I screamed one last time over the sound of groaning machinery and whirling shadows.

"Because I couldn't." His voice was now in my head. "You're needed here. You're not human."

"Then what am I? A demon?" I laughed at the absurdity of how it sounded.

"Almost," he replied. The gate opened and a ring of slats moved aside to form one large octagonal hole. I scrambled to the forest floor as quickly as I could manage while I watched Thom fall head first into the abyss. The Dybbuk were sucked into the vacuum behind him. The gate roared, absorbing the steady influx of shadows.

"What now?" I called to Sam. "The book doesn't say how to close it."

"Now it's your turn." He gave me a hideous smile and pushed.

I fell backwards, knocking my legs against the sides before falling into the hole, catching myself a few times as I reached out for anything to grab onto, only to lose my grip. My fingers finally hooked on to a thick root exposed in the dirt.

"Ian!" I yelled as I fastened myself to my only lifeline and dangled like a fish on a line. "Help!"

Below, I imagined Thom's body, a tiny speck caught in an endless fall, but there was only darkness. The sky turned from a cool gray and then to blue as the Dybbuk torpedoed passed me on its way down the dreary depths.

My arms weren't strong enough to carry my weight up to the surface. "Ian!" I screamed once more.

When I saw his face pop over the side, I was relieved.

"Hurry. I don't think I can hold on much longer."

He looked to his left and then to his right. Then past me. I waited for him to flash me his classic impish smile. Instead, he straightened his back and started talking to Sam.

"Please. I can't." I leaned my head against my arm. There was still more energy pulsing beneath the sigils. In theory, it would be enough to catapult me out of here if I trusted the power enough to do as I imagined.

I kept watching for signs that Ian was in the middle

of bargaining for my life. It looked more like two buddies catching up, complete with shoulder bumping and knowing laughs. His eyes met mine once again and they were devoid of all emotion. The relationship we had shared these last few weeks meant nothing. That is when I saw the red glow in his eyes and the comprehension was crippling. Large skeletal wings unfurled from his back. It had been a lie all along.

All I wanted to do was let the anguish wash over me until it forced me down into the pit. Maybe I could catch Thom on my way down the rabbit hole and apologize about not trusting him.

"Goodbye, Gem," Ian said without a hint of concern. Part of me was devising complex fantasies in which Ian created an elaborate subterfuge in front of Sam in order to ultimately save me.

"Ian, please." I poured every emotion I had into that plea.

"It's been nice." His voice was cold and sounded older than the seventeen-year-old angst-ridden slacker he portrayed. He flicked something at me, raising my hopes, only to get nicked by the tail of a fading cigarette butt. He looked right past me and then laughed at something Sam said. Before my mind could even catch up to my heart and grasp what had actually just happened, Ian was gone.

That was when the rumbling began from beneath. The tremors struck with the force of an earthquake, their power increasing with every ripple until the walls of the chamber threatened to collapse. The pit belched sulfur. Steam hit me with a face full of clay. Rocks clouded my vision and filled my mouth with the organic taste of earth.

"I don't think so," I said as I began to clamber up the length of the root.

There is no way I'm letting them get away with this.

The muscles in my triceps quivered from the stress of pulling my weight and my palms were being rubbed raw from the friction. Sweat dripped down my back as I struggled to get out of there.

Tarzan made this look a lot easier.

The air now was choking and visibility was nil. The chittering sounds were growing louder with each blast of pressure and the sounds of clawing filled me with visions of the monkey-like creatures of the Dybbuk on the other side of the veil.

Something clipped my shoulder as it flew passed and I lost my grip, sending me right back down to where I had started. The sounds of bees swarming was followed by hundreds of things flying passed me and out into the dusk-colored sky. I looked up and caught sight of a humanoid creature with slick red skin and oversized avian eyes like black pools. It was hanging upside down, its clawed feet gripping the side of the wall.

I tried to think of my next step. There was still an unexpended kernel of power resting within me.

I could use it to summon help.

The moment to try anything had passed when the grotesque creature with its shiny black beak pounced on top of me and began pecking at my head. I thrashed around, trying to hold on as it yanked out chunks of hair and tapped at my skull. My scalp burned and I began to scream. I threw a stray punch and the creature unleashed more of its power at me as it beat its thorned wings against my body. Tears ran down my cheeks as I realized that my life was going to end this horribly. Betrayed by the one person I had trusted enough to sleep with. Pecked to death by some beast as the rest of the world was subjected to a worse fate.

My eyes searched the heavens.

Now would be a good time for the powers that be to intervene.

The monster grabbed my arms and began poking at the flesh. It ran the tip of its beak up and down my forearm and gave me a questioning look as if all of sudden he recognized me from somewhere. It tilted its bird head in surprise.

That was when a shadow bulleted straight into the creature, slamming it up against the far side of the pit. The sound of crunching bone echoed all around us. The Dybbuk released the creature to the depths of the chasm and flew back towards me into an embrace. Wispy black tendrils curled around my limbs and began lifting me up.

"Ghosty?" I asked.

It kept me steady and safe until resting me at Charlotte's side before reforming into its familiar pillar-like stature. It stayed there while I pleaded to my best friend's unconscious form to wake up. I checked for a pulse and found one but it was weak. Around us the woods were empty. Ian and Sam were long gone. The pit was no longer rumbling but still spewed the egg- filled stench.

"What should I do?" I didn't know who I was asking.

Ghosty just stood there, as expected. I ran to the pit and picked up the amulet, expecting it to close without the magical device. It didn't.

Instead, a colossal horse, white as a dove, galloped out. Its rider reigned it into a stop before me. He wore a suit of polished armor, his helmet was tucked beneath his arm and a thin gold circlet adorned his head. He would have been beautiful had terror not oozed from every pore. I shivered when he smiled, put the helmet on and grabbed his bow in the other hand. He held up one finger, kicked the side of the horse and then he was off.

"That probably wasn't a good thing." I looked to Ghosty.

It morphed a human head and nodded in agreement. It was the first time he had really communicated with me and I would have smiled if things hadn't turned to such shit. I hunkered down next to Charlotte's motionless body, her breathing had changed and appeared stronger.

Could I get her home?

I couldn't be sure that my dad was back to normal. Ghosty's presence indicated that it was still possible for some Dybbuk to stay. So I waited.

When Charlotte woke up, she screamed. "My dress." She began to wipe away the dirt but the fabric was streaked with mud and grass stains.

"Charlotte, you're okay!" I threw my arms around her and squeezed.

"Wow." She rubbed the back of her head. "What an asshole. That like hurt. A lot."

"Tell me you're alright."

"I'm fine."

"Can you walk?"

"Yeah."

When we got closer to my back yard, I saw two forms standing just beyond the reach of the security lamps. Even cloaked in darkness, I knew it was Sam and Ian watching the chaos in the streets, illuminated by the surrounding inferno. I squashed the urge to vomit.

"Wait," I whispered, holding Charlotte back behind one of the larger maple trees.

"Is that him?" Charlotte asked. "Cuz if it is, wow, I am totally going to kick him in the balls."

I saw one of them turn their heads in our direction.

"Quiet. We're gonna get even. I promise." I drew us down further to the ground and out of their line of sight. "There's just one thing."

"If you're going to hit me on the head, no way."

We watched as demons of every shape and size molested humans in the street, tearing at their clothing and skin as they cackled and hooted into the night air. The sound of glass breaking and alarms blaring was the added chorus to the misery.

"I don't think I'll need to. I'm asking your permission. Sam said something, that you're the lamb. But you're not dead. So I'm assuming it means that you just have a certain kind of supped-up power I can use. It's your essence," I said, recalling how the tattoos always sprung to life in her presence.

"Are you sure?" she asked. Our faces were close and I could see the uncertainty in her eyes.

"No. I'm not. I don't know about half the things going on around here. But shouldn't we at least try to stop it? I don't think it can get much more fucked up than this."

274

"Okay. Go for it. Make sure you really hit Sam. Punk."

"Just tell me if it becomes too much."

We sat back-to-back and locked hands. I stirred the small ball of energy that had lodged itself within my Third Eye. Charlotte relaxed into my body as the flow of power began to pour through me.

"You okay?" I asked. It was killer, trying to hold the power and talk to Charlotte at the same time, but I needed to know how she was handling it before I could go on.

"Yeah." Her voice sounded dreamy. "Give them hell."

I looked down at the sigils on my arm. They were cold and empty. The power I was using now was like the power I drew from the club. Human essence. Bit by bit, I was sucking down Charlotte's soul.

CHAPTER TWENTY-SIX

My heart had chilled down to its core. I spun Charlotte's power through me as I watched Ian and Sam, with pure hatred bleeding out from every fiber of my being. I gathered all the animosity into the pure clean energy from Charlotte and wove them together into a tapestry of destruction.

Overhead, the dome the Dybbuk had erected was gone. In its place was thousands of demons, spreading off into the distance, searching for greener pastures than the broken town of Harrisport.

When the power threatened to suffocate me, I stood up and let Charlotte's tranquil form slide down. Electricity buzzed through me and I could smell the distinct ionic smell surrounding me. I took one deep breath. Here there were no more incantations or demons. This was pure power, and all I knew was that I had to let go of it soon or else it would consume me like the sun had Icarus.

What happened next was pure and quick. I let the

power focus through the necklace. It compounded into a force beyond nature, ripping through the tree trunk until it whipped both Sam and Ian to the ground.

I took one step. Then another. Before I knew it, I was standing above them. My two worst enemies.

"You played me. This whole time." My voice boomed with the force of electricity trying to escape the conduit.

The two of them lay there at the mercy of my hold. I hammered the beams of light further into them. I knew what I had to do next. I peeled back each layer of the veil until I was directly in the Otherworld. I began to push Sam's contorted body through it. He twisted in pain and screamed. "Don't do this. We can work together," he pleaded.

"It must really hurt if you're bargaining with me now. Sorry. I'm through with you." With one last burst, he disappeared.

With only Ian left, I was able to pour everything I had into just him. "Don't you know that saying about a woman scorned?" I said.

His eyes flashed from blue to red and then back again. I pinned his arms and legs out to his sides.

"You're going to regret this." He gave me that knowing smirk. The kind a guy gives when he's trying to tell you he knows what you look like naked.

"I doubt it," I said and thrust the last of the power into him. I wanted to obliterate him. No Otherworld or endless Drifts for Ian. I was going to blast him into oblivion.

My body grew weak and I infused myself with more power. The urge to see this through was foremost in my mind. Ian's body convulsed beneath the power. Smoke rose from his hands in an ironic display of stigmata.

There was a blip in the line. I felt it once. Then again. Then a third time. Something was jarring my connection to Charlotte. I chanced a glimpse behind me and saw Ghosty's form flying back and forth between the power that was tethering me to my friend.

"Stop it," I yelled. "You're going to ruin everything." I tried to keep pushing at Ian but he was strong. His decay was slow and I didn't know how much power I needed or how long it would take.

Just then, the Dybbuk jumped in the path of the electricity. It absorbed more and more until it unraveled what was in me, leaving me an empty shell. I collapsed to the ground next to Ian and watched as Ghosty imploded in an inferno of blue flames.

I crawled on my hands and knees until I found her. I wrapped my arms under her shoulders and dragged her as far as I could towards the porch. Ian's body was gone, leaving an imprint in the grass where he had lain. The smoke began to clear away. I sat on the grass in the comforting light of the yard, resting Charlotte's head on my lap. I began to stroke the hair away from her eyes and was nearly broken at what I saw.

All along her neck and around her face, dark red veins pulsated above her skin. Her lips were pale white and her eyes were clouded in ash.

"Charlotte?" I whispered.

I ran my hands over her skin in silent prayer, caressing each line, pleading for them to disappear. In my tearful haze, I caught sight of two bare feet in the grass out of the corner of my eye. Still alight in the glow of magic was Brian's ghost, standing above us.

"I'm finally losing my mind," I said.

"Gem, do you think I'd let that happen?" He was wearing the same Zoso shirt. The aura of blue light that surrounded him began to dissipate, leaving a translucent glow to his phantom form. He looked down like the weight of the world rested on his shoulders. "I tried to warn you. About Ian. It's just hard when you're stuck like that."

He crouched down beside and examined Charlotte.

"This is all my fault," I cried.

"I could tell you it's not just to make you feel better."

"It was you. This whole time you were right here and I didn't even know. You saved me from Sam and now you saved me from myself."

"It wouldn't have happened at all if I had gotten you away from Ian."

"I didn't know who you were talking about. There was Ian and Thom. I kept thinking it was Thom. Ian kept-"

"He kept planting seeds of doubt about him. It was part of the plan. To get you to use your powers to open the chamber. Make it seem like that would be the only way to get rid of the Dybbuk." His voice croaked when he uttered the last word.

"So how are you here now?"

"Unfinished business. I was stuck here because I thought it was my fault. That the accident was a heinous mistake that could have been avoided if I wasn't such a self-centered jerk."

"It was the truck."

"Yeah but I was stupid, and texting. And then you took the blame for everything. It was too much. I had to stay here and help you."

Charlotte began to stir in my lap. "Gem? Is it over?" she asked but her voice echoed through my head.

"Sam's gone." I rubbed the worry lines from her forehead.

She opened her eyes. "I can't see. And I can hear you. In my brain." There was fear in her voice. Her eyes were coated in a milky white film.

"Shh. Just rest. I'll figure it out."

"Gemma?" My dad's voice rang across the lawn. He hustled down the wooden stairs. "What happened?"

I turned to Brian, expecting him to help me out. My dad placed his hand on my shoulder. "Are you alright? Let's get Charlotte in the house."

"Yeah. You're right." I waited for him to say something about Brian's presence but I doubted he could see him at all. Just like he hadn't seen any of the Dybbuk. He scooped Charlotte into his arms and took her inside.

"You coming?" I asked Brian. "Or is this it?"

My heart was prepared for anything right now. When everything was said and done, I would be the one left crying. Sparing me from one last grief wouldn't have changed who I was becoming.

"I'm not going anywhere. We still need to close the gate. Put back everything that came out."

The two of us followed our father into the house side by side to find Charlotte already on the couch, tucked beneath a mountain of blankets. The sound of rushing water and clanking pots told me that Dad was already fidgeting in the kitchen.

"Dad, we need to talk," I called out to him from across the house.

There was no answer, only the continuous busyness of the clicking gas range pilot and the slamming of cabinet doors. I settled down on the stool of the breakfast bar, Brian took his usual spot beside me. The small gesture filled me with a paradox of emotions. It was comforting to have him there and, at the same time, it cut through me like a knife.

"Dad. Please stop."

He turned away from the boiling pot of water and stood opposite me. I looked for any hints of lingering evil. There was none. None of the manic behavior that I had attributed to post- accident insomnia. He was back to his silence, his judgmental looks that only hinted at his true feelings.

"What is it?" He wrung the water out of a dishrag and into the sink before smacking it against the stainless steel basin.

"I'm not sure you know what's going on. It's bad and I need your help."

"And Charlotte?"

I pulled my sleeve up, bearing not only the tattoos but also a piece of my soul that I would have rather kept hidden. The sigils, although inert, shone an iridescent blue black beneath the high intensity light of the halogen bulb hanging above us. The look of recognition was hard for my dad to cover up.

"Ask him about Mom," Brian said.

I shot Brian a 'what the hell look' then realized how crazy I must seem if my dad couldn't see him.

"Listen, pumpkin," my dad started. "I know it's been rough for you but I need to deal with Charlotte. I don't think it's safe to take her out to the hospital."

He went over to the kitchen window and peeked through the cafe curtains, the ones I found in Target after Brian set the vintage ones ablaze in a volcano experiment gone wrong.

"Dad, it won't matter if Charlotte is fine or not if we don't solve my problem." I decided to go for it and took Brian's advice. "Tell me about Mom."

"It's dark out there." He rubbed both palms over his red- rimmed eyes. Not demonic red. Just tired. "I can't even get up the news on the radio. But I feel it deep in my gut. It's bad out there."

"Then you know why you have to tell me. I need to fix it. This is all my fault." I looked back to check on Charlotte. From where I was sitting, her skin looked better and she was still asleep. Sleep was good. That's when the brain shut everything else down and worked on healing itself.

"How do you figure that?" He leaned against the counter.

That's when it all came out. I told him about the Dybbuk. The grimoire. The book club where I spent my time summoning demons of the Otherworld, not reading Vonnegut. The chamber. The only parts I left out of my confession were the Drifts and Ian's betrayal.

"I guess this isn't a surprise." He walked over to the range and turned down the flame. Steam was rising from our large pasta pot. Tongs in hand, he stirred the water then pulled out a skeleton key and dropped it onto a kitchen towel.

"Your mother froze this in a block of ice. I joked with her, telling her most wives froze their credit cards when they knew they'd been doing too much shopping.

"She said 'Ethan, when the time comes, you'll know it.' And it was never mentioned again. That was a few months before she up and disappeared. Every time I pulled out a steak for dinner, it would taunt me, that foggy hunk of ice. But I didn't touch it.

"The night we came home with Brian from the hospital, the bell rang. It was the perfect summer's day so we expected there to be some visitors. Neighbors. Your grandmother came up from Georgia and made a pitcher of sun-kissed tea. We had Brian in a Moses basket, sitting on the porch in the back with us as we sat, sipping it from tall glasses. Your mom went ahead and answered it. I never saw who was at the door that day. But when she came back, she had you in her arms.

"She said you were her daughter and that your name was Gemma. I asked her the obvious questions. Who, what, how? She just said, 'You don't want to know. Not really.' And I think she was right. I had a feeling about what she was doing all the time we were married. Secret meetings. Going off into the woods with her friends. But I loved her and didn't want to seem like some macho guy telling her what to do. Thought it would drive her away." He laughed bitterly at the last part.

He handed me the key while I stared off in shock. Thom had known. My mom and dad had known. This epic-sized secret had been hidden from me for my entire life. I looked down at the simple silver key in my hand.

"Does this mean you're not my father?" I asked.

"I'm afraid not, pumpkin," he answered. The fact that he didn't go into a whole sitcom dad talk about how he'll always be my dad no matter what clued me in to how he really felt and why he had been so absent ever since Brian's death. His only child.

"What now?" I pushed every unwanted thought into the lockbox in my head where I kept everything I didn't want to think about.

"It's the key to her closet."

I started down the hallway with Brian trailing behind me.

My father's room had been cleaned. It was back to all its OCD glory. To the left was the hallway that led to the master bath. To the right was the bed, a door on either side. The one to the right was his walk-in. To the left was hers. It hadn't occurred to me that it had been locked all these years.

"You sure about this?" I asked Brian. I was getting some pretty heeby-jeeby vibes coming off the door.

"Whatever you need to close the chamber is in there."

"Can I ask how you know this?"

"One of the perks of being a ghost." He smiled.

I shoved the key in the lock and turned. The woosh of a seal being broken was followed by the scent of lavender. She always wore it. It made me sick to my stomach.

Inside it was a time capsule. The silk blouses she was so fond of hung in a row of color-coordinated perfection. Clear acrylic boxes showcasing all her favorite shoes lined the floor below dozens of hangers filled with the same pair of black slacks. She was never one to mommy it up with sweats or jeans.

"I don't see it," I said. "It's just all her boring clothes."

I knelt down on the plush cream carpeting and pushed aside the tower of shoeboxes. I opened her drawers and rummaged through scarves and hosiery. Then the next drawer full of white camisoles and yoga pants. My frustration was building with every minute. There were demons out there running amok while Charlotte lay unconscious on the couch.

"Brian, a little help?"

"Chill. If you haven't noticed, I'm not exactly solid. Just keep looking."

He was very much like a hologram. The kind with static coming through in certain areas, like a weak TV signal.

I crawled to the back of the closet. There was a patch of carpeting that didn't look like it was part of the same continuous piece. I tucked my fingers underneath the corners and wedged it free. And there it was. A trapdoor.

CHAPTER TWENTY-SEVEN

Most houses in the area couldn't boast a finished basement. Or an unfinished one. With the flooding that can happen anywhere from October through April, it would only serve as a hassle, leaving most residents content with a crawl space. Finding a twelve-by-twelve stone room beneath my parents' bedroom baffled me. I was expecting a hidey-hole where my mother stashed her most intimate things. Love letters from high school boyfriends. A pack of cigarettes.

The descent was anything but easy. The rope ladder twisted and swayed if I didn't hold myself completely rigid as I searched with my foot for each rung in the dark. I felt the cool breeze of Brian rush past and a single light bulb came on.

"I thought you couldn't touch anything. Doesn't include light switches, huh?" I said as my feet found solid ground.

"Nah. That's more of a ghost thing."

The windowless room was cool and there wasn't

much space to stretch. A small green leather journal sat on an antique secretary. To the right of it was a bookshelf, bursting with books of the occult, the old and new testaments, in both Hebrew and Latin, the Apocrypha.

I ran my index finger along one of the shelves, picking up a thick layer of dirt. I sat on the upholstered tuffet and flipped through the pages of what appeared to be my mother's journal. Each page was filled with a sigil, a date, and a brief description of her encounter with the celestial or demonic being.

"I don't remember her having any tattoos," I grumbled. "And I don't know what we're looking for." I slammed the book shut and leaned back against the cool wall.

"She always wore those stupid blouses. And we were young. I doubt we'd have noticed or cared," Brian said, hovering beside me, attempting to thumb through the contents of the bookshelf.

"But it would explain why Principal Kelly freaked out when she saw mine. She said Mom and her were friends."

I opened all the tiny compartments and found nothing of interest until I checked the large drawer in the center. Inside, was the grimoire. It looked exactly like the one that was missing although there could very well have been copies all over the universe for all I knew. It was worn in the same spots and had the same ink stain on the first page.

"This is too weird," I said, placing the book in my lap.

"What is it?"

"The grimoire. It's missing. So this has to be a copy.

I don't know how this is going to help me."

My butt was getting sore and I remembered the amulet I had shoved in my back pocket after my failed attempt to close the chamber.

After I had set it on the table, Brian said, "It looks like the symbol on the cover."

I turned the book over and saw that he was right. "It still doesn't give me any idea of what to do next."

"Well, let's think about it."

I rolled my eyes at him.

"Come on, Gem. You want to save the world or what?"

"Not really." I shuddered beneath his glare. "Okay fine."

"To open the gate what did you need?"

"The amulet, the lamb, and binding Thom."

"Are you sure the binding was part of it?"

"I wouldn't know." My brother's talent for deductive reasoning hadn't left him on the other side.

"So then, if the universe is composed of opposites, dark and light, good and evil, the only thing we need is the opposite of a lamb."

"Someone with no innocence left," I said.

"Exactly."

"Don't you think we're stretching it? I mean, there has to be instructions somewhere here."

"Suit yourself but it'll only get worse out there."

I felt time slipping through my fingers and I was angry that this burden had somehow fallen to me. It wasn't fair that I had to deal with all this demon crap. That's when the idea hit me. "What if I were to use a demon?"

"Makes sense." He was now behind me, examining

the sconces on the wall and the faint hint of chalk line caked on the wall. "So do you think all of this has anything to do with why Mom left?"

"Doesn't matter." I took the amulet and the grimoire and started up the ladder. "We've got work to do."

Charlotte looked rested. The angry thick lines were receding and the rose color tint had returned to her lips. She was sitting, propped up by pillows, in a cloud of shredded red chiffon, and flipping through channel after channel of static.

"You look much better," I said.

"I feel totally better. Ever wonder how a dead battery feels. Ugh."

"I guess you just needed some rest."

"I still can't see." Her voice was lower. I sat beside her and saw that her eyes were still a sickening cloudy white. "I mean, I can see, it's just not normal. Like how I'm used to seeing."

"I'm so sorry, Char. This is all my fault." I wanted more than anything to blame this on Sam or Ian. It just didn't feel right. I would like to think that I could have said no at any time. Even Thom said that the rest was up to me. He also said that demons knew how to toy with people.

I should have listened to him then.

What did I know?

"She said it had to happen."

"Who?"

"The lovely lady. In my dreams. She was filled with light." She looked away towards the window, lost in thought. "They need you on their side. I'm the one who will see what you can't."

"I think you need some more rest." I was worried that she had lost part of mind along with whatever eyesight had abandoned her.

"The light. I will see the light amidst your darkness." Her melodic voice filled me with more self-loathing. That she could be so positive after everything. "She said to embrace your darkness if you are to ever know light."

My hopes for Charlotte sank when I heard her rattle on about light and dark. All I saw were grays and though they varied in intensity, it weighed down on everything. I thought I had seen good in Ian. I thought I had seen the bad in Thom. And then there was my mother and her secret life. Me. I wasn't quite sure what was good and evil, if ever such a thing even existed.

"It's alright. I'm going to make it right."

"She knows you will," Charlotte sang on. "It's all in your head." She tapped the small indentation on her forehead. The french-tipped nail of her index finger had cracked.

"We should go," Brian said.

"We don't exactly have plan," I whispered in his direction.

"You should listen to your brother," Charlotte said.

"Can you see him?"

"Totally. Just not the same way you do. Go back to the chamber. Use what's left of Thom's journal. She said so."

I had forgotten the slip of parchment tucked snugly against my chest. There was a good chance that it had been ruined by now, just like the rest of the book. I unfurled the scrap of paper. There was part of a sigil but the true name was illegible, Thom's smooth cursive had bled beyond recognition.

"You think this is it?" I asked Brian as I walked away from the pain of Charlotte's situation. I showed him the scrap of paper.

"Is it safe?" he asked.

"Don't know who it is but I guess we'll find out soon."

"Then what are we waiting for?"

Charlotte insisted on coming with us. She made strange small sounds and comments all along the way, seeing and hearing things that neither myself nor my ghost of a brother could make out. The crackling rage of the forest fire engulfing the surrounding forest was all that consumed me.

"Almost there," I huffed. I was nearly out of breath from carrying the brunt of Charlotte's weight as Brian hovered inches above the ground right behind us. Overhead, the branches rustled as unseen creatures tangled in them. I waved my phone overhead, catching sight of a long sinewy arm and slate-colored flaps of skin.

"We need to hurry," Brian said.

When we got to the pit, it looked cold and empty, devoid of any activity, sinister or not. The temperature plummeted as soon as we entered the summoning ring, in direct contrast to the smoky heat that pursued us deep into the trees. The gray ash around the perimeter kicked up into the breeze, dancing along the small quivering blue beam, making it difficult to see and breath.

"It has to be now," Charlotte said, lowering her body to the floor. She began to palm the ground, searching for something in the dark, moving on to her knees and crawling frantically in circles. Then she stopped. Dead still. Her neck whipped around and she stared at me with those luminous sick eyes. "Now!"

I pulled out the scrap of paper and smoothed it onto a large boulder. There were no candles, no salt. I was winging this and hoping for the best. What choice did I have? Leave the sadistic creatures loose in my town or suffer my own consequences.

I searched for the familiar thread of power that lingered deep within my chest. Always. My gaze turned to Brian. He hovered over Charlotte's weak form, frozen in the terrified afterthought of her scream, and gave me a warm smile. The kind that always told me he knew I was doing the right thing, like when I was five years old and went back to the corner store to return the rainbow erasers I had stolen from the low-lying Lucite crates that ran along the aisles of the stationary section.

Overhead the sky held blood red remnants of sunset, choking on layers of thick smoke. Leaves curled up and crackled as if they were aware of their impending incineration. I looked at Brian one more time for reassurance before I opened my mouth and let the power that had built up within me slip free.

"Is it working?" Brian asked.

I hesitated to speak, fearing the moment would be ruined along with the connection to whichever mysterious entity I was about to get in touch with. I shrugged my shoulders and said, "I have no idea."

The pit remained empty and I could feel the sweat trickling down my back as the intensity of the fire was drawing nearer. I held on to the connection, hoping that it would soon burst open with energy and produce the demon I was hoping for.

Frantically, I looked back down at the page and then to Charlotte, who was still caught within the grip of her fit, motionless, just like the rest of the surroundings. All the while, I waited for the magic to come.

CHAPTER TWENTY-EIGHT

"Are you sure you did it right?" Brian asked.

"Of course I did it right." My voice squeaked nervously. "I think. This one's different. No sigil. No true name. I kind of had to run blind for this one. Oops, sorry Char." I cringed at the faux pas. "But it had to have done something. I felt it work." I thought back to the glowing sensation that had boiled within the stone of my necklace.

Just then, Charlotte cackled into the night sky and rolled on the ground in a fit of laughter.

"Char, are you okay?"

"It worked. They're coming," she was able to squeeze out before being overcome with another fit of hysterics.

My feet trembled as the ground beneath began to shake. Images of elephants stampeding through the African plains entered my mind as the sounds of hundreds of feet pounding the earth grew closer.

"You might want to get out of the way, Gem,"

Brian yelled as he motioned for me to move away from the pit. I grabbed Charlotte by the waist and dragged her along with me until we were sheltered up against a large oak tree.

Then the hoard appeared. It all happened in slow motion. Every last demon was drawn back into the gate as if some magnet was luring them back. In the air, some attempted to grab onto branches in order to avoid another lifetime of imprisonment. One after another, they walked in reverse down the sides of the abyss. They numbered in the hundreds, like a swarm of black locusts that could no longer prey on Harrisport.

There was a loud crack. I looked up and saw the tree beside us go down in one fell swoop as the demons clinging onto it were slammed down to the ground. Charlotte huddled closer into the safety of my chest and I wrapped my arms around her.

"It's going to be okay. We're safe," I whispered to her.

Then the rain poured down in buckets and it was hard to see with the water pouring down my face. My jeans soaked through within a matter of seconds and I tried my best to wipe away the layers of hair so that I could watch as the last of the invaders were forced back to their underworld.

I didn't take my eyes off them. I needed to make sure every last one went back. That's when I felt a large hand on my shoulders. Fingers digging into my muscle forced me to release my hold on Charlotte.

"What the hell!" I screamed. Rain filled my mouth, leaving my words sputtering out.

"Indeed." I turned to see Sam's familiar bald head

right next to mine. His eyes blazed with anger. "You're going to pay for this." He yanked at my necklace, breaking the clasp.

"How?"

"Your mistake, Gemma, as usual, is thinking that you know everything. It appears I'm going to have to take you with me," he said, grabbing my ankle.

"Gem, don't leave me here like this," Charlotte said, weeping.

I dug my heels into the ground and thrust my hands into the mud, trying to stay put but the magic pulling Sam in was too strong. My body slid across the old summoning circle. The slick cool mud drenched my clothing and coated my face. It was too hard to fight it. I sobbed until my body collapsed and my strength left me. I was willing to give in.

"Don't do it, Gem." Brian's voice carried over the pattering of the torrential downpour. I lifted my head and saw Sam's body between my feet, halfway in the base of the gate's mouth. With the last of my strength, I gave one hard kick to his face and sent him careening into the black.

The ground began to shake and I scrambled back to Charlotte, who by now looked like a sad wet kitten. The flat interlocking pieces of the gate began to spiral back together until the hole was no more.

As if on cue, the rain stopped and silence followed. Full dark had already settled in but the familiar pin-pricked sky was back, no longer obstructed by the hideous creatures.

"It's over." I sighed with relief.

"Looks like it." Brian looked up with me. "There's the big dipper." He pointed.

"Let's go home." I stood up and pulled Charlotte along with me, even though the idea of getting her all the way back to my house was daunting. *Just do it, Gem.*

It's alright, Gem. I can manage myself.

Our eyes met at the unspoken words. In the light of the full moon, I could see that Charlotte's eyes had reverted to their original lustrous sapphire color.

"You're really okay?" I asked.

"Yeah. I think so. Except for the mud." She looked down at her tattered dress and tried to smooth off the caked dirt but only made it worse with more streaks.

"I think we could both use a shower." I locked arms with her while Brian followed us back to the house.

It was hard to tell the extent of the damage at this time of night but it was evident from the charred smell drifting through the air that the rain had put out all the fires. We went straight to the house and while Charlotte was in the shower, I helped my dad clean up the mess. Most of the papers he had been obsessing about the last few weeks turned out to be nothing but garbage.

"I can't believe I wasted so much time on this nonsense," he said while I swept the kitchen floor.

"I'm sure it'll help somehow," I reassured him.

Brian was sitting on his chair at the counter. So far Charlotte and I were the only ones who could see him and I liked it that way. It made things easier to compartmentalize. I could stick him along with the sigils in the box in my brain where I kept things that I couldn't talk about with anyone else. Like Charlotte's head games.

"You've got to tell him," Brian said.

"Tell him what?" I muttered under my breath.

"Were you talking to me, pumpkin?" My dad looked up from the blueprints on the table.

"Huh? No, sorry. I was just thinking out loud."

He smiled and went back to rolling the surveys into the cardboard tubing.

"Tell him it wasn't you driving."

I didn't answer, instead moved the broom back and forth in a nervous frenzy.

"This isn't about you." Brian followed me down the hall. "I don't think I can go wherever it is that I'm supposed to go if I have this kind of unfinished business hanging over my soul."

"You think this is a good time to bring this shit up?" I whispered. "It's done and buried. And from the looks of things around here, I don't want to set Dad back any more than he already has been already by these demons that have been feeding on his soul this entire time."

"Please, Gem. Just get it out. We'll all be better for it."

"I'm fine."

"Don't be like that, Gem. I know when you're lying. Remember. We're twins."

"Not really." My dad's hurtful revelation about my parentage echoed in my head.

"Yes, really. We've been together since the beginning. Through Mom leaving and Dad being just as distant. There's nothing I wouldn't do for you. That's why I know you're going to tell Dad the truth.

Because you would do anything for me."

Gem, you better get in here.

Can you please stop invading my head? At least make a ringer sound so that I know you're about to talk.

Okay. Ring Ring. Gemma, this is Charlotte speaking. Get your ass in your room now.

"I promise I'll tell him, Brian. Tomorrow." I left the broom leaning against the wall and went into my bedroom.

Charlotte was dressed in a pair of my sweats, a thin gauzy t-shirt, and extra thick, fuzzy white socks.

"What's going on?" I asked.

"You've got take a look at this. I mean all I can say is wow."

She handed me an envelope. The creamy white paper was rich and the gold wax seal on the back showed a lion's head. I ran my index finger underneath and pulled out a card. Written on it were three words in metallic pewter calligraphy.

It's not over.

Below them was a signature. Ian.

"You would think I'd get more of an explanation. Or maybe an apology. I don't know. You'd think after sleeping with me and then ripping my heart out, he'd have more to say." The paper crumbled in my curling fist as tears spilled down my cheeks.

"Gemma, I hate seeing you like this."

"Me, too," Brian said. I hadn't even known he was standing behind me this whole time.

"I'm just so tired." I threw myself onto the bed. Images of Ian and me assaulted my thoughts. Holding hands in front of the yew tree. Swimming in the lagoon. Smiling in class. Saving me from Allison.

Losing ourselves in the music. "I can't. It hurts so much." My anguish flooded the pillowcase and I pressed my face further into the bed.

"Shh. It's alright." Charlotte ran her hand through my hair.

"It hurts so much," I cried.

"I know." Her touch was comforting. She kept running her hand over my head and down my back until everything was gone.

I am on top of a large mountain. Below me the desert is endless. Its red-hued sand blows on in on an endless storm, dumping more and more onto the rolling dunes. The earth is red. The sky is red. And the sun is a brilliant white so strong it hurts to look. But I'm not looking up. My eyes are fixed upon the horizon at the wall. I can't see anything yet but I can feel the evil power that is gathering far beyond the walls of sand and stone.

The air is thick and restless, caught in the task of moving all the sand to the base of the mountain. I look down and then back to the hazy line where earth and sky meet. It is turning darker. I hear the sound of the ocean even though my thoughts tell me there is no water to be found for miles.

Then it happens. A wave of red-black crashes down, flattening the dunes. It pools at the base of the mountain and laps up against the chalky rock. Blood.

Bits and pieces of the mountain slough off and are devoured by the angry liquid. I look back to where it came from. The sound of horses. Four of them. I cannot see them but my mind is telling me there are four. One comes into view. His rider pushes him to the point of exhaustion but there is victory in his posture. The white horse. He is here. It's not over.

* * *

I woke up drenched, sweat running down the back of my neck. I pushed away the damp curls that clung to my face and noticed two things. Charlotte was snoring away in my bed and the sun was pouring into my room. Something that I had missed for a while.

Without thinking, I threw on some sweats, tied my running shoes and headed out for my run. On my way out the door, I passed Brian and waved. He returned it with a smile and I was off onto the damp dirt path that was so familiar to me. I had neglected it.

Each time the ball of my foot hit the ground, I imagined punching Ian in the face, one after another until my head cleared, and the anger left every cell in my body. I had found some peace, even if it was temporary.

When I got back, Charlotte, my dad, and an invisible Brian were waiting for me on the deck. There were eggs, bacon and toast.

"I know it's chilly out but I thought we could all use some fresh air," my dad said, pouring everyone a glass of orange juice.

"Yeah. Wow. Your dad can really cook," Charlotte said, digging right into her plate.

I sat down and looked over at Brian. He would never be a part of our family anymore. It was selfish of me to keep him here just because it made me feel better. I had to let go.

"Dad, there's something I need to tell you."

"Sure, pumpkin." He put down his fork and knife and looked up at me.

"It's about Brian." I thought it was going to be easy to let go of the burden but the words seemed to be getting caught in my throat.

"What about him?" he asked. The uncomfortable situation was agitating him. I could tell by the way the crease in his forehead was deepening and he nudged his glasses up with one finger.

I looked down at my plate. "He was the one driving," I said.

"Driving?" he asked.

"The accident. He was the one driving. I switched spots with him before any help came. I didn't want him getting blamed for it. I didn't want anyone thinking badly of him."

"Are you sure? Because you didn't seem to remember all that much."

"My memory was fine. I didn't want to talk about it so I pretended like I didn't remember. We were in the car and Allison was texting him and before we knew it, the truck blindsided us. That's the truth."

"I don't know what to say," he replied.

"You don't have to say anything. I just thought you should know."

"Wow, Dr. Pope, these eggs are killer," Charlotte said.

With that, we continued to eat in silence. I peeked up from the corner of my eye and saw Brian smile. But he was still there.

CHAPTER TWENTY-NINE

Brian didn't disappear or go into the light like we thought he would. He was there every day when I woke up. We spent our days volunteering (I actually did the work) with the town clean up during the day. At night we returned to our routine of searching through Mom's things while I cried.

I did as much as I could. Cleaning out branches. Piling up trash. Reorganizing the school library. Sweeping up glass. Anything to keep my mind occupied. I couldn't let myself think about what happened with Ian until I was alone in bed and I could let go of all the tears.

It was three more weeks before we were able to return to school. Everyone in town pitched in as much as they could to clean up the mess and the Senator was able to get a lot of government aid when Harrisport was declared a disaster recovery area. The story on the news went that we had been hit with major cataclysmic weather phenomena, one after another. Which wasn't too far from the truth.

I poked my head into his room. He seemed lost in thought, his face turned to the window. His eyes caught mine in the reflection. "Hey, sis."

"Hey. So do you want to come with me? Or will you hang out here all day?"

"I'm not sure." He looked back out the window. Our view of the forest was untarnished by the fire but I could feel it in my bones, as well as where the gate was and where every demon had left its taint.

"Come on. It'll be fun. You can do a running commentary. It'll be like that show. You know, the one with the high school boy and he narrates his own life."

"Gem, I thought I'd be gone right now."

"Yeah, but you're here. So let's go pretend like we're normal teenagers."

"It hurts to be here."

All I wanted to do was reach out to him but as soon as I did, my fingers went passed right through his form.

"We'll figure it out," I said. "I'm sure I can summon the right angel who'll tell us what we need to do."

"No, I don't want you doing that stuff anymore. It's not safe. For you or anyone else. Look what happened to Charlotte."

"I kind of think she lucked out. I mean, who else on this planet can communicate telepathically. Brian, I know you're probably scared. I am too. I know they didn't all get locked back in the chamber. The one on the white horse. He's still out there. So we can just ignore that if you want."

"Then it's only the beginning."

"One day at a time," I said, slinging my bag across my chest. "So let's make today count."

He looked at me. "Since when are you the smart and optimistic one?"

"I lost everything. I'm not going to let that happen again. Not if I can help it. And that includes you."

We left his room together and I knew that nothing could bring me down.

It was strange being in homeroom without Thom. The mood in the classroom reflected the sentiments of the town itself; a bit depressed but ready to overcome.

When Ian walked in, my heart dropped to the floor. I could feel him stomp on it as he walked past my desk. I couldn't help myself and followed his body as it sat right next to Allison. The two of them smiled at each other and were speaking in hushed tones. I felt like an outsider looking in.

"Stop torturing yourself," Brian said.

"I'm not. But what is he doing here?"

The boy sitting behind me, Dave or Doug, gave me a funny look. I couldn't tell which one he was since he had an identical twin brother (I know, shame on you, Gemma) and it was already too late in the year to ask without looking stupid so all I did was smile and turn back to my journal. I was trying to catalogue the names of the demons and angels I already knew for my own purposes and I was trying to elaborate on Thom's sigil in an effort to find a way to bring him back when Principal Kelly walked in.

"Good morning, class. I'm sorry to inform you that

Mr. Flynn is no longer with us. He has been missing since the fires and no one knows of his whereabouts. We're looking for a replacement but in the meantime, I will fill in for homeroom and there will be no AP English classes until further notice. It shouldn't take more than a week. Now let me call roll."

She sat down on the desk and went through the list of names. When she got to mine, I could have sworn she looked at Brian and smiled.

When the bell rang, Principal Kelly asked me to stay behind.

"Is there something you need?"

"I need to thank you. He told me what you did."

"Who?"

"Thom. Who else?"

"I thought you didn't practice anymore."

"There's nothing like having your life threatened by a hoard of demons to get your witchcraft switched on."

"Is he okay?"

"No. He's stuck there. I can't get him out."

"You knew who he was all along. It's all my fault. I let the wrong people tell me what to do."

"Did you think I would hire some college student as a teacher? He just didn't have credentials and that's the story I ran with to get him in here to check on all of you, just in case any of the parents snooped around. Anyway, don't be too hard on yourself. It'll all work out."

"You seem very sure of that."

"As you get older, you realize the universe has its way of delivering the answers right to you. What you don't realize is how many people you saved."

"It won't matter soon. Something bad is coming. Much worse than before. I feel it coming and I don't know how to stop it."

"Trust in yourself. That's all anyone can do. I'm here if you need me." She gave me a warm motherly smile.

"Thanks."

"And it's nice seeing you too, Brian."

"You too, Principal Kelly," Brian and I said at the same time.

"Keep an eye on your sister."

"Will do."

We were free to leave and I was eager to get to my next class, bringing the end of the day one step closer. As soon as I turned the corner, I ran straight into a wall. A human wall.

"Sorry," I said, all flustered as I tried to gather my journal and papers from the floor.

"No biggie." I looked up to see Ian's deep blue eyes. Seeing the confident twinkle in his eye that had once appealed to me grated against my mind.

"Excuse me," I said, about to go on my way. "Wait a second. I need to ask you something."

"You sure you want to know the answers?" he replied.

I didn't let him deter me that easily. "How come you're still here?" I looked him straight in the eye. I needed to confront him head on or I was never going to get over him.

"Oh, you think I'm a demon." He started to laugh. "Sorry, wrong team. I'm one of them." He pointed his finger up to the ceiling.

"Figures," I spat and left him in the hallway before

he could see the redness in my face.

That Saturday night, my dad decided to join me to go see Charlotte's play. Turns out everyone showed up. Even the Senator and his wife, who wanted to show solidarity after the traumatic events that changed everyone's reality. No one could explain the mysterious dome that had held the townspeople prisoners. There were theories about aliens and terrorists but the story that stuck was more strange weather.

We took our seats in the front row. Charlotte had reserved us as guests along with her parents and although I didn't really want to sit next to them, my dad had a good enough time talking about Moab Labs and the new technology they were releasing soon. I took that as my cue to zone out and was surprised by the ringing that caught my attention as soon as I stared up at the stage.

Ring Ring. This is Charlotte. Come in, Gem.

Hey, Charlotte. I'm glad I brought my dad to buffer me from the Senator.

Oh, don't be so scared of him. He can smell fear.

So do I say break a leg?

Thanks Gem. I'm so psyched. Wow. Gotta go.

That was when the lights dimmed, the curtains pulled back and I watched in fascination as Charlotte transformed into a performer. She was beautiful. I couldn't get over how, in all our time as friends, I had never known she could sing. It was a pleasant way to spend an hour and we all lingered after the show to hand Charlotte flowers and stroke her ego.

On our way out, Allison and Ian were standing by

the large red exit sign of the school auditorium. It was weird case of deja vu. Only this time the two of them were laughing together and I felt like the butt of some secret joke.

"See you tomorrow, freak," Allison said.

My dad didn't seem to notice but Brian did. I watched as his anger boiled over and left him illuminated like a poltergeist.

"Leave her alone, Ally. She's my sister."

"Brian?" The color left her face and she dropped Ian's hand like a hot potato.

"Yeah, it's me. And I came here to tell you to leave her alone. It wasn't her fault. She wasn't the one driving."

"But I waited. I bought the perfect blue dress for our date. And I waited on the couch and you never showed up." She was crying now.

"I know you were. I tried to get back for you but it wasn't meant to be. I was driving and I was checking your texts and I didn't see the truck coming. It's my fault. I'm sorry I left you alone but you'll find someone new at college and you'll have the life you've always dreamed of. Just not with me."

With those last words, the light faded and she couldn't see him any longer.

"Brian, please. Please come back." Her voice was hoarse and ragged.

I pulled her to me and hugged her. She hugged me back. Maybe everything wasn't so forgone. Things could still change. The future was there and I just had to take it.